Falling
Trust No One. Believe Nothing.
Jennifer Grant

For Andrew and Langston

My absolute reasons for getting up each day. Read your hearts out. Keep your curiosity. Always. I love you both eternally.

Author's Note

This story was born from grief, and the loss of a childhood friend who was taken from this world far too soon. We were only twenty-one. I can still remember the call, the silence, the unfairness of it all.

Some of what you'll read is imagined, other parts are drawn from truth. But the thread that runs through it all is the regret of unfinished goodbyes and the struggle to make peace with something that never felt final.

Falling is my attempt to honor a friend who deserved more time, and to finally close a chapter that has remained open too long.

Playlist

mehro – "like you're god"
Aurora – "The Seed"
Anna Mieke – "Warped Window"
Aoife Wolf – "They Say I've Got a Fever"
Haunted Like Human – "Run Devil Run"
Ethel Cain – "Hard Times"
Colter Wall – "The Devil Wears a Suit and Tie"
Steve Earle – "Meet Me in the Alleyway"
Laura Gibson – "Li'l Red Riding Hood"
Laura Marling – "Devil's Resting Place"
mehro – "pirate song"
Pearce Roswell – "Second Plate"
Tommee Profitt, Sam Tinnesz, maryjo – "Garden"
Red Hot Chili Peppers – "Under the Bridge"

I too, have been a mourner. Sorrow deep
Its lava-tide around my pathway roll'd...
All joy grew dim before my tearful eye,
Which but the shadow of the grave could see;
There was no brightness in the earth or sky,
There was no sunshine in the world for me.
~Mary Ann H. Dodd Shutts

Chapter One

"He's gone," she says, her voice cold and detached, a tone that I have come to expect. "Jumped."

Silence passes between us, only broken by the rustling of papers on the other end of the line. She must be at her desk, distant and distracted, far away in every sense as she delivers the news.

I was always taught to be a good girl, and in my house that meant not reacting. To remain stoic. Cold. Not to draw too much attention to ourselves. Mama is, and has always been, an emotionless void. Lacking in any sort of warmth.

Mama knew Jay. And she knew him well. Our small town had only one clinic, and as the sole licensed nurse on staff, she knew just about everyone. As well as every bump, bruise, and hemorrhoid they ever had. Jay would often show up at our front door in the afternoons, and we would just sit on the front stoop, talking about everything—or sometimes, nothing at all.

"Sawyer?"

The decades-old grandfather clock loudly chimes in the background, a sound that lulled me to sleep on many overnight visits with Grams and Poppy.

I release a slow breath of air, steadying myself before responding. "When is the funeral?"

"Saturday," she says, her tone remaining cold and steady. "I take it I should be expecting you? I'll clean up your room."

"I'll be there Friday evening. I'll leave as soon as I can after work."

Christmas lights twinkle, creating a dance of red and green that casts twisted shadows onto the walls. 2:30 AM. I haven't been able to sleep for the past three nights—the workdays becoming exceedingly long as memories of him haunt me, roaming through me like ghosts. I slide the wrapped gift back and forth across the the desk, its wide-grinning Santas taunting me like an itch beneath my skin. I sigh loudly, the noise slicing through the heavy air as I slide my feet back into the slippers and shuffle into the kitchen.

The tea kettle hisses and gurgles. I open cabinet doors, searching for the glazed ceramic mug that I sloppily crafted so many years ago. It was one of my first real attempts at art—lumpy, uneven. But some might say it's got...character. I shove glassware left and right, ordered design and straight lines with front-facing handles abandoned for disordered chaos months ago. Mama always believed that I had some sort of obsessive-compulsive disorder, and perhaps she's right, but something snapped inside of me like a rubber band the second that autumn settled in, leaving cabinets in disarray and layers of dust lingering on shelves. A yawn escapes—no, erupts—as my fingers grasp the handle and gently place the mug onto the countertop.

Two teabags loosely fill the hinged wooden box, both of which are the same elderberry and lemon flavor that I always buy. Familiarity makes me feel safe, I suppose. I reach for one of the packets, ripping open the paper and dropping the sachet of tea into the mug. Steam curls and rising as boiling water fills to the rim. I add a dash of honey to sweeten what I'll never drink and make my way back to the desk.

Tears pull at the corners of my eyes from the blue glare of the screen, each blink burning with searing pain. I rub at them, pressing my spine into the high-backed chair as it groans beneath my restless shifting. Flickers of color dance on the white painted ceiling, a happy little display of holiday spirit that I'm sure most would enjoy. Now, it just makes me angry, the way red is overpowering in a display of false cheer. Why do red and green get to be the official colors of Christmas? What about lavender, carnation pink, or old, reliable navy blue?

I jolt upright, reach for the electrical plug and yank it hard. The dark wraps around me like a blanket, and I ease back into the smooth leather, my pulse returning to its normal still and unfaltered beat.

I blow at the curling steam and slide the mug to the corner of the desk. I don't even like tea. Never have. And I'm not quite sure why I even make it. A shadow passes through the thinly veiled curtains, illuminated by the glow of a low-hung moon. But it disappears as quickly as it came, leaving only the sound of a thousand crickets that sing in the night.

The obituary reads lifeless and dull. Flat. Cold. Raised by his grandparents after his mother chased a high for way too long, I suppose no one actually knew the real Jay—the layers of depth, imagination, and dreams that ran much deeper than the surface. They make him out to be nothing more than some guy with a troubled past who loved music and played in the high school band. I click at the mouse, scrolling through a few more lazy articles and empty condolences from distant family that hadn't reached out to him in years. My breath catches. I click. Something stirs in the pit of my stomach as I fall deep into unfamiliar territory.

I blink hard. My eyes flit across the screen with urgency. My pulse picks up speed. Cryptic usernames reveal secrets of a fateful night less than a week gone. Cade10699, the user who claims that Jay was pushed, mockingly referring to those who scattered from the scene as *"pussies."* My hand trembles as I yank open the drawer, frantically rifling through keys that unlock nothing I remember, dull scissors and crumpled up receipts. A blank scrap of paper emerges, along with a pen barely hanging onto its last few drops of ink. I slam the drawer shut with a sharp *crack*, violently shaking the pen and scribbling the series of letters and numbers down as fast as my hands can move.

Cade10699: I was there. He didn't fall. He was pushed. Bunch of pussies ran like cockroaches. LMAO
DarkZephyr01: Delete. Immediately.
KaMiKaZ3: man STFU
Cade10699: they closed the case. all gravy baby.

I push back from the desk, sinking into the depths of black leather as I stare into the void above. At the crooked trail of holes left when I tried to hang a light fixture on my own. Dread twists in my gut like a knife, and I gnaw at the inside of my cheek, biting down as the staccato beat of a drum echoes loud in my skull. My eyes squeeze tight, and all around me static cracks like fractured snow. I swallow the unease as I push away from the desk and rise. My breaths are slow. Deliberate. The hallway stretches long and dark ahead of me, crumpled sheets awaiting like a tomb.

I slip beneath satin and pull the comforter around me like some sort of protective cocoon. Nothing feels real anymore—not this bed, not this house, and not the chorus of crickets outside that hum their mocking tune. A soul once full of adventure and unbreakable friendship is now stripped bare. Nothing but a hollow void.

Light streams through the curtains. The neighbors suddenly threw a bunch of farm animals in their backyard. And unfortunately for me, their rooster is my daily alarm. I stretch my arms across the bed, slowly letting consciousness roll in.

Cade10699.

I jolt upright on the bed, heart racing, peeling back the covers and swinging my legs over the side. Cold wooden planks bite into my toes as I race to the living room, dropping hard into the groaning chair. My fingers tremble as I slide the mouse back and forth, frantically scanning the screen for the proof that was there just hours ago. I rub at the sleep sticking to my lashes like glue, a slight "pfft" hanging from my lips. Obituary. Social media posts from former classmates who never said a single word to him. Funeral arrangements, detailed and sterile, forcing bile to rise in the back of my throat. Nothing more. Nothing less. Sinister truths, vanished into the abyss where all dark web things go. Hidden from daylight.

Chapter Two

Traffic slows to a crawl as the parade of red lights in front of me sway right, then left, searching for the lane that will magically open in front of us. My exit is just another half mile ahead. Highway 27. A route that I've taken countless times. A route once framed with citrus groves and majestic oak trees, now a wasteland of concrete slabs and chain store shopping plazas. With just two weeks left until Christmas, people rush to holiday parades and light displays, crowding in stores to fill their carts with so-called holiday cheer. But this holiday is bleak and gray, with the sun setting much too early, the pitter-patter of rain tapping steady on the glass, and my best friend ripped from me in some bitter, twisted fate. I inch my way through cars that honk steadily, irritation bubbling over their holiday spirit, and take that hairpin curve driven a hundred times before. My fingers curl tight around the wheel, though I wish I could leave the memories behind forever. Wish it didn't hurt this much.

As the road opens up and lights fade behind, I crack the window just slightly. Heat has taken over the inside of the car, clinging to my neck like some suffocating weight. I lean closer to the window, drawing a slow breath before choking on it and quickly sealing myself inside again. Cow shit. Pungent. A bitter reminder that I am headed home.

As the red lights fade out into the background and darkness swallows the path ahead, I sink again into the warmed cushion, my fingers fumbling to turn up the radio and drown out my own thoughts, focusing solely on a chorus of Eartha Kitt's "Santa Baby."

Silence just hurts. Silence is when every thought claws its way to the surface, leaving this insatiable urge to scratch beneath the skin. So, from now on, I'll just drown it out. Life is full of choices. And I can simply choose to not participate in the past. Jay's memory will not be buried six feet under in some tacky casket, in a town where time doesn't move. A place where the silence stretches for miles and people claim to know you—even when they don't.

I veer onto Highway 60 as dread coils tight around my throat. An unrelenting force. The car slows to well below the posted limit and my thoughts begin to race again. Fast. I turn the radio volume up—louder and louder—as a voice blasts through the speakers. Car accidents. Injuries. Fat settlement checks that lawyers bleed dry. The words hammer into my skull until I let out a wail. Until my voice finally breaks through the chaotic sound.

I left home at eighteen. Never looked back. Jay came to visit me on weekends. I tried to convince him to come with me, to leave the past behind, but he felt some obligation to stay. To take care of the grandparents who adopted him when his mother chased a high in shadowed corners. We both had ghosts that haunted us, and that's probably what kept us so close. This need to protect the other. But I wasn't there when Jay needed me the most. I couldn't protect him. And I just don't know if that's something I can live with.

The edge of town takes shape in front of me. And the rain finally breaks as the Christmas lights near Main glow like some beacon of festive cheer—or existential dread depending on how you look at it. Parade floats line the old Citrus and Chemical Bank parking lot as traffic comes to a standstill again. I grip the wheel tighter, white knuckling as I swallow down something bitter, like old pennies or burnt coffee, and pull into the familiar Shop 'n Go.

Prisms of light dance as my boots stomp into a slick mix of oil and rainwater that puddles on the pavement. I slam the door shut behind me as high pitched laughter pierces the air, and a glowing neon sign flashes "OPEN" in garish red, illuminating her thick curls like something straight out of an eighties shampoo ad. Elizabeth Ryan. Head cheerleader and the town golden girl with a path paved straight to the Ivy League. The definition of privilege. Still—she chose life at the local community college with her high school sweetheart, the best wide receiver our town had, leading our division 6A football team to victory. It was a good run for several years before he accepted an invitation to join Ohio State and left Elizabeth broken back at home. I almost feel sorry for her. Just a little. Not enough to make a grand gesture or anything. And not enough to actually speak to her. I reach for the cold metal handle, my free hand balled tightly inside my sleeve as I fight the chill racing up my spine.

Fluorescents flicker and hum above, and shiny tiles that sparkle with dirt *crunch* beneath my boots as I keep my head low and make my way toward the back corner of the store. A shiver races through me as the air from the cooler seeps through the fibers of my sweater, sinking its claws in as I quickly grab a six-pack of something probably awful. With my gaze still focused on the shiny squares at my feet, I make my way back to the front, falling into a line five deep as his voice booms toward the front doors, casually greeting a group of young boys with skateboards tucked tightly under their arms. William Fisher—or, as we kids always preferred to call him, *Brown*.

Brown has owned this corner store for as long as I can remember. According to Mama, I crossed the busy highway in nothing but a saggy diaper and my birthday suit just to buy candy from Brown when I was barely able to walk. Mama does like to tell old wives' tales, though. Like how she quit smoking for me, though I recall her sneaking out back every Friday night, a Marlboro Red pinched between her fingers, a glass of something amber dangling in her other hand. I suppose I can't really blame her. My fingertips curl tighter around the cardboard handle.

Something about this town makes you want to forget everything you've ever known. To let the earth swallow you. To bury all of the shattered dreams and dirty secrets this town holds. My boots shuffle forward as I slide the beer onto the counter. Muffled voices suddenly become clear as the flickering fluorescent bulb above nips at my vision.

"I'll be damned, it can't be—" he quips, sliding his glasses down his nose in exaggerated fashion. "Is this our little Sawyer?"

"Brown—" I muster out, my throat tight, water pooling in the corner of my eye. Fragile. That's what I feel like. Don't set her down wrong or she'll break. Don't look at her wrong or she'll break. Just a fragile, delicate shell of a human, unable to form any sense of connection with anyone in my life—well, anyone except for Jay.

"Oh sweetheart, I heard—you here for the services tomorrow?"

I nod. Words stick in my throat. This is the first real conversation I've had about his death. But nothing about this seems real. Not his passing, not this town, and certainly not this blinding maze of buzzing fluorescents and flickering signs that hum like they're alive. "I am. Short trip."

"Real shame what happened. His grandfolks are real broken up about it from what I hear, too. Your mama doing okay?"

My shoulders rise and fall as my breath catches in my throat. "I suppose I'll find out soon enough," I sigh, the weight of returning home pressing hard. "Headed there tonight."

"Well, you tell her hello and give her a big hug for me. You know, you're lookin' more and more like her every day."

My hand rakes through freshly dyed hair—the box said #21, *Bright Black*, whatever that means. I wrap a strand around a finger and twirl at it, pretending the dark strands of hair will hide the fact I'm a spitting image of her. A throat clears from behind somewhere as I reach deep into the pocket of my jeans, pulling several wadded-up bills as most of them flutter to the floor. I crouch, resting my ass onto the heels of my boots as I scoop up the mess, finally popping my head back over the counter. I place one neatly folded twenty onto the counter, pushing it toward Brown, narrowly escaping the judgement of everyone in line.

"So, what's all the commotion about?" I ask. "Traffic isn't moving at all. No one can get downtown."

"Christmas parade. You been gone so long you already forgot?" he asks.

A small grunt builds within my chest as I reply, "Of course."

Brown hands me the change, lightly cupping his hand around mine and squeezing tight. "Sawyer, you take care of yourself. And don't you drown yourself in this garbage."

I slowly nod, blinking away the tears that keep trying to escape.

"You staying long?" he asks.

One of the skateboard boys groans in annoyance behind me. "Just a few days," I answer, slipping the change into the tip jar and sliding the beer from the counter.

"Come back and say hello. Okay?"

I muster a smile and dangle the treasure of beer at my side, quickly making my way toward the glass doors as the icy chill smacks me hard in the face. "I will!" I call out over my shoulder as I make my way back onto slick pavement, my feet picking up speed as I head south. Away from my car and straight toward Stuart Street at Nye Jordan Park—the park where Jay and I used to get high every Friday night, sharing our darkest secrets and laying them bare. Just two kids filled with hope. That hope was taken from Jay, though. Taken by Cade10699. And I'm going to find whoever it is behind that name and take back what was stolen.

The treeline streaks past, just a smudge of shadows as darkened clouds shift, paving the way for a blanket of stars in the night sky. You can see them better out here—less pollution than where I live. I try to count them, but with each spin they melt into a whirlpool of light. One big comet spinning endlessly, chasing its tail like a dog.

"The park is closed!" a voice thunders from the tennis court.

A beam of light slices through the dark and lands square in my eyes. The merry-go-round suddenly acts as a puke centrifuge. I swallow down bile, dragging myself upright and forcing the world back into place. I throw a hand in the air—a half-hearted attempt to block the light that must be a thousand lumens strong.

"I was just leaving!" I call out, doing my best impression of someone *not* completely inebriated. But the moment I straighten my legs, the ground tilts and my body slumps again over metal rails.

The light sharpens as footsteps draw closer, slicing through the grass like they've got something to prove.

"Ma'am, have you had anything to—fuck, is that you, Sawyer?"

"Turn that goddamn light off and I'll let you know," I huff, pulling myself upright once again. I stick the landing this time.

The loud *click* of a flashlight cuts through the air. My eyes adjust to the sudden darkness, slowly taking in the familiar, rounded features of his face. Disappointment washes over me with an audible sigh. "Wes—"

"Damn girl, nobody's seen you since graduation. Where the hell have you been?"

"Just trying to keep a low profile, you know. Don't want to get a ticket for loitering in my own town," I smirk. I know I can wedge myself just beneath his skin, at least enough to make him squirm. "Or mistaken for a threat by some bored cop and get tackled at the Shop 'n Go."

"You always did have a mouth on ya," he pushes like he has something to prove.

Unbelievable. His hairline, much thinner than before, beads with sweat as the middle button on his shirt fights the urge to pop. Wes couldn't outrun a turtle to save his life, much less a criminal. But all of the men in his family have worked in law enforcement in some capacity over the years, so I suppose his new career path wasn't exactly a choice, but rather an expectation.

"Am I being held on charges?" I ask, the last word stuttering up my throat.

"God no, Sawyer. Just chill the fuck out," he orders, cracking a grin.

I hop down from the merry-go-round, metal *squeaking* loudly in protest as the backing of the high school marching band plays a boisterous medley of Christmas classics. Or butchers them. The last nearly-empty can of beer tumbles to the ground at my feet. "So—I'm free to go then?"

"Yes ma'am. Free as a bird—" he clears at his throat, puffing out his chest like my neighbor's rooster, flexing like he's got something to prove. "But you aren't driving anywhere."

"Shit, Wes! Of course not," I yell, heavy and sloppy, obvious to anyone passing by.

I fold myself in half, stumbling left again as I lift the empty box, slowly grabbing cans and tossing them back inside. He just stands there. Watching. Breathing. Thick and heavy. Like he just climbed a flight of stairs, or maybe a whole damn mountain. I straighten my spine, slowly making my way toward his more-than-ample frame.

"You—like what you see?"

I pull my bottom lip into my teeth. Rub off the dirt on my hands. The dirt that soiled the denim on each knee from a tumble onto damp, muddy ground. His breathing grows louder now, like a bear that just woke up and is already pissed off.

Does he even know how loud it is? It's incredibly disturbing.

"Always have—" he confesses as the corner of his mouth pulls into a smirk. "Plenty of room in the back seat." He nods toward the cop car parked on the street, a beacon of red and blue, alerting literally everyone to my presence.

"Jesus Christ, Wes!" I smack at his arm. Hard. "I'm not trying to fuck you. I need a damn ride to the car."

"Oh!" His cheeks flush red, glowing even in the dark. "But we're *not* going to your car. Where you stayin'?"

My gaze falls to the ground at my feet. The usual shade of green replaced now by sodden sludge and slick decay that seep into your bones. "Mama's house."

"Off Clower?"

My shoulders fall along with my resolve. I kick at something beneath my boot—a broken branch, maybe, though it squishes like spoiled meat or maybe a bloated toad. "Yeah," hangs from my lips in barely a whisper.

"Come on, Sawyer. Throw that shit in the trash and just get in the car."

"Do I have to ride in the back, though?"

"Yeah, Sawyer," he begins. "I can't risk—"

"I know, I know," I interrupt. "Let's just go."

His hand lifts like he means to steady me, but I flinch, yanking my arm back and stumbling left. Again. A groan scrapes its way out through clenched teeth, then slowly sinks into silence again.

Welcome home, Sawyer.

14

Chapter Three

Keys fumble in the dark as I put on quite the show for the neighbors. Mama never did fix the porch light. Might as well just hang a sign that says *rob me* on the front of the house. A few more swipes, a few more nicks in the muted shade of beige that she swore was "homey," and the lock finally *clicks* its release.

Inside, the house is swallowed by shadow. No greeting but a faint *tick-tick-tick* that echoes down the hall like water dripping through cracked stone. I raise my hand in front of me, not far enough apparently, as my shin slams into something hard.

"Fuck!" I yell out.

She must have rearranged the furniture again.

I crouch down, firmly rubbing at the skin as the pain slowly subsides. Still nothing. No footsteps *creaking* over warped floorboards. No television blaring football games in overtime or movies where the husband is secretly the killer. No clatter of dishes or cabinet doors. Not a sound other than the *tick-tick-tick* of that godforsaken clock.

"Mama?"

The floor begins to rock and sway beneath my feet, and the walls spin like a centrifuge.

Left. My bedroom is to the left. Bathroom down the hall.

I dig my toes into the heel of each boot, slipping them off and kicking them into the void just before my gut flips, like just before that drop on a rollercoaster you didn't mean to ride. I stagger down the hall and collapse to my knees, wrapping my arms around with quiet desperation.

The retching comes in waves, splashes back against the bowl fast and hard. I press my forehead onto cool porcelain as I gasp for air. The room spins. The sweetness of rose-scented soap lingers beneath cigarettes and the sour stench of vomit. A light flickers on as my breath comes in shudders.

"Jesus Christ, Sawyer," she bites.

My breath stammers sharp and uneven. Something sour coils again. Deep. Like a storm drain backing up. One last retch and I push out the last of it. At least for now. I rock back onto my heels and rake my fingers through the knots in my hair, as if I can claw my way out of this body. Or claw my way out of his house.

"You done?" she asks.

"Why? You going to give me a lecture?" I shift my weight back, slowly straightening my spine and slapping a palm onto the counter for support, legs trembling beneath me like a fawn. "Little late for parenting, don't you think?" I draw a shaky breath, my pulse returning to its normal lull.

Her angry gaze slices right through me, a lifeless palette of green and gold, ripping open the wound that I carefully stitched together over the last few years.

"Go to bed, Sawyer. Funeral's at eleven," she orders, flicking off the light with one final switch. Ringlets of hair dance on her shoulders as she melts into shadow, disappointment trailing in her wake.

I turn to the mirror, but a stranger watches back. Dark circles sink beneath wide pupils, and sun-kissed skin is now ashen and parched. I peel the sweater over my head, the tank top beneath clinging and slick with sweat. I claw hair from my face and make my way down the hall, fingertips gliding along the textured paint until they land on the switch. I flip it. Light floods the room.

My eyes adjust, then roll. A groan slips as I take in the scene. Piles of boxes, remnants of her decades-old shopping addiction, are stacked like barricades around the room. My things, probably tossed like trash without a second thought.

A sharp *meow* pierces the silence. A ribbon of black fur weaves between my legs.

"Salem," I whisper. "Hi sweet girl, I missed you."

I make my way over to the bed, shifting boxes and tossing piles of nicotine-stained clothes onto the floor. The bed frame groans beneath me as I throw myself onto the mattress, shimmying beneath pink sheets with tiny, yellow embroidered flowers that are older than me.

The ceiling spins.

One...two....three times around.

Nauseating.

The sun kisses my bare shoulders, now a bright shade of pink. Temperatures hover in the low nineties, and summer hasn't even arrived yet. Florida summers can be relentless, and most locals flee to the coast, spending long days drifting down natural springs or taking refuge in the saltwater of the Gulf.

Each day, I walk the same stretch of road home. Pass the same crooked slab of sidewalk I've tripped over a hundred times that the city refuses to fix. The same tree that smashed into Frank Giordano's house, still unrepaired because he's too cheap to do anything about it. It's true. Everyone swears he's in the mob or something, but Mama says there's no way. Says no man who duct-tapes his windows back together is busting kneecaps or playing anyone's boss. She's probably right, but I still like hearing the rumors. It's fun pretending something worth gossiping about actually happens in this town.

Mrs. Manley, the crossing guard posted daily at Woodlawn and Clower, grins so wide that I catch the gap where her missing molar used to be.

"Hello Sawyer! How was school today?" she asks, head bobbing with enthusiasm.

"Same as always." I force a half smile, nudging a pebble with my toes. "Lots of homework."

It's the same exchange every afternoon—her question, my shrug, both of us reading a script from the same boring film. She hoists her red stop sign into the air, bounding into the street with the shrill blow of her whistle. One single car idles in wait. I pick up speed as my new sneakers, the ones I just had to have, rub skin raw on the back of each heel.

"Be safe, Sawyer!" she calls out from over my shoulder.

Halfway there.

Mama works late, and most nights she's out for drinks with her coworkers long after their shift ends, which means the house stays empty after school. I don't throw wild parties. I don't even invite anyone over. Don't really care much for people, if I'm honest. Besides, the house is—silent. Not the peaceful kind, but the hollow kind that just kind of seeps in slow. There's no laughter echoing down the hall, no clinking of silverware or muffled voices gathered in the living room. And I'm not ungrateful. The water runs. The A/C blows. The fridge keeps soda cold enough. It's just not the sort of silence a kid should grow up in, that's all.

Green eyes glow behind the trunk of an oak tree as paws *crunch* softly through leaves. A tail flicks with curiosity. Right. Then left. I pin to the sidewalk as the ball of fur approaches, each step careful and deliberate. I rest a knee onto the pavement as quiet *meows* carry through the air.

"Is that your cat?" a voice calls out from across the Clower street.

My head snaps left. I don't think I've seen his face before, but people tend to blur together at school. "No! I just found it here."

"Want some help?" he offers.

"Sure," I say loudly as he rushes to cross Clower.

He looks to be around my age. Carries a nearly-empty black canvas backpack slung over one shoulder. Rounded glasses slide down his nose as droplets of sweat bead along his hairline. His skin has a deep tan and his hair is buzzed into a fresh fade. He beelines for me, dropping the backpack into the grass and crouching onto his knees beside me.

"He looks hungry," the boy offers. The back of his hand lifts toward the cat's nose. Gently. Slowly.

I lean forward, my head narrowly missing the ground by inches as I closely inspect. "I think it's a girl. Unless someone chopped its balls off—"

He wiggles an arm free, quickly sliding a flannel sleeve down his other arm, too.

"Wha—" I stutter out. "What are you doing?"

Slowly, he reaches forward, creating a blanket of soft fabric between his palms. He gently places it over the ball of black fur before scooping quiet *meows* into his arms.

"You're taking it home?" I ask.

"No. *You* are taking it home." He rises swiftly, black canvas bag hanging over one shoulder, frail black cat cradled under his arm. He strides forward—then halts abruptly, glancing back. "Where do you live, anyway?"

I trudge forward. "Harbor Way." I lift my fingers into the air, pointing in the direction of the new housing development just up Clower

Street. Though mostly still in developmental phase, the mounds of dirt and freshly poured concrete will soon become a beacon of hope for the more economically challenged locals.

"I live on Sailpoint." He turns back, tucking precious cargo tightly, boots thundering with purpose. "Let's go."

Four tiny paws land squarely on my chest in one swooping pounce. My body folds in surprise.

"Salem," I whisper.

She *purrs*, and her paws gently knead at my skin like a baker with a deadline. Cats seem to inherently know when we need them, and then behave like an ungrateful houseguest the rest of the time, silently judging everything that we do.

"I miss him, too." I gently place my fingertips onto the sides of her neck, rubbing as her eyes close tight. My head drops onto the pillow, the scent of mothballs and cedar enveloping me as the ceiling spins above. Unease churns again—deep in the pit of my stomach.

Her hand collides with mine, setting off like a firework up my spine. I flinch, pulling my hand toward me and cupping it for protection.

"You're going to put a hole in those tights," she snaps.

I glance down where a fresh thread gleams as it dangles on my thigh. "Huh—"

"And that dress—where did you find that? Shoved in the back of your closet? That thing looks like it's been balled up in a corner since before your Daddy left."

My palm glides over the fabric of the dress. Cotton. Black. Sweetheart neckline. Respectable length. Seemed like a perfectly fine choice for a funeral. Sure, it has a few wrinkles—I smooth my hand over the fabric—but are there more rules to funeral attire that I'm not aware of?

"I don't believe this is a Paris fashion show," I hiss, reaching for the dangling thread of nylon and giving a hard yank, exposing a large patch of bare skin just above my knee.

Her quiet *shh* slips out before she can stop it. I pull my bottom lip between my teeth and bite down hard. I can never win with her, though I still argue like a petulant child—me begging her to see things in my perspective and her begging me to see things in hers.

I swallow against the solid knot in my throat, and heat creeps its way up the back of my neck while I battle the dry grit on my tongue. After emptying the last of my stomach's contents this morning, every part of me feels parched and drained. I remember a water fountain in the lobby, the sting of Pine-Sol filling my lungs while the sun's glare bounced off its metal surface, searing my eyes the second I walked in. "I'll be right back" I whisper low, leaning forward. But my body locks the instant cinnamon perfume reaches me, its scent sharp, sweet and impossible to forget.

Jeanne Scott. Jay's grandmother. The woman who singlehandedly picked up the pieces of her broken child and raised Jay as her own. Dressed in a rich tweed fabric, a single white rose, splashed with lavender, is pinned to the front of her dress. A paper dangles from her fingertips, and Jay's face is front and center. Arms folded across his chest. Eyes still clinging to something like hope.

"Sawyer?" she whispers, voice wrapped in honey, yet the polite throat clear that follows *cracks* through me like a gunshot to the chest.

My shoulders flinch, and my knees knock against the pew in front of us. Some man with only a thinning ring of white hair turns. Narrows his eyes. Scowls.

I don't even know who this man is. And I'll bet a hundred bucks Jay didn't either.

"Yes?"

Jeanne drops down beside me. Cinnamon invades the air now, slowly wrapping its fingers around my throat. Her palm lifts to my back, rubbing tiny circles as I fight the urge to scratch.

"I'm sure you have a few words to share."

Heat spreads through me, slow and steady, as I pick at the mangled cuticle on my left thumb. Cinnamon closes in, tightens its grip until the air runs thin. "I don't—"

"I saved a spot for you—right after Tanya gives her speech." She gulps air as if she's drowning, and a silver ringlet of hair slips from its pin. "I figure you have plenty of memories to share with everyone."

Cinnamon reaches its dirty claws down my throat now. I blink. A gnat flits between us. Jeanne bats her hand in irritation before smoothing imaginary wrinkles from her dress. "Well, honey"—she claws once more at the tiny speck of black—"say something."

"Tanya is here?" I ask, my voice cracking as hushed whispers grind to a halt.

Jeanne reaches behind me, steadying the back of my arm. "Sawyer." Her face shifts, disappointment settling in. Just like Mama's when she speaks to me.

"He *hated* her," I protest.

"Yes, he did. But God would want us to forgive, Sawyer."

"Well, *God* isn't real," I hiss, pressing my spine into the hard pew and letting out a sharp breath. "But Jay was—Jay was real. And *he* hated her."

She sighs, pity softening her gaze. Murmurs slowly fill the room again, a decades-old church that neither Jay or I ever attended. "Sawyer—are you going to speak?"

Fire rages beneath the surface of my skin. Tanya was the kind of mother no child asks for, sick with an addiction that she never even tried to break. It was a weight that Jay carried until it nearly drowned him.

"No."

"He would want you to," she offers, voice barely a whisper.

"*He* wouldn't want any of this," I snap.

My gaze locks forward. Steady. Focused. Fixated on Gabe Shephard and his butchered rendition of "Wind Beneath My Wings."

Jay would have hated every second of this three-ring disaster.

Cinnamon slowly fades as Gabe finishes his song, and I release a slow breath, shutting my eyes tight. Maybe when they open, none of this will be real, and Jay will be beside me laughing at the insanity of it all. The room comes into view again—and there is Jeanne. Only the rustle of tweed and the sharp *tap-tap* of heels can be heard as she makes her way to the podium. Hushed whispers fall silent as all eyes focus ahead.

"First, I want to thank all of you for being here to celebrate the joy that Jay brought to all of our lives," she begins.

A celebration. His life was cut short. He barely started living, yet we're throwing a party. Jeanne continues on, dabbing at her eyes with a tissue every few sentences. My gaze flickers left, anywhere but the ornate wooden casket that sits front and center. Closed, of course. No proper goodbye. Just polished wood and whispered condolences.

Kaleidoscopes of glass filter light from above, splintering into a cross that falls sharp on my chest. A sharp swat to my knee. I turn to find a scowl etched across her face.

"Stop being difficult," she snips.

My fingers lace together, tight—cutting off circulation as I fight the urge to talk back.

Put the pain in the box, Sawyer. Lock it away.

"And now Jay's mother would like to say a few words," Jeanne says, slowly backing away from the podium as footsteps grow louder behind me.

And there she is. The woman of the hour. Mother of the year. Bundled up in a faux fur coat, shoes barely visible beneath the hem. Her bleached hair, streaked with dark roots, piled high on top of her head, framing her sunken eyes rimmed with dark circles.

"Today, we bury my son." She clears the rasp in her throat before continuing. Thick gold bangles *clink* loudly on her wrist. I glance down at my fingers, still laced tightly, knuckles turning white. "This loss has been de—" she stumbles, swallowing hard before forcing out, "—vastating."

Of course she's three sheets to the wind. My lips pull tight as heat crawls up my spine and spills to the tips of my ears. I rush to my feet as bile rises again. My stomach convulses in heaves that feel like some cruel punishment. And the sharp tang of metallic crawls its way from my throat.

Out.

I draw a slow breath in, push a longer one out.

Now. I need out.

I make my way toward the doors as something wet slides down my cheek. Maybe tears. Or sweat. Maybe something even worse. Faces pass in a blur. Almost there.

Five more steps. One...two...three...

Fingers wrap tightly around my arm, almost yanking my damn shoulder out of socket as he pulls me to the side.

"Wes?"

His expression blurs beneath the wet veil of my lashes, and my chest aches with some strong mix of defiance and the need for something I can't name. My fingers twitch at my sides, fighting the urge to shove him away.

"Come on, Sawyer. Stay." He leans in close, voice a soothing whisper in my ear. "For Jay."

My gaze falls to his khaki pants, ironed with a perfect crease down the front of each leg, then rises to the simple black button-up shirt. Must be off duty today. I give in. My shoulders pin to the wall at his side. Neither of us speaks another word as Tanya finishes making a complete mockery of Jay's entire life.

A sharp ringing floods my ears. It comes and goes, but I like it. Drowns out the voices, leaving only a shrill, deafening chorus in my head. Wes nudges at my arm. I nudge back. A few more strangers speak, maybe distant family members or friends of Jeanne. As annoying as Wes is, I'm actually glad he's by my side. That's twice he's pulled me back from the edge. I guess I owe him.

Suddenly, voices carry and legs stretch. Chatter grows louder by the second. A few of Jay's bandmates stop to look at me with pity as they awkwardly pat at my arm.

"You doing okay this morning?" Wes asks, his voice slicing through sideways glances, cheap gossip and idle talk.

I nod. That's all I can give right now.

"Need a ride back to your car?"

Another nod.

His hand slaps at my back with a firmness. I appreciate it. Much more than pity.

"I'll be right back," I whisper.

My feet drag me forward, pulling me toward the front of the church as fractured light rains down in a kaleidoscope of colors, painting me in stained glass hues. My breath catches, stuttering up my throat as the lacquered cherry wood casket comes into view. The floor tilts, walls close in, and my shoe snags on something, sending me sprawling into an empty pew. I catch myself just before I hit the ground, like some sort of roadkill splatter at the funeral of my only friend. That will really give them something to gossip about. Another step. Then another. My fingers rise, sliding gently along the polished trim. The only sounds are the ringing in my ears and my own shallow breaths.

"Terrible what happened," a voice booms from my right.

My patience, already stretched thin like a rubber band, suddenly snaps. "Was it? Do you actually believe you have a clue what happened that night?" My gaze breaks from the casket to find his eyes, flecked with gold yet somehow cruel, piercing straight into mine. A groan rumbles low in my chest. "You." I look down at my hands again, fingertips pressed to shiny lacquer as I wait for something to happen. Maybe for Jay to wake up and say this was all just a cruel joke.

"I'm just here to give support, Sawyer. I'm not your enemy," he says, tone dripping with arrogance and mock concern.

Colton Landry. Most locals just know him as "Colt." The spoiled, rich kid who was constantly in trouble for something—bullying, skipping class, breaking into the country club—and now the gleam of a badge peaks from beneath the jacket of his suit. The ringing returns fast, filling my head with a chorus of high-pitched tones.

"Sawyer—"

My eyes press tight.

"Sawyer, are you going to speak?" he asks.

"Why does everyone keep asking me that?" I snap, eyes jolting open as my fists curl at my sides. "What else is there to say?"

His palms lift in defense, and he takes a step back from the animal he just unleashed in me. "Just seeing if I can help—that's all."

"No one can help." My chin lifts, meeting his gaze head-on. "Can you bring him back? Can you reverse time?"

He blinks. And blinks again. Even skates his tongue over the corner of his mouth like he enjoys this. Like he gets some sick satisfaction by pushing people to the edge.

I narrow my eyes onto him. "Then go back to the precinct. Kick your feet up with the rest of the useless cops in this town."

Hands reach from behind, landing squarely on my shoulders. My head snaps.

"It's time," a voice whispers close.

Cinnamon closes around me again. I glance toward the church doors where Wes still stands, arms crossed and back leaned against the wall. Unease fills me, crawling slowly up my limbs. I turn back. Only Jeanne stands beside me now, arm stretched and waiting.

A pitter-patter of rain falls on opened umbrellas, gathered closely around a freshly dug grave. A steady cadence drills into my ears as the heel of my right shoe sinks into muddy ground. I wish it would swallow me whole, pull me under, away from hollow condolences and fake grief. I yank my sunglasses down, shielding my eyes as wetness pricks at the corners.

Jeanne offers a single white rose. I swallow hard, gently reaching for the stem and slowly twisting it—right, then left. Tanya claws at her neck, unsteady on her feet as she fights whatever demon she swallowed this morning. A cold snap rips through me as the wind forces a quick goodbye. Jeanne's hand lifts to my back, gently nudging me forward. I wiggle my right heel free, carefully stepping onto the balls of my feet as

I make my way forward, toward everything dead. The leaves, crisp and brown, that once had trees to hang from. Pale, lifeless faces of people he never knew. The stark, twisted branches of oak trees that scrape at a gray canvas sky. The pitters of rain that land with soft *thuds* into a muddy grave.

The treeline spins as something twists tight beneath my ribs.

Pastor Hill.

The casket.

Him.

The world stops. Wind stills. Leaves stick. Faces blur. I toss the single white rose into the earth as dirt swallows it whole. The gathered crowd slowly thins. I glance over my left shoulder. Wes stands dutifully, not far behind me.

"How long will you be in town?" a voice booms from my right.

I jump, fear twisting quickly into disdain. "Why the hell are you even here?" I snap.

His lips curl into a smile. A fucking smile.

"I attend the services of all the victims I work cases for," he replies. "Just paying my respects, Sawyer." His arms fold across his chest as his stance widens, like a wolf claiming its territory. Plotting. Scheming.

My eyes narrow as I pull the sunglasses from my nose, dangling them at my side now. "You worked this case?"

His chest puffs as a smug grin spreads across his face like wildfire. "Sawyer—I'm the lead detective on the force. Of course I worked the case."

Tightness pulls at my chest, and my heart slams against my ribs. I turn back toward the grave—two men quickly tossing mounds of dirt before the sky breaks loose again. My eyes squeeze shut.

"Bonfire out at Connersville tonight. You should come. You know—be around people. It'll be good for you."

I bite into my tongue. Hard. The taste of copper fills my mouth. Strands of black whip across my face as another gust of wind bites at my skin. "Don't count on it," I snip.

Silence. Only the *thud* of shovels, dirt piling high. I turn, jaw clenched, marching toward Wes as his gaze softens.

Chapter Four

With a population around twenty thousand, it's nearly impossible to go unrecognized in this town. Everyone knows everyone, and no matter how much time and distance I put between us, being here pulls me right back into the same tired stories and small-town gossip I tried to escape.

Connersville Road—this time of year nothing but dead earth, cow patties, and a gray December sky. I swallow, something coiling tight around my throat.

Jay attended the weekend debauchery over the last few months, often sharing his new adventures over lengthy phone calls as I held my tongue. The same assholes that turned their backs at school, suddenly embracing him as fall settled over the town.

I slam the car door shut behind me and head toward the centuries-old patch of oak trees that line the road. Carefully, I step over the low-lying fence, trudging forward as slick mud coats my boots like a paste. Music *booms* in the distance, leading me through the thick treeline as branches snap beneath my feet. Something scurries fast beneath a web of spanish moss. And I can almost swear that something else whispers my name.

Shrill laughter pierces the treeline as I push my way forward, through the footpath carved only from decades of teenage boredom. I pull my coat tightly around my chest, fastening one more button around my collar. My hands stuff deep into my pockets, joints aching with cold.

The familiar, old truck sits at the water's edge, its once-bright paint now faded under a patina of rust, each weathered scar telling stories of decades gone by. Most are gathered closely around the flames on a frame of thick logs used as makeshift seating while red plastic cups are passed between hands. Elizabeth Ryan's golden curls toss in the wind like a movie scene, her smile straight out of a toothpaste commercial as Carter Smith slips a hand between her thighs.

I stop sudden, drawing a slow breath as the treeline begins to spin again. Something pulls at my coat from behind. Pins me right here, the soles of my boots sinking slow into soft ground. Paranormal investigators say cold spots are evidence of ghosts. But this isn't cold. And it's not a ghost. It's *him*. It's his voice that whispers at my neck with warm breath. "I promise to find them. I promise to make them pay," I breathe, letting the words escape softly.

"Sawyer!" a voice rings out.

My eyes narrow into slits, combing the darkness as the figure settles into view. Beatrice Walker waves her hand high into the air, a wide smile flashing her perfectly straight teeth. Jay and I just called her *Birdie*. Named after her great-grandmother, she never did take to the classic southern name. That—and she gossips. A lot. But Birdie's sharp, cuts through the bullshit with ease, and for that, she's gold in my book. And perhaps her innate ability to know everyone, and everything, could prove useful. I push forward, my boots picking up speed as I bound toward Birdie's welcome wave.

Her arms reach around my neck, pulling me forward as she closes in on me. She squeezes tight enough to leave her fruit-scented perfume stuck in my hair. I give a few perfectly firm pats at her back. I mean, we were never close enough to cause this much of a scene. She finally releases me. I push out a breath.

"When did you get back in town?" she practically screeches.

"Oh—yesterday, I think." I blink, trying hard to sort out the days. "Yeah. Yesterday."

Her expression turns solemn, slurring as she concentrates carefully on each word. "Of course. I—I'm sorry, Sawyer. How could I be so thoughtless."

My gaze falls. I slowly roll a snapped twig beneath the toe of my boot.

Don't lose it, Sawyer. Not here. Not now.

"Want something to drink?" She gestures toward the cooler at her side, cracking open the top and revealing the ample supply of cheap beer and half-forgotten mixers. At least, enough to wipe them all out by midnight.

I lean forward, folding myself in half as I reach for a can, wincing as my palm wraps around icy metal. I need to play the part. Pretend to be their friend until they spill all of the secrets they hold tight. The tab *hisses* as I pull it back. I down the bitter stuff fast, face twisting before I muster a smile. "How have you been?" I ask, my cheeks burning as the wind slaps at my skin. I pull the hoodie of my coat up high onto my head, tucking my ears in tight for warmth. Birdie pulls the knitted cap from her head, strands of shimmering blue cascading over her shoulders. She quickly pulls another beer from the cooler, slamming the lid shut and throwing her arm behind my back. She gently guides me toward unfamiliar faces gathered on thick oak logs as the chill floods my veins.

We take a seat close to Elizabeth and Carter, with Wes lingering closely at their side. Birdie excitedly yaps about something in my ear—something about a runaway reindeer, cute guy in a reindeer costume or a reindeer that attacked a cute guy. I don't know. Hard to hear over the clattering of my own teeth in my skull. I rub my palms against my thighs as vapor curls from each breath.

My head snaps over my left shoulder, scanning the waterfront where only Colt stands, tossing rocks that skip across the surface of the old phosphate pit, now home to some of the best bass fishing around.

"Sawyer?"

My head whips right. Birdie stares blankly, awaiting my reply. "What?" I choke out.

"Were you not paying attention to anything I said?" she asks, twisting at a strand of freshly-dyed blue hair. She giggles. "Something up with you two?" She glances toward the water's edge.

"God no!" I huff in disgust, my head shaking right and left. "He's the same awful prick he's always been."

Her lips curl slightly, a mischievous look in her bright blue eyes. "He's hot, Sawyer. You can't deny that." Her eyes devour him like prey as my stomach churns.

"Hey, listen—I saw something." I pause, words sticking in my throat the moment I remember how she earned her name. Birdie's eyes grow wide as she leans in close. And Elizabeth practically climbs into Carter's lap now, the two locking lips like war-torn lovers. I toss back cheap beer, shifting my focus back to Jay and pulling a folded piece of paper from deep in the pocket of my coat. Carefully, I unfold it, smoothing out creases as I push it toward her hand. "Do you recognize any of those names?"

Her eyes scan the scribbled ink, a deep V forming between her brows. "Never seen them before."

A sigh slips out, and vapor curls into the air like a ghost. If Birdie's never seen those names, odds are no one has.

"Why do you ask?" she pushes.

"It's nothing." I shrug, quickly folding the paper again and stuffing it back into the coat.

Colt joins the group now, raking a hand through dark hair as he seats himself directly across the flames. All eyes turn toward him. Of course they do. I hate that he's so damn good-looking. Even more, I hate that he knows it.

"So, what are you up to these days?" I ask, steering Birdie's attention back to me.

"Oh! I'm the shift manager down at Coffee on Main—you should come in!" She grins widely. "I'm there Monday through Saturday every week."

Reluctantly, I return the smile, grateful for the warm welcome home. It's probably the only one I'll get. "Yeah. Sure. I'll stop in this week."

Her hands clasp together in excitement. It's genuine with Birdie. That's what makes her so well-liked. The girl could find a daisy in a pile of cow shit.

"You made it," his voice slides from above like honey poured over whiskey. My gaze shifts and pins to his. Chestnut eyes gleam with arrogance, and a checkered flannel shirt clings to his chest. He pushes a bottle of winter ale toward me. I take only seconds to consider it before practically ripping the beer from his hand.

"Thanks," I snip.

Birdie nervously glances between us before jumping to her feet. "Sawyer, I'll see you soon?"

"Yeah."

She takes off toward the inky treeline, joining a circle gathered just beyond where the light of the flames can reach.

Colt drops down onto the log beside me. My ass hurts. My hands hurt. And I'm quickly running out of patience. But impatience in this sleepy town will get you nowhere, like searching for sweet tea and cornbread in New York. "What are you even doing out here? Aren't you the law?" Sarcasm drips from my tongue—and there goes that smile again. I hate him. I hate him with every fiber of my being.

"I am." Sarcasm seeps through his lips. "But I'd much rather everyone have a safe spot to drink than spend the evening hauling everyone into the station."

I toss back the beer, but it does little to soothe against the biting cold.

"Come on Sawyer. You used to join us out here. You leave town and just, what—forget about all of us?"

"Tried to." I sink my right hand into my pocket, fingers gently grabbing at the only shred of truth that I have. The urge to question him itches at me. But, I don't trust him. Not even a little bit. I push the paper down into the fold again, peeling my hand out fast.

"Where are you staying while you're in town?" His hand drops to my thigh. My skin crawls in disgust. "Out at your mama's house?"

"It's really none of your business," I snap, leaning back and yanking my thigh from beneath his palm.

"God Sawyer, you still holding onto shit from a million years ago? We're not kids anymore." He pauses, waiting for a sign, a word, something. "I'm not here to hurt you."

I toss back the rest of my beer, rolling the tension from my neck. I slide the hoodie from my head again, the cold air like a slap. I start again. "I'm sorry—it's just weird being back."

He smells good. Like expensive cologne, the kind that smells like leather, bergamot and musk. God, I hate it.

His hand falls again to my thigh. I leave it there.

"Things have changed, Sawyer."

"Of course they have," I choke out.

"I didn't mean it like that," he replies, his voice deep and velvety, like a weighted blanket easing the tension from my chest.

"I know." My head snaps left, a half-hearted attempt to hide my tears.

His fingers brush at my ear, gently tucking wild strands of hair safely behind. Warmth slowly crawls, filling in the cracks and welcoming his touch. I push up from the tree trunk that's been my reluctant throne, and my right ass cheek tingles with pins and needles as I stumble to my feet. "I don't plan on staying long." Truth. Cold and simple. Because I *will* find the assholes that pushed Jay off that bridge if it kills me. And I'll do it with or without Colton Landry's help.

He reaches for my hand. My breath hitches, catches in my throat. And my lips tremble slightly as shrieks of laughter pierce the air. Probably just the cold. I pull my hand from his, quickly shoving the beer in its place.

"Mama's."

I don't know why I said it, why the word spilled out of my mouth. I don't want him around me. Colt Landry represents everything corrupt in this town, and I don't believe for a second that anything has changed.

An earth-shattering grin spreads like wildfire, his tongue skating over the corner of his lips. "Still out there off 555 and the old ball fields?" he asks.

"Don't get any ideas, Landry." I lean in close, stand on the tips of my toes to whisper in his ear. "Boys aren't invited to the sleepover."

"Oh, come on—" His hand flies to his heart. Feet stumble back. "You're breaking my heart."

My palm lifts to his arm, giving him a sharp shove out of the way. "I gotta go," I hiss, turning back toward the treeline to fumble my way back to the car.

"Careful, Sawyer," he calls out.

FALLING

His gaze presses into my back, his presence inescapable.

Chapter Five

My palms slide against the sheets. Legs stretch. Light spills from the curtains. Elbows dig into the mattress, dragging me upright inch by inch. I pull my knees close to my chest and wrap my arms tight. My eyes adjust. I rub at the crust in the corners. A *groan* rumbles from somewhere deep within my chest.

Salem pounces onto the bed, nuzzling into my shins.

"You hungry?" My fingers gently scratch at her head.

She *purrs* in reply.

A yawn rips out of me. Loud. Polite as a middle finger in church. "Okay girl—I'm coming, I'm coming."

I swing my legs to the side of the bed, my right foot landing squarely onto a box filled with junk. In my eyes, at least. I kick it aside. My feet land with a hard *thud* on cold tile. I shuffle toward the overnight bag, clothes spilling from the top like biscuit dough oozing out of one of those cans that damn near gives you a heart attack when it pops. My fingers find the wool socks I packed and toss them aside until I spot the cozy slippers buried at the bottom of the bag. I toss them onto the floor and slide my feet in, instant relief from the cold that nips at my toes.

The house is bright now, *too* bright, with memories of childhood rushing back like wildfire licking up dry grass. The same tired furniture in the same dusty corners, threadbare cushions with *groaning* springs beneath. No sign of Christmas. No balsam fir. No sparkling lights to fill the room.

Salem weaves at my feet—in and out—her tail flicking with impatient hunger.

The pantry door gapes open, and pure chaos spills from the shelves. My eyes flit. I push onto the balls of my feet, stretching high to grab a can of tuna mush that teeters off the edge of its shelf. The tab *pops* loud as Salem *meows* eagerly, the fishy aroma reeking like a bait shop dumpster in mid-July. I empty it into her bowl as she greedily laps up the sludge.

The coffee pot is full. I reach for a mug, quickly pouring enough caffeine to jolt me back to life. Hopefully. Steam curls, and the scent of burnt coffee beans slowly wraps around me. My nose twists. I yank open the refrigerator door, inspecting the shelves for creamer, or anything to sweeten the bitter stuff. Of course there's nothing but takeout leftovers and old, expired milk.

I shuffle toward the sliding glass doors, sliding the panel along the track and stepping onto the back porch. Cold slaps me across the face, a sharp sting that sends a chill crawling up my spine. But it's nothing compared to the gaze I feel locked on me now.

"How long are you planning on staying?" she asks, voice rough as gravel, tone like ice.

I toss the bitter black liquid down my throat. It swallows down like dirt, thick as regret. "Not long."

A cigarette dangles between her fingers, and smoke curls lazily into the air. The smell is nauseating. I cough into my fist, barely masking my disgust.

"I need that bedroom for storage," she snips.

"Didn't take you long to clear my things out, did it?" I fire back.

She lifts the cigarette to her lips, the ember flaring bright as she drags in another breath of nicotine death. Smoke spills between us now, settling like a wall...and a weapon.

"What did you think would happen, Sawyer?" she snaps. Loud enough to cut through the morning stillness. Loud enough for the neighbors to hear.

I swallow down more dirt.

"You left. Plain and simple. You don't get to just walk in here and expect things to be the same. Do you?" A huff escapes her chest as she presses back into her chair. "You can't be that stupid."

"I left because you couldn't be a mother!" I yell. Fuck the neighbors. Fuck their listening ears. Fuck this place. I gulp down the remaining coffee, dangling the empty mug at my side.

"Watch your tone," she warns. "I gave you everything you ever needed. I even quit smoking for you girls. Don't you ever forget that."

"You quit smoking for two years," I snap. "If that's all you've got, I feel sorry for you."

"What else did you want, Sawyer?"

I stare blankly, clawing at a piece of hair tickling at my ear. "Love." My eyes prick with wetness. I blink it away. "That's it."

She kills the last drag of her Marlboro incense, adding it to the bowl, ashes an inch deep. "You have until Christmas in this house. Do you understand?"

My jaw locks. Head drags right, then left. I slam the mug onto another box overflowing with a collection of cheap junk. "Don't worry. I could never spend another holiday in this house with *you*."

I storm toward the sliding glass door, fling it open and push inside. Blood rushing. Face turning red. Jaw clenched tight. The door slams hard behind me, rattling in its frame and sealing her away.

Whitewashed brick greets patrons under another dreary sky, a faded black awning shielding me from the steady pitter-patter of rain. I pull my coat tightly around my chest, dragging my muddy boots across cracked pavement beneath.

Blackwood Social sits at the corner of Broadway and Main, a bar that has changed ownership, and names, countless times over the decades. Across the street, the old courthouse, steeped in history, stands as a library and memorial to lives cut short. Out front, a sprawling oak tree looms, its gnarled branches a silent witness to the town's darkest sins.

I draw a slow breath in. It rattles. Unsteady on its feet. Slowly, I release it. A cloud of vapor curls from my lips. I shove the door open with a sharp push, the sudden rush of noise and light crashing over me like a tidal wave.

Inside, a fireplace glows, logs *hissing* and *popping* as its warmth creeps into my aching joints, stiff with a chill that no coat can fix. Music booms from the speakers in exaggerated country twang, with one lone day-drinking cowboy butchering karaoke, dragging each mangled note through whiskey-soaked air. Peanut shells litter the floor, metal-backed stools surround high-top tables, and Christmas lights in colorful hues cast a glow on shiplap walls. Scattered patrons devour french fries nestled into little newspaper boats, greedily licking salt from their fingertips. Another craft beer joint clinging to relevance. Another name destined to fade.

A woman tends the bar that lines the back wall, yellow hair pinned to the top of her head and sun-kissed wisdom caressing her skin. Another ragged breath and I lift my chin, heading straight in her direction.

11:00 AM. In a city that goes to bed early each night, businesses remain steady during the day. I pull out a bar stool as its metal rakes the floor like a petulant child. My arms wiggle free from the heavy coat, draping it across the back of the stool as I slide onto the hard, cold seat.

"What are ya havin' honey?" her voice croaks from behind the bar.

A name tag clings to her chest—*Penny*.

A yawn slips through. I couldn't spend another minute in that house this morning, and so I sat quietly by Jay's grave, spending the hours watching raindrops sink into freshly piled dirt. My stomach rumbles. Cold lingers in my fingertips.

"Whiskey," I reply.

"Neat or on the rocks?"

I blink. I don't drink whiskey. Never have. But, I believe rocks are ice, and neat is nothing but a slow burn that will ease every ache, every horrible memory, from your bones. "Neat."

"You want anything from the lunch menu?"

My bottom lip pulls into my teeth, mouth watering as the scent of meat and mushrooms fills the air. "I'll have a burger. Medium-well."

"I'll get that right in for ya. Give us about fifteen minutes." Penny quickly gets to work, filling glasses with fizzing soda and one lowball whiskey for me. She slides the glass across the weathered wood, now slick with lacquer, and I catch it with ease, throwing it back fast to dull the jittery ache settled in my gut.

Fear and alcohol kind of go hand in hand. You can be drunk on both, just the same—but only one can soothe the soul, being just the tonic that restless bones need.

Metal scrapes to my left. Deafening. Uncomfortable. I turn. His tongue pushes into his cheek, arrogance gleaming in his eyes.

My eyes roll back. "Now, to what do I owe the pleasure? Funny how I seem to run into you everywhere that I go."

A cocky grin spreads slowly, his eyes never wavering from mine. "Maybe it's destiny. Written in the stars." He chews at a piece of gum in the back of his teeth.

"Or maybe you're just bored and need something to do." I toss back more liquid death. "Don't you ever work? Aren't you the town sheriff or something?"

His stupid grin grows wider. "Detective, Sawyer."

"Whatever."

He slides onto the seat beside me, waving a finger in the air to capture Penny's attention. Ringlets of yellow have already slipped from their pins as she rushes to serve greasy patties and ice-cold beers to wide eyes and watering mouths.

"Make yourself comfortable," I snip. I rake my fingers through dampened strands of black, wishing I had waited another hour by the grave.

"You know, Sawyer—I'm not the enemy here. You can talk to me."

Colt shrugs off his blazer, revealing a fitted black shirt stretched over a defined chest. His badge gleams in the glow of Christmas lights strung across the walls. Four walls. Closing in. Suffocating me inch by inch. I look away, slowly swirling the whiskey in my glass, watching it circle and crash like ocean waves against the rim. Colt clears at his throat to my left. I toss back the smooth and oaky drink, drowning out thoughts I don't want to face.

Penny returns with one mouth-watering burger basket in one hand, one newspaper boat of fries in the other. My spine straightens eagerly as she slides greasy perfection my way. Her elbows land on the bar. She slides forward, cleavage flashed at Colt like bait on a hook. "Handsome, you havin' lunch today?" she asks. Her voice is different now. Smoother. Silkier. Drips like honey down your throat.

Colt entertains her advances, giving a disgusting wink and that devastating smile. "You know what—I think I will." His head whips toward me, that smug, cocky grin still plastered across his face. His gaze locks with mine. "I'll have what Sawyer here ordered."

"Whiskey too, honey?"

His gaze breaks. Finally. "Yes, ma'am."

Penny straightens, quickly getting back to work, half her hair now falling loose.

"How do you do it, Landry?" My lips pull tight, head shaking in disbelief. "How do you manage to fit through the door with a head that damn big?"

His palms slap onto the bar, a low chuckle grumbling from his chest. His chest muscles flex against the fabric. I shift away, unable to mask my face twisting with irritation.

"Come on, Sawyer. No more games." He holds up two fingers into the air. "Scout's honor."

I turn back. His grin fades gradually, his features softening under the dim glow of light. Stubble frames a sculpted jaw, and clean lines reveal just how much time this man spends perfecting the reflection in the mirror.

"You were never a Boy Scout, Landry. And it's three fingers. Not two."

"You're right." He leans back, resting an elbow onto the barstool back. Smirking. He spins abruptly until his badge locks eyes with me. "But I do respect them a lot."

"You might have been a grade ahead of me, but I've known you since we were kids. I know more about you than you think, Landry. Unfortunately."

His fingers brush at my ear again as he tucks a loose strand behind.

"That might work on other women, but it won't work with me," I snip.

I focus solely on the burger now, stomach rumbling again as grease and salt taunt at my nose. One thick patty piled high with all the fixings. Bacon, lettuce, and tomato. Much too big to fit into my hands. I wrap my fingers around it as best I can, savagely sinking in teeth like a lion to its kill.

"I'm not playing any games with you, Sawyer. Believe what you want, but you're a very beautiful woman. Every head in this bar steals glances your way when you aren't paying attention."

I soften. My resolve. My anger.

"Why are you all damp anyway?" he asks. "Don't you own an umbrella?"

I place the burger into the basket again, grabbing a thin napkin to wipe the grease from my fingertips. It shreds in my hands. "I went to the grave this morning." I press my spine into the chair back, waving the white flag between us.

Penny slides another whiskey in front of Colt. He doesn't move this time.

"Sawyer, why are you torturing yourself? You have to let him go."

"No!" My hands fall to my lap, gaze follows next. "No," I whisper. "I can't."

He reaches for the glass of whiskey, throwing it back in one fell swoop. My gaze shifts to the wall behind the bar, a mirror catching my reflection. I shift away. The woman who stares back unrecognizable now.

"Alright."

I meet his gaze head on now. Confused at the sudden shift in the air. "Alright? That's it?"

"That's it," he confirms. "I know he was your best friend. I know. As much as any other guy wanted you, they were never going to win."

"Please," I scoff. "What other guy ever wanted me?"

The corner of his lip curls, that hint of his golden boy smile returning. "I did."

"Don't be ridiculous, Landry. I'm not in the mood." I dive into the burger again, tomatoes slipping from the grease.

"I'm serious, Sawyer. I wouldn't joke with you about that. Promise."

Penny returns, sliding another tasty burger Colt's way. My resolve melts. I don't have the energy anyway.

"Landry—" I begin, words dying as quickly as they came. I reach for the newspaper boat of fries and stuff one in my mouth. The salt hits sharp on my tongue.

"Ellis—" he says, voice deep like velvet.

It eases something inside of me. Maybe it's just the whiskey. Probably. I swallow, let my hands fall back to my lap.

"Spit it out already," he pushes.

I wipe my fingertips onto the fabric of my jeans, grease stain forming at the knee, and shove my hand deep into the coat pocket behind me. I pull the crumpled paper, quickly unfolding it before I change my mind. I push it toward him. "Do you recognize any of the names?" I swallow at the lump of regret that already sticks in my throat. "Usernames. They have to mean something."

Colt takes the crumpled paper from my hands, his tongue skating over his bottom lip as he scans the page. He clears at his throat. "Nope. Not a clue." He pushes the paper back toward me now. I carefully fold it back like some creased gospel, a holy manuscript.

"That's it? Aren't you a detective?"

"What's so important, Sawyer? Why are you still here? Everyone knows you couldn't wait to get out of this town. He's gone. Now look,

I know you're having a rough time with that, but you've got to let him go. For your own sanity."

"Something doesn't add up," my mouth vomits before I can blink. "Someone gave me the names and said they had something to do with Jay. Before he died." I pick at a cuticle on my left hand. A little white lie can't hurt. I need Colt on my side, unfortunately. I'm sure there has to be some police database that he can search.

"Sawyer—"

I meet his gaze. He looks at me with pity now. Everyone does.

"At least try to get out and enjoy yourself while you're back home. I know this shit has your head spinning in circles. I can see it. But none of this is going to bring him back."

My lips pull tight. I can't trust him. Not yet. "You're right," I lie.

His eyes widen in disbelief. "That's it? No smart ass remarks? You're slippin' Ellis."

"I'm tired." And I am. But I won't stop. With or without him.

I push at the basket—half eaten burger still inside. I don't have time for this, every second here a waste. I wave my hand high into the air, desperate to grab Penny's attention.

"I've got it," Colt orders. "Go rest. Try to enjoy your time home. It's almost Christmas for God's sake."

A smile gently pulls at my cheeks, grateful for the offer. "Alright."

I reach for my coat, slipping my arms back inside as I head toward Main Street, toward the lingering ghost that watches as I desperately search for answers.

48

Chapter Six

Last week of eighth grade. The heat is heavy. Oppressive. Each breath drags slow through my chest. The porch fan spins above but barely helps. And a box fan that I dug out of the junk pile in the garage whirs loudly behind the screened porch door. I think it belonged to Grams. Mama was in a hurry to clean Gram and Poppy's house after they died, and threw most everything they had into a big mound.

A blister bubbles underneath my right foot. The porch boards are hot enough to fry an egg on, but the strap on my sandal snapped this morning, so bare feet it is.

I wiggle my toes. The shirt I wore to school is untucked, the cotton fabric drenched as it plasters to my back. I settle into the old rocking chair, stretching until my heels rest on the wooden rail. I pop open the cold can of soda in my hand.

I rock slow as the chair practically groans beneath me. Salem, my new friend, lies curled in my lap, faint purrs humming like a sweet song. One paw slightly twitches in her sleep.

"You always sit out here like that?" a voice calls from the end of the driveway.

I don't flinch. Recognize the voice as he slowly makes his way toward the porch.

"Most days," I call back.

"Tried to catch you on the way from school, but guess I just missed you. Wanted to see how the cat is doing, that's all."

He reaches the steps that lead up to the porch and stops suddenly, glancing down to kick a small pebble out of the way. His glasses slide down his nose. He takes them off, gives his face a quick wipe with the hem of his shirt, then places them back on. He seems nervous. Chews on his bottom lip.

"Wanna come up?"

He nods and makes his way up the steps, winding past me and Salem, letting his backpack fall with a *thud* as he plops down at my side.

"How's the stray?" he asks, nodding at the ball of fur sleeping in my lap. "I take it you two are getting along okay?"

"Well—she eats a lot. Mama was pretty mad at first, but I think she kinda likes Salem now," I say, gently rubbing behind the cat's ears.

"Salem? That it's name?" he asks. "Isn't that for boys?"

I clear at my throat before correcting him. "It's *gender neutral.* Besides, there's no rules when it comes to animal names. You could literally name a dog Salami Face and no one would care."

"Justice McFur," he adds.

"Bagel Lord," I joke.

"Dumpster Dan," he grins. "You know, because he eats everything like a dumpster?"

"Glen" I say. "No wait...Todd. Todd is much better."

Our eyes meet. His glasses slide down again. Laughter finally bubbles to the surface, hearty and full.

"Okay, but now I need to meet a lizard named Todd," he giggles.

"Or a fish named Craig," I toss in, lips pulling tight as I narrow my eyes onto him. "What's *your* name, anyway?"

"Jay."

"I'm just Sawyer," I shrug. "Nothing as cool as Salami Face."

"Well, I think Sawyer is very pretty."

I pull my knees to my chest and wrap my arms tight. I'm not sure if he meant the name or me.

"School should be illegal when it reaches triple digits," he continues. "I mean, other schools have snow days. We could literally burn alive."

I put on my best Principle Cooper face. Hold a finger in the air. "To be successful at life, one must begin early." My hand flies over my heart. "Creating a path of discipline and dedication to achieve all dreams."

He smacks at my arm. Salem snorts and lifts her tiny head for a moment before curling up tight again.

"I think Mr. Cooper has heatstroke," he continues. "Told me I was insightful today."

"Guess we're all hallucinating now," I say.

His head jerks sudden. Eyes widen. "You going to the dance thing on Friday?" he asks eagerly. "Last one of the year."

Something about that word settles heavy and thick. Dance. "God, no. Sounds like my version of hell."

"Cool." He smiles as he replies. "I thought I was the only one with taste."

"Of course, I'll miss Coach Tate throwin' it back in those God-awful pants," I laugh. "Or Ms. Cole watching everyone with her nose all scrunched up like this." I wrinkle my nose tight, crinkling it into tiny cracks as he smiles along.

"You know, she told me I write like someone twice my age," he interrupts. "I'm not sure if she meant genius or mid-life burnout."

"Probably both," I answer.

"Figures," he smirks.

A dog barks somewhere down the block. And the sun sinks lower, practically beating on our skin and boiling us alive.

"You're weird," he says.

My eyes flit to his, not sure how to take it. He stares down, playing with the stitching of his shoelace.

"You're sweating through your eyebrows," I add.

He looks up. Our eyes finally meet. His lips pull at his cheeks. So do mine.

"Hey—" he begins, wiping away a bead of sweat that trickles down. "You know, I have a pool at home."

"Congratulations," I add, letting my head fall and rest onto the back of the chair.

"I meant...you should come over sometime and swim. My grandparents don't mind. Honestly, they'll just be happy that someone's using it."

Salem twitches, then rises to her tiny paws and jumps toward Jay, landing squarely in his lap.

"She likes you," I say.

We don't talk much more. Just rock and sweat and sigh. Occasionally complain. But it's comfortable. Hard to explain.

"I'm getting a car next year," he blurts suddenly. "Nothing new. Just an old Caddy my grandfather used to drive. But it's clean. Paint looks good as new."

My shoulders fold into themselves. "My Daddy was supposed to teach me how to drive." I claw at damp tendrils that stick like paste to my temple. "He kinda left, though. And I don't think Mama will."

"I can teach you," he offers, voice rising with excitement.

"Really?"

"How about driving lessons every Saturday this summer?" he asks.

"Sure," I say.

"But *only* if you stay and swim after."

I grin wide. A breeze blows through the porch, whispering against damp skin like the sky changed its mind. Happens a lot during sticky Florida afternoons.

"Okay. You've got a deal."

Marble statuesque lions flank heavy, wooden doors, their stone eyes unblinking as electric neon hums from above. I pull my coat tightly around my chest, my boots stuck to the pavement below. The rain has brought an unsettling cold, a suffocating chill that blankets over the town as fireplaces roar behind shuttered windows. I blink. Footsteps approach from behind. Fast. Too close A force brushing my shoulder, leaving me unsteady on my feet. Slurred, rowdy voices slice through the air, my face contorts as irritation bubbles beneath my skin and a pack of men hurry toward the doors.

"Sorry," a man calls over his shoulder. Dismissive and hollow.

I shift my weight from the right boot to the left, folding my arms across my chest and rubbing at my arms for warmth. The doors swing open. Music spills onto the pavement.

County Line Road stretches exactly eight miles. It's just a vast wasteland of empty warehouses and stalled construction. I suppose that's exactly what draws in oversexed teens hiding from watchful eyes. To my right, a scrapyard of gutted cars dumped for parts. To my left, a light flickers, casting shadows on a weathered cross. A shiver wracks my spine. My teeth clench against the cold.

"You coming, miss?" a deep voice booms from just within the opened doors.

I swallow down a bitter warning, sharp as broken glass, as my heels finally lift from the pavement.

The doors slam shut behind me, sealing me in a neon tomb. The air is thick with smoke and heat, and steady bass blares from speakers across the bar. Deafening. *Almost* drowning out the group of rowdy bachelors gathered by the stage.

The Honey Trap, the only gentleman's club close to town, has been in existence since before I was born. A family affair, I suppose. My mother, a dancer to help pay the bills through nursing school. My father, one of the club's finest patrons.

I rake the barstool across the floor, sliding onto the seat and peeling my arms from my coat. I drape it over the back, ignoring uncomfortable stares from the right.

"You drinking tonight?"

A tight-fitting shirt features a silhouette of exaggerated female cuves, the body glistening in thick drops of honey that seem to pool at the hem. Ill-fitting lingerie barely covers her bottom—legs shifting slightly for warmth. She teeters toward me, legs trembling like a fawn on heels much too high.

"I'll just have a beer. Whatever's on draft is fine," I shout over bass that rattles the walls.

A man slithers onto the seat beside me. Old. Liquor hanging from his breath. I ignore him, fixing my gaze straight ahead.

"Let me get that for you, sweetheart," his voice croaks from my right.

My lips pull tight, heat crawling up the back of my neck in utter disgust. I turn. "Go back to your cave," I hiss.

His face flickers, shock, then something darker. "You fucking bitch," he snaps.

My eyes roll back as he climbs off the stool, shoving the chair hard and heading toward whatever dark corner he crawled from.

The bartender slides a foaming glass of amber in front of me, sympathy glistening in her eyes. "Ignore him. He's in here almost every night. If he gets too rowdy, Tank'll throw him out."

My chin shifts to the left, eyes landing again on the large man in a suit, a thick-necked menace, arms crossed, guarding the entrance like a bank vault.

A muffled DJ yells into a microphone, voice nearly swallowed by the screech of electric guitar. I spin on my seat. A dancer enters sultrily on the lit stage, grinning wide as the bachelors cause a scene, raising crinkled bills high into the air. A weight presses on my ribs, emptiness slowly creeping in. I spin back toward the bar, greedily gulping back watered-down beer, the foam gently tickling at my lips. My eyes shut tight, forcing out every uncomfortable memory, every sound. The ringing, though—it stays. A steady chorus, a deafening sound I can't seem to shake.

I throw back the beer now. Cold going down, before the slow burn settles in. The kind that makes bad decisions sound good. I lick the foam from my lips and slam the glass onto the counter, bar sealed under plexiglass, a graveyard of dollar bills scrawled with confessions and Polaroids yellowed with time.

Drunken cheers erupt as the group of bachelors roar their approval behind me. I turn to find the dancer now crouched as they shove dirty money her way, fingers lingering way too long, eyes roaming everywhere but her face. A loud sigh slips out as I slide myself from the seat, boots scraping against the floor. I reach deep into my coat pocket, pull out wadded-up bills and toss them onto the bar. I move toward the stage, steps careful and deliberate, following the dancer's glassy-eyed stare as she disappears behind thick, smoke-stained curtains.

To my left is an office where a man with stringy hair shuffles papers and puffs on a cigar. To my right, excited chatter filters through a slightly cracked door. I shift, chin high and eyes forward.

No one turns. A man with arched brows and defined lips lightly dusts glitter onto a dancer's shoulders as hushed whispers hang from their lips. Another woman sits on the floor, only a strip of black fabric barely covering her hips as she claws at stiff, hairsprayed curls.

I scan the room. Lockers line a narrow, dark hallway to my right, familiar features peeking through shadows as high heels *tap* across the floor. My boots stick like glue, irritation bubbling as breaths stutter up my throat. Old memories flooding back fast. Unease settling heavy in my gut. I push off the toes of my boots, forcing myself toward the dim hallway.

Her gaze, expressionless and flat, stares straight as she fumbles with a stubborn lock. I clear at my throat. Her head snaps toward me, gaze sharp with hate.

"What are you doing here, Sawyer?" she asks, my name like shards of glass in her mouth. Familiar grayish-blue eyes stare back. The same as mine. The same as Mama's.

"I'm not staying," I bite back. "Don't worry."

"Then why in the fuck are you here?"

The floor slightly tilts. Faces blur around me. "Jay. The funeral was Saturday."

Her features soften. Only a bit. Only for a second. It quickly dies. "So why are you still here? And what the hell do you want from me?"

Skylar and I both grew up in Mama's house. She was older, a few grades ahead, a fact that she never let me forget. But aside from the blood in our veins and Mama's cold blue eyes, there isn't much else we have in common.

"Could you at least put a shirt on?" I hiss.

"They're tits, Sawyer. Get over yourself."

Frustration gnaws at me, and I gnaw at my cuticle. I knew better than to drive out here, knew better than to expect anything from blood. "Something happened with Jay."

"I know, Sawyer. Literally, everyone knows."

"No," I argue, my head shaking left and right. My chest tightens as my gaze flits to the floor, waiting out the spinning of dirty tiles as I steady my trembling knees. "He didn't jump, Skylar."

A laugh escapes her throat. Ugly. Taunting. "God, you are still the same. Never change. Nothing but drama with you." Hostility cuts through her contoured cheeks and harshly lined lips. "*You* are the reason Daddy left. And *you* are the reason Mama was left alone."

"That isn't fair," I choke out. "You know I couldn't stay. You know how she treated us."

"She was hurt because of you. Because you couldn't keep your mouth shut and leave well enough alone."

Tears sting at the corners of my eyes, her words a dagger, blade hovering mere inches from my chest. Sisters by the blood in our veins only, strangers in every other sense. "You left, too, Skylar," I protest. "You can't possibly blame me."

"I had a baby, Sawyer. Christ, I have a whole family to think about now. I don't have time for your bullshit anymore."

Her gaze falls flat, like she lost all fucks for the family she once had. She turns back to the locker, fumbling again until the lock finally *clicks*. Useless. That's all this was. A wasted trip, and even more wasted pleas.

"My bullshit?" I scoff under my breath, cheeks flushing hot. "You have a *worthless* man at home that lets you work as a stripper to pay *his* bills. Now, that's bullshit, Skylar."

I don't feel bad. I don't have remorse because it's true. Shawn knocked her up at only seventeen, dragging her into the same dead-end trap so many others fall into. He's nothing but a bum. The kind of father who thinks watching his own kids is babysitting, who expects a hot meal on the table the second he walks through the door.

Her head snaps toward me, daggers shooting my way now. "Get out."

I meet her stare head-on as I shake with disbelief, fists clenching and trembling at my sides. Copper spills into my mouth. My teeth sink into my tongue.

"Get. Out." Her lips tighten as she raises her arm and points a finger at the door. "Do not come back. I don't want anything to do with you ever again. In fact, no one does."

My body shakes, heart thrashes violently against my ribcage. I shove my fists deep into the coat pockets as I storm back across the dressing room and push a shoulder into the door. Heat crawls from my feet to my neck, searing slowly as it rises to the surface like something unearthed from the grave.

Chapter Seven

Just a few short blocks from the historical courthouse sits the police station, a mid-century concrete fortress, a hundred years of grime ground into its bones. A wall of raw concrete, jutted pebbles catching the light, tinted glass doors with a worn mat beneath, surrounding palm trees and brown grass clinging to life.

I've never stepped inside, though I know everyone well. At least Mama does. A wind gust pricks at my skin, needling beneath my coat. I shift my weight, rock right then left, swallowing down sandpaper in my throat.

A glass door swings open hard—and a woman in a fitted suit brushes past, her heels like a metronome down the steps. I twist. My head snaps over my shoulder as she disappears down Broadway Avenue. So put together, so polished. A far cry from my tangled hair, stained jeans, and scuffed military boots worn thin from years of wear.

I face forward, fingers raking through strands of black in a losing fight with the wind. An icy hand closes around the cold metal bar as I push my way inside.

Inside is cold. Sterile. Like the break room of a place you'd never want to work. A simple blue desk sits below a bullet proof window, glossed terrazo stretches throughout, and a single strand of garland, lit with colorful holiday lights, frames the room in bleak holiday cheer. I push through the faint scent of disinfectant and boredom, toward the smudged frame of glass.

Sherry Kirkland sits behind the window, shoveling yogurt into her mouth with her lunchbag spilled open at her side. Empty wrappers litter over weathered pine.

Sherry was friends with Mama. Something like a million years ago. Two friends who went to nursing school together, only one able to handle needles and blood. I used to hear stories of wild nights and innocent fun. But that was before everything changed. Before the light drained from Mama's eyes, leaving Skylar and I broken and alone.

She looks up, sliding the glass window open as she gulps down curdled milk. "Sawyer? What are you doing back in town?" she asks.

"I need to see the Chief," I blurt out, voice echoing off freshly painted white walls.

"Everything okay, honey? Your mama alright?" she asks, thick sludge creating a resounding *glurp* in her throat.

"Mama's fine. I just need to speak with someone in charge, that's all. Please. It's important."

She wipes greasy fingers onto the fabric of her dress, swiftly reaching for the handle of a glossy, outdated phone. Decades of secrets. Heavy, hidden, and humming on the line.

Sherry turns, spinning out of view as she mutters something under her breath. My gaze shifts to the weathered toes of my boots. My right shoelace is untied, the fabric coated in grief-soaked earth fresh from Jay's grave. My heel taps at the speckled floor as heat whispers up my neck. I slide my arms from the thick coat, making my way toward the uncomfortable folding chairs lined against the wall. I sling the heavy coat aside and sink fast into the chair. Sherry leans forward, yellowed curls falling beyond the window frame, phone dangling from her hand.

"The Chief isn't in right now, but they're gonna send someone out to get 'ya," she offers, lips pulling with quiet pity, skin crinkling around her eyes.

I nod, brief and silent, slight satisfaction filling my chest. My fingers lace together in my lap, and my eyes scan the cold, cramped room. A heavy blue door secures uniformed officers beyond, and only a small diamond of glass gives a glimpse of whatever's behind. Along the far wall, a heavy oak shelf displays years of awards, their plaques coated in dust with time.

I stretch, heels protesting against the speckled gloss in loud, echoed *squeaks*. Too sharp. Too loud. My head falls back onto the sterile wall as I rest my eyelids. Heat spills through me, wrapping tight, burning to the tips of my ears. I rub at my palms, now sticky and fevered with the knuckles turning white.

Footsteps thunder down the hallway, just beyond the locked blue door. They pause briefly as a loud *buzz clicks,* and Wes barrels through the door, green shirt crisp with perfect creases, badge gleaming in flourescent light. My spine straightens as a breath eases out and my shoulders fall with relief.

"Sawyer—everything okay? Did something happen?"

His cheeks are blushed from the heat that spills from the lobby vents, his eyes clouded with concern.

"Wes, I need to talk to the Chief. It's about Jay," I plea, my voice cracking as his name tumbles out.

He slides onto the chair beside me, palm finding the small of my back. White walls spin. Heat closes in tight.

"The case was closed, Sawyer. I know it's hard to let him go, but we did everything we could."

His palm rubs in small circles. Too close to my skin. And too long. I flinch, shifting my weight toward the empty chair on my left.

"I have evidence, Wes." I reach for the pocket of my coat, slung across the chair back now, my fingers finding the neatly folded paper and swiftly pulling it out. I unfold the careful creases and practically shove it toward him now. "Look. These names—they were there. That night. They were all there."

His eyes widen, his weight shifts back.

"Please Wes...let me talk to the Chief."

He stands, and his head gives a subtle nod toward the painted blue door. He lifts his arm, curling his fingers into his palm as he gestures for me to follow. "Come on."

My legs straighten slow, knees trembling in fear. I've got one shot. One final plea for help. I can't do this alone. I draw a slow breath, following close behind as we enter a fluorescent-lit hall. More sterile walls. More locked doors. Wes glances over his shoulder, nodding as he confirms that I'm still behind. My boots echo off the pristine floors as we turn another corner. A broken water fountain, push plate jammed so it never shuts off. A watercolor painting of Peace river. More plaques that commemorate years of service lining another wall. Toward the end, an open door. A chance to make things right.

He looks up from behind the desk, a mess of papers jumbled in his hands.

"Fuck. Not you." A sigh barrels from my chest, shoulders drop with defeat. I glance toward Wes now, standing wide-eyed with his mouth agape. "I asked for the Chief. Not *him*."

A throat clears. My gaze shifts.

"Sawyer, the Chief isn't in today. There's a press conference across the street at noon. You know...important matters," he mutters, sharp and dismissive. He shuffles papers around as he pushes back in his chair, lacing his fingers behind his head like he's bored.

I slam the creased paper down onto the desk, a resounding *smack* echoing down the hallway. My fists curl at my sides, anger seething in my chest.

"Sit down, Sawyer." His features soften, the deep V between his brows disappearing from sight. "Take a breath."

I yank the chair back, sliding onto the seat as a sliver of something like hope seeps back into my lungs.

"Wes—give us a minute," he orders, head nodding toward the open door.

"No," I interrupt. "He stays."

Silence. Then widened eyes. Colt obviously struggles with defiance. Always has. Wes takes the seat to my left as his labored breaths pulse against the bulletproof vest.

"Alright. Let's hear it," he says, voice soothing and soft as he rests his elbows on top of the desk.

I nod toward the scribbled ink as the words come tumbling out, like the contents of my stomach after eating bad fish. "Those names—usernames, game handles, whatever they are—admitted to killing Jay. I saw it. It wasn't an accident, Colt." My fingers lace in my lap, gaze shifting down as a whisper chokes out now. "He didn't jump."

Silence passes between us as a steady beat thumps from above. Fan blades spin in circles, like an injured dog chasing its tail. Goosebumps prick at my skin. A jolt of something electric rockets up my spine.

"Say something—someone," I plead.

Another throat clear. Colt lifts the paper, briefly scanning over the names. I can almost swear his lips pull into a goddamn smirk as Wes shifts uncomfortably in his seat.

"Where did you see this?" he asks.

"I—" I sink back in defeat. "I don't know. It disappeared."

"Sawyer, what am I supposed to do with this?"

"You're *supposed* to re-open the case!" I shout, my cheeks flushing red with heat. "Don't you hear what I'm telling you? You're a fucking detective! I'm telling you he was pushed. Why is no one listening to me?"

His palms lift in defense. His head shakes with disbelief. "You need to calm down and take a deep breath."

"Do *not* tell me to calm down," I snap through clenched teeth. "My best friend was murdered. And the very people that were supposed to protect him, who took an oath to keep this town safe, simply gave up. *You* gave up." My gaze shifts left. "Wes?"

"I—" he stammers.

His shoulders rise and fall, his plump cheeks blushed with regret. Frustration gnaws in my gut as Jay's voice whispers up my neck.

"The case was closed. You have to let it go, Sawyer. You're trying to stir up trouble, and if you don't lower your voice in this office, I'll have to escort you out," Colt says coldly.

Fingers curl again, knuckles turning white. Rage stirs beneath my ribs, every destructive impulse now boiling over the pot. My fists slam onto the scattered papers and files.

"You will do everything except for your job, Colt!" My screams echo loud as curious footsteps rush toward the door. "Jay was murdered and you closed the case! Look at that paper—" my voice quiets with a desperate plea as my finger taps at the page. "They did it."

"Sawyer—" he warns, "get your hands *off* the desk."

My hands fall again, twitching at my sides, trembling knees beneath. Heat spills to my ears, and my pulse thrashes beneath my skin. "Or what—"

"Escort her out," he orders Wes, any remnant of compassion completely drained from his eyes.

"Come on Sawyer," Wes soothes. "Let's go."

My jaw loosens in utter disbelief, wetness pricks and trickles hot down my cheek. "I can't believe you." My head shakes. Shoulders fall with defeat. "Actually, you know what? I can. You're still the same piece of shit you were in high school, only now you have that *fucking badge*."

"Get her out," his voices booms like thunder. "Now."

I rip the paper from the desk and stuff it deep into my coat. Wes grips at my elbow and leads me back toward the door. One last glance, and I yank my arm from his grasp, storming toward the fortress walls outside.

My elbow slams into the door as everything spills out of me, gasping for a breath of air as tears finally release. It all floods like a dam breaking loose. Sorrow. Frustration. Gnawing defeat. I slump onto the top step, arms resting heavy on my knees, burying my face in my hands. I let it all loose. All of it. Raw, loud, and ugly. A damn pitiful sight for anyone passing by.

"Sawyer—come on, I can't stand seeing you like this."

I lift my head, face red-streaked and swollen, desperately crying for help. "Why isn't he listening, Wes? He was murdered and no one fucking cares."

His palm rubs circles onto my back again, comforting, soothing, warmth radiating with every gentle motion.

"Here—" he reaches for my coat. "Put this on before you freeze to death."

I slide my arms in, lean my head into his uniformed chest.

"If you can give him something, anything, then maybe we could look into it. But a paper with scribbled names, Sawyer—" he sighs, draping an arm across my shoulders and pulling me in tight. "We just can't do anything with that. I'm sorry. I know that's not the answer you wanted."

My nose sniffles, cheeks sting from the cold. "I know."

"You need rest, Sawyer. Have you had any sleep since you've been home?"

I pull away from him now, swiping at my tear-streaked face. "Not really. Not much."

"You need to take care of yourself. You can't help anyone if you run out of steam," he soothes.

"You don't think I'm crazy?"

A low chuckle escapes from his chest. "Well, Sawyer...I definitely think you're crazy."

My face twists. A flash of something close to hurt sneaks through before I can slam it back down. I know he's only joking, but it still stings sharper than I want to admit.

"Come on now, I'm only teasing you. Give us something to work with, and I promise...we'll do everything we can to help." His palm ruffles at my tangled hair as his lips curl into a smile. "Besides, if you don't get off these steps, I might have to arrest you for loitering. And that comes with a pretty hefty fine."

My eyes pinch at the corners as a laugh tumbles out and startles us both. The first in a long while. I almost forgot what it feels like.

He rises to his feet, offering a hand between us. I reach. Grateful. That's three times now he's pulled me back from the edge.

"Go on, now."

I manage a half-smile, the best I've got. It's all I can give. My legs move now, fast and determined down the pavement. A no-fail mission stretching out ahead.

FALLING

Chapter Eight

My palms slide against the crumpled sheets, my body drenched, sweat coating my skin like sticky morning dew. I throw back the bedding, stretching my legs out long. Darkness pins to the window, a chorus of crickets screaming a sermon just beyond the glass. Mama never could stand the cold, and she always ran the heat non-stop if it ever dropped below 70 degrees. A *groan* churns from somewhere deep. Steeped in exhaustion.

I managed a few hours of sleep, at least enough to keep me going another day. But without the help of Wes or Colt, I'm just not sure where to turn next.

I'm trying, Jay. Please—give me something. Anything.

A shadow moves just beyond the bedroom door, only the slight glow of a candle left burning to dimly light the hall.

"Salem?"

A *meow* stirs at my feet. Her tiny paws kneading like a baker handling dough as her eyes glow green and her tail flicks with satisfaction.

"There you are, girl."

I rise on the bed, peeling the damp flowered sheets from my body in some urgent need to escape. Mama stirs in the kitchen. Her slippers shuffle loud across the floors. My fingers reach for the nightstand, slipping my phone from the scuffed pine. 8:45 PM. Another restless night filled with anything but sleep.

It takes approximately ten minutes to travel from one side of town to the other, and if I hurry, I can make it with plenty of time before close. I shift, throwing my legs over the side of the bed and jumping to my feet. Carefully, quietly, I tip toe toward the strewn pile of clothes in the corner, sliding each leg into warm denim, with a thick, cable-knit sweater pulled over my head. I stumble left, then straighten again. This house feels like a black hole, time stopped, slowly pulling until I'm stretched too thin.

I push toward the foyer, taking careful steps to avoid another fight. Light spills from the kitchen, and her voice grates like a fork dragging across a porcelain plate. Impossible to ignore.

"You just gonna come and go as you please?"

A heavy sigh spills from my mouth. I spin fast on my heels as heat spreads quicker than fire ants in summer grass. "I didn't know I still needed your permission. I've lived on my own for almost four years now, Mama. When will you treat me like an adult?" I flinch at my outburst. Hate that I'm letting her win.

"When you start acting like one. And as long as you stay in my house, I expect to know when you come and go," she barks. Her voice a low, almost guttural growl.

"I told you...I'm not staying long."

Her gaze pins to me now, cigarette dangling in her hand. A phlegmy, crackling sound escapes her throat. I stop. For just a moment. Wondering if she is okay.

"I'm just visiting an old friend. I swear. We just want to catch up for a few days," I reply, offering an unspoken truce.

Her gaze could turn a person to stone. A deep V cuts between her brows, her words like a warning. "Lock the door behind you."

I turn, her stare climbing my back, cold and deliberate. An invisible tether that ties between us, never letting me escape.

A light drizzle falls, then sinks into thirsty ground. I swing open the car door fast, stepping into the damp night and pulling the hood of my coat over my head. The hum of fluorescents flickers just beyond. And the last car idles nearby, its headlights bouncing off the storefront glass.

I make a run for it. Reach the locked door. Brown stirs just beyond the streaked panes of glass, wiping at counters with a mop tucked beneath one arm. The lights flicker before the electric hum dies, leaving only the blue glow of a single neon sign washing over my skin. I claw at my hair, carefully tucking strands behind my ear before the wind scatters them wild again. My breath clouds then slowly fades. I purse my lips, blowing the perfect vapor ring. A hint of a smile tugs at my cheek. Jay and I used to do this on early December walks to school.

My fingers curl at my side. I lift a fist to the glass, then freeze. A breath of defeat slips out, and my shoulders slump with the weight of every slow-moving day this town's ever thrown at me.

A southern magnolia branch groans as a gust tears through, then everything settles silent again. The faint glow of red and green dimly lights Main Street, each light post topped with a plastic wreath, the town's idea of holiday cheer. This quiet stretch of streets is pretty much dead to the world, every business closed for another early night.

I tap a toe on cracked pavement. Trapped. That's what it feels like. Stuck in the very town that chewed me up and spat me out, leaving an open wound that still burns raw.

Behind me, a soft *click*, followed by bells that chime against tempered glass.

"Sawyer?"

My head flits over my shoulder, and a sigh rolls out in a soft *whoosh*. "Hi Brown," I reply, teeth chattering loud from the chill.

"Well, what in the world are you doing out here alone?"

My jaw unclenches. Words die in my throat. Rain pounds harder now, hammering against gutters that swallow it beneath. My gaze shifts toward the sky, black as ink, anger loose and raw over the town.

My lips pull tight. I suppose I don't really know what I'm doing here. Drowning myself in beer and whiskey until everything fades to black? Chasing a buzz that makes everything sting a little less sharp?

The door pushes open, spilling warmth and light into the cold.

"It's raining like a cow pissin' on a flat rock. You better get in here before you catch a cold."

I step forward toward Brown's outstretched arm, his palm up, fingers curling in invitation. The weight inside of me eases as he guides me gently by the back.

Behind me, the door *clicks* shut. Locked. Safe. I shrug the wet and heavy coat from my arms.

"Here—let me take that for ya'," he offers, draping it from a coat stand where his crumpled brown hat rests. It's a long-standing fixture in this place.

"Thanks, Brown."

"Everything okay, Sawyer? Your mama doing alright?"

I nod. My fingers clasp. Damp hair clings at my neck like Saran wrap stretched too damn tight. A stutter chokes out. "I'm not really sure, Brown. I mean, Mama's doing fine. I guess."

"But you're not—" he begins.

His words hang there like dead weight, waiting on an answer I don't have. My chest rises and falls, bones thawing slow like a Thanksgiving turkey before the big day. More fluorescent hums above as wetness pricks at the corner of my eye.

"Grab a couple beers from that cooler over there," he offers, pointing toward the back of the store. Like I haven't been here a hundred times before. Like I didn't practically grow up in front of his eyes.

"I thought you hated the stuff," I reply, eyes widening in surprise.

Brown was never one for the drink. He lost his wife to the bottle years ago, at least half a decade, never quite healing from the loss. Patsy Fisher was loved by everyone in town, always going out of her way for others, whether they deserved it or not. Patsy never judged anyone, and it's easy to see why Brown loved her so much. But even Patsy had demons that she just coudn't beat. Maybe we all do. I suppose we've all become masters at hiding things. And trust? Damn near impossible.

Brown chuckles, cutting through the tension hanging over us, hanging over me.

"One or two isn't gonna kill ya," he says, his face turning serious. "As long as you aren't three sheets to the wind, hittin' the bottle like a screen door in a hurricane."

My boots are caked in mud, freshly mopped floor gleaming all around me. I freeze, knowing Brown spent who knows how long making the place spotless. And here I am, ready to turn it back into a mess.

"Well, go ahead," he coaxes, his voice soothing. Familiar. Like the slow, steady rock of a porch swing, with Jay still sitting at my side. "Don't worry about the floors. They'll just get dirty again tomorrow."

My lips tug at my cheeks and relief washes over my skin. Carefully, I step through puddled water, heading straight for the beer cooler doors. A radio station plays muffled Christmas music through speakers above. And for some reason, I don't really mind. A hum even pushes through pursed lips. I stop and scan the glass as my toes tap at the slick tile in a steady beat. I yank open the door, gaze landing on December in a bottle, spiced winter ale with a cinnamon and nutmeg malt. My tongue skates over my lips as anticipation hangs like the spark of a match just before the glow of a flame. I press onto the balls of my feet, fingertips just barely reaching two bottles that *clink* in my hand. They hang at my side as the cooler door swings closed and I shuffle back to the front of the store.

One slightly burnt hot dog spins on rollers in a *hiss*, it's salty, meaty scent wrapping around me. My gut rumbles like a rock rolling down a gravel path.

"You hungry?" he asks, fingers already reaching for a crisp, toasted bun. "Come on around here. You can't go skippin' meals now. You've gotten scrawny as a chicken bone left on a supper plate."

I join him on the other side of the counter, even a light skip to my gait. I slide the beers onto the peeling laminate, and push up onto the stool. It wobbles slightly on the uneven floor. Brown pushes the warm, charred meat toward me now, and my fingers greedily reach for the late-night snack, even though my stomach warns me it's probably a bad idea. I hesitate only a beat before I shove an oversized bite past my lips, feet swinging carelessly below.

"Well, I've gotta say...I'm a little surprised by the visit. Happy to see 'ya. Just surprised is all."

His fingers wrap around a cold bottle, lining the cap to the counter's edge, popping it with one swift beat. The sound ricochets in my head, like a hammer banged onto metal. Sharp. Jarring.

"Having a nice visit with your mama?" he asks.

The hot dog bun clings to my throat. Only a muffled reply hangs from my lips. Brown chuckles again, amusement sparking in his eyes like fireworks exploding in delight. I swallow down the salt and grease in an undignified gulp as spiced ginger and cinnamon crash over my tongue.

"Well—" he says, placing his elbows onto the counter as he leans forward. The wood *creaks* slightly beneath his weight. "You eat like you got the devil on your heels, girl."

My shoulders rise, then fall, considering that maybe he's right. You know...if you believe in that sort of thing.

"Maybe I do," I agree.

My feet resume their carefree swinging, the rubber of my boots creating soft *thuds* against the wood.

"Brown—" I begin, pausing as he drops down onto a stool, popping the top on the second bottle of beer. "What would you say if I told you Jay was murdered?"

His weight shifts. The stool lets out a soft *creak* that settles beneath him.

My gaze shifts above where the ceiling fan spins in a quiet rhythm. Doing nothing but pushing stale air in lazy circles. It gently knocks on beat, like a shallow pulse settling into my bones.

Brown clears at his throat. My eyes meet his now. Wide and thoughtful, but definitely not surprised.

"I guess I'd say that's a real shame."

"Uh-huh," I reply, stuffing another bite into my mouth and swallowing in a loud *gulp*. "They admitted to it. I saw it with my own eyes. Swear."

"Well, I think you should probably tell someone. Call the police station and let them know."

I swallow down the oversized bite like salvation, ketchup oozing as it sticks to the corner of my mouth. I swipe it with a fingertip. Red lingers like fresh paint. "They don't believe me. They refuse to re-open the case. Won't even hear me out."

I suck the ketchup from my fingertip, a resounding *smack* following as it bursts, tangy and sharp.

"I guess you'll have to crack the case yourself," he replies. His nails tap onto the chipped laminate in a smooth legato beat.

"Mmhmm," I agree. "And I've got their names, too."

His breath hangs in anticipation as he shifts in his seat, leaning in close to whisper low as if we aren't the only people inside. "They from town?"

"Well—I don't exactly know, I suppose. But I have their usernames from some weird, hidden corner of the internet. They admitted he was pushed."

"Did you tell your mama? She knows just about everyone in this town," he offers.

My spine sinks in defeat as I gently place the half-eaten hot dog down. "She hates me, Brown. I can barely stand being in that house with her. I mean, she doesn't care about anything I have to say."

"Oh sweetheart, I'm sure that's not true. You're blood after all. Family's there through thick and thin."

"No," I spit out. Defiant and final. "It's different now. She blames me for Daddy leaving. Looks at me with nothing but hate in her eyes."

He leans forward again, even closer this time, his voice threaded with quiet concern. "Maybe you should kill her."

Every muscle in my body stiffens, locking into place fast. A shock races sharp up my spine. My jaw drops slightly, frozen in disbelief. And my eyes lock wide open, an itch forming from my unblinking stare.

"What?" I breathe, voice barely there.

"I just said that maybe you should tell her."

The high-pitched *hum* fades slowly, the *thumping* beat of the spinning blades above returning.

"She just isn't the same, Brown. Not since Daddy left." I toss back another swig of the spicy ale. "And the cops won't even listen. Practically kicked me out of the station."

"Well, sometimes the only person you can count on is yourself. You're just gonna have to dig in and figure this out. But I know you can handle it. You're made of something tougher than most folks around here."

I pause, carefully hanging onto his reply. He's right. There's really no other choice at this point. I can't stay past Christmas with Mama, and I can't give up, even if everyone around me refuses to help.

"I will, Brown," I reply, determined and resolute, the gas station meal filling me with a rough, newfound grit. "I'm not leaving here until they pay for what they did. Jay deserves that much. He deserves peace."

"Ahh...there she is. That stubborn girl who never let anything get in her way."

"She's still in there," I assure him. "Just loses her way sometimes." I swipe my palms along my jeans, quickly hopping down from the counter and landing back on my feet. "Hey...thanks for the warm meal. I'll let you get back to closing up since I've got an early day ahead of me."

Another soft chuckle. His eyes crinkle with the kind of joy that's contagious, slips out easy and pulls you right in.

"Well, I enjoyed the company. It was a nice surprise. The nights stretch long sometimes, Sawyer, a little too long if ya' know what I mean."

"I do," I say with a nod.

I head straight for the coat rack, sliding my arms into damp sleeves and cinching the coat tight. I hesitate for a brief moment, turning back as he watches, making sure I get out safe. The world slows to a stop in this store. It's like some sort of gravitational singularity, where happy memories of Jay linger and loop. "We should do this again. Say—tomorrow night?"

"I'll save you a hot dog. Warm and pipin' hot."

I draw in a quiet breath, then let it ease from my lungs. A smile stretches wide enough to pull at my cheeks and soften the hard knot that sticks in my chest. Brown feels almost like a second father. One who sticks around. Shows up. Doesn't just up and vanish when things get rough. And though he isn't blood, right now—he's the only reason I can stand still. The only reason I can fight whatever hell is coming next.

Chapter Nine

The sun peeks behind a gray sky. I tilt my gaze upward, arms loosening at my sides. Close my eyes tight against the sun, now peeking from behind the clouds like it's not sure it belongs. A door swings open in front of me. Loud chatter spills onto the pavement and the industrial growl of coffee grinders echoes off the walls. Elizabeth Ryan grins, tightly gripping a paper coffee cup, steam curling in her hands. A quiet giggle bubbles to the surface.

"Feels good, doesn't it?" she beams.

She's as pretty as she was in high school, maybe prettier, with her blonde curls piled high onto her head. A few tendrils frame her soft features, and deep cherry red lines her lips. She blows at the steaming coffee lid, kissed by red just below the rim.

Jay had a thing for Elizabeth once. I got really mad about it at the time. Maybe it was jealousy. It was the first time I can remember feeling that anxious rot tearing through my chest. Jay and I never defined what exactly we were, though I know he felt something for me. Something more than what we said it was. Spilled his guts as we sat on his bedroom carpet, sharing all of our favorite songs. I kind of always knew. I mean, he would sneak glances at the fit of my summer shorts, and his heart would thump really fast when our bodies moved close. I considered it. Felt something real between us. Something heavy with want. But I never entertained any of it. Couldn't. Jay was all I had in this world, and I couldn't lose his friendship to tangled-up feelings and frivolous fights.

A shadow swallows the pavement like looming death, the sun disappearing as quickly as it came.

"Of course," she says." A sigh slips out. Thin and tired. "I guess it was nice while it lasted."

Her eyes catch the light, bright as some far-off tropical ocean. Easy to see why Jay stole glances her way, why almost every boy in school did. Maybe she isn't so bad. Maybe in another life we could have actually been friends.

"Yeah. It was," I manage.

"Well—take care, Sawyer. Maybe I'll see you around?" she asks.

The knot returns to my chest. Because I *don't* want to see her around. But it isn't because of Elizabeth, it's the reminder of everything rotten in this town. Every wound just eating at my flesh.

"Yeah. Probably," I muster.

Elizabeth disappears down the sidewalk, sipping her coffee as if the essence of life itself is contained in that cup.

I yank open the coffee shop door, a modest wreath of real pine adorning the glass, and step into a wall of warmth steeped in roasted beans and vanilla. Padded benches hug one wall, every table claimed by locals hammering on laptops like they have a deadline at noon. Birdie moves faster than butter on a hot biscuit behind the counter, a saying my Daddy must have worn out a hundred times, hauling industrial sized bags of coffee into the grinder, wiping up spills before they can stain.

She spots me mid-wipe, her eyes growing wide. "Sawyer!"

The rag hits the counter, and her arm shoots skyward, waving like she's flagging a damn rescue boat. My lips pull tight, gaze dropping low. All the sudden attention lands heavy and strange, like being shoved onto a stage when you're just the understudy who never learned their lines.

I weave through the crowd until I'm close enough for Birdie's hand to catch mine. Her fingers flutter as she yanks me in, letting out a squeal sharp enough to peel paint from the walls. She releases me, only for a second before placing her hands onto my shoulders and giving a gentle shake. It's like she's making sure I'm real.

"I'm so glad you stopped in! Let me get you a coffee. Anything you want—cappuccino, Americano. Oh! We have a new cranberry tea that everyone literally raves over."

"Birdie, you don't have to—"

She promptly cuts me off. "Nope. I'm making you a drink. Done deal, so it's best you tell me what you like."

It's been a while since I had a decent cup of coffee, and the frothy cappuccino being made behind the counter does smell tempting, like the hint of vanilla bean that cuts through the steam.

"Cappuccino," I say, another smile tugging at my lips. It almost feels strange in the wake of Jay's death—like I'm breaking some unspoken rule. "With just a splash of vanilla?"

"You got it."

Birdie quickly makes her way behind the counter, brewing espresso and frothing milk as if a celebrity just walked in the front door. She really is a comfort, like a brilliant rainbow after a summer storm.

I reach deep into the coat pocket and pull out the folded paper. One more time. Just one more try. I know eyewitness testimony is usually strongest on the first go, not that she witnessed a crime, but hell—maybe another look could trigger something. A memory. A clue. Just anything.

Birdie slides the steaming cappuccino across the counter, a heart drawn in black ink on the cup, my name right below it. The warm scent of vanilla drifts right under my nose. "You're the best," I say, flashing a grin. I set the paper onto the counter, right on a splash of steamed milk that almost swallows the scrawled ink. "Hey Birdie? Would you mind taking one more look at these names?"

"Sure," she says, propping her elbows onto the counter. Her eyes flick over the creased, stained page. Slowly, her head shakes side to side, lips pulling tight as she thinks. "Sorry Sawyer, I really have no clue who they could be."

My shoulders slump as I reach for the damp paper, folding it again with care.

"Did you ever think that 10699 might be a birthday?" she quips. "I don't know, just throwing it out there, maybe something might stick."

I blow softly at the steam curling from the cup's spout before bringing it to my lips, savoring the rich vanilla like a warm patch of sun. Birdie's suggestion does make sense, and it's a possibility I haven't yet considered, though it feels like something I should've.

"No. That's great. It's something, Birdie. At least a place to start."

"You should ask the other barista, too." She nods in the direction of a young woman with raven black hair like mine, with a sleeve of colorful tattoos that decorate her left arm. She pours what appears to be coffee flavored ice cream into a clear plastic cup, smiling ear to ear as she hands it to a young girl excitedly snapping pictures on her phone. "Vee!" she calls, waving the raven-haired woman our way. "Can you take a look at this? See if anything stands out. If you recognize the names."

Vee puzzles a moment as an impatient customer waits, arms crossed, at the counter's end.

"I gotta go, Sawyer," Birdie pipes as she puts on her best manager face. She calls out over her shoulder, "Let me know if you find anything out!"

Vee scans the stained ink, shrugging as she croaks out an "I'm sorry" and quickly gets back to work. I let the coffee rest between my palms, the hint of a smile pulling at my cheeks again. Because at least I have something. At least I have hope.

My fingers grip the wheel tight, brow furrowed as I steer down the narrow, bumpy dirt road. Decades-old tree roots snake from the ground like the gnarled fingers of some beast trying to claw its way out. A clearing. Then, a sharp turn right onto pebbled ground, a makeshift driveway for the oddly-painted Tiffany-blue house. A gutter hangs, broken from the roof's edge, and the skirting is slowly rotting from the Florida rains. Still, colorful Christmas lights hint at holiday cheer in an otherwise desolate side of town.

I turn the key, quieting the engine as I second guess everything. My forehead falls to the top of the wheel, still gripped tightly in my hands. I don't want to be here. Not at this house and not in this town. I just want to leave the past behind, even if everyone else can't. But Birdie's words ring loud in my head, and it's a possibility I can grasp, a possibility that I could hand over to Wes and Colt.

My chest rises and falls, a slow breath quieting my racing pulse. I shove open the car door, reluctantly, swallowing my pride as I head toward the battered front porch.

The narrow steps *creak* and *groan* beneath my boots, the planks of wood clinging to life as they sag beneath each step. Toys in faded shades of pink and baby blue scatter across the deck, and a broken doorbell droops from a jutted black box. I stop, just shy of the door frame, swallowing hard as I raise a curled fist to the grimy paint, pounding with urgency as the thunder of steps near.

She pushes open the door, a baby resting on her hip, almost knocking me off my feet. "What is it now, Sawyer?"

"Can I at least come in?

She pulls her lips tight, seemingly swallowing down poisonous words. A moment passes, and she finally caves, stepping back and nodding me inside.

My nephew, River, sprawls across the sagging cushions of a worn and faded couch. Lost in a daydream or whatever spills from the television. Skylar struggles to lift the baby from her hip, squirming in a sagging diaper and pink flowered shirt, trying to get her tiny kicking feet into a worn high chair. Tiny fists pound onto the tray below like a demand.

"You had another baby—" I manage. My feet press into the floor in genuine surprise.

"No Sawyer," she snips, eyes rolling back hard. "I manage a baby daycare while working another full-time job."

"I didn't know. I'm sorry."

"Of course you didn't," she snaps, dropping a bowl of cereal rings onto the tray.

"What's her name?"

She hesitates, but finally gives an inch. "Raelynn."

"Where's Shawn?" I ask.

I scan the house, eyes flitting fast. A half-dead rosemary plant in the kitchen window. Dishes piled high in the sink. A month's worth of unopened mail scattered over the counter, like no one's ever coming home.

"Playing pool with the guys."

Her irritation bobbles to the surface like it's trying to start something. And I'm not in the mood to dredge up worn-out fights we've already beaten to death. Her relationship with Shawn has always been tumultuous, breaking up every few months, getting back together each time Shawn promises to change. He's always worked odd jobs here and there, but nothing ever stuck. And a life of dealing street drugs seemed to always pull him back in.

"Skylar, I need a favor—" I begin.

She shoots another threatening gaze.

"I want to take a look at your senior yearbook. I just need maybe ten minutes and then I'll be out of your way."

Her face puzzles. Arms drop to her sides. "For what?" she asks.

"Do you remember the paper I showed you? The names that might be connected to Jay?"

She slowly nods, and her eyes widen as she hangs on every word.

"Well, Birdie thinks one of them could possibly be a birthday. And if it's true...that means that they would have graduated with you."

She straightens her spine, unfurling with curiosity. Her tousled hair is slipping loose from its messy bun. She rips the elastic from thick strands as she bends forward, securing wild curls back into place. Curls that she definitely got from Mama's side of the family.

"Alright," she concedes. "You've got ten minutes."

If there's one thing that piques my sister's interest, it's gossip so bloated with drama that it practically bursts at the seams. My lips pull, a smile of victory tugging at my mouth as she disappears through the kitchen.

Raelynn babbles happily as she fists sweetened oat rings, shoving sticky fingers into her mouth, though most of it falls onto the floor.

I shift my focus to River now, joining him on the tired couch as springs poke at me from beneath.

"So...how's it going little man?" I ask, though he probably has no idea who the hell I am.

River's gaze is pinned to a cartooned superhero, red juice staining his lips. His feet shove into my thigh, pushing me into the arm of the couch in festered annoyance. I pull my knees to my chest, hugging myself tight as I scan over the room.

Photos in mismatched frames hang on the walls, and toy trucks and colorful building bricks sprawl over worn, carpeted floor. A gaping hole punches through thin sheets of drywall, just one of several remnants of Shawn's angry fists.

Skylar returns, roughly dropping the class yearbook onto a coffee table with a scuffed red oak frame.

"Here. I don't know what you think you're going to find in there, but knock yourself out." Skylar returns to Raelynn, now fussy in her chair.

I snatch the book onto my lap as if fire threatens to burn its every page, flipping through glossy photos of familiar halls and bleachers, lingering on each face with hopeful words printed beneath their smiles.

"Cade...Cade...who are you?" I whisper. I turn each and every page with a fierce determination, but it fades quick as I reach the end. There is no Cade. Maybe the numbers mean something else.

Something like despair sinks in my gut as my spine presses into the cushion. But I give it one last try. Just one more attempt. Slower this time, I start from the beginning of the class photos, carefully considering each name, pausing as I reach the ones beginning with a K. There, a familiar face stares back at me. A shaved head and hollow eyes that unearth something chilling and bone-deep beneath my skin.

Bryce Kincaid.

The promising athlete that fumbled everything and tormented everyone. Skylar spoke of him often, though mostly with disdain. I don't know much about him, or his family, but it's a well known fact that he comes from money. *Old money.* The kind that afforded them a newly-built, sprawling estate on the other side of town. The side of town where forced laughs and designer suits fill the country club's rooms.

I snap the yearbook shut, tossing it back onto the table as hope burns white hot beneath my ribs. I rush to my feet, hurrying toward the kitchen with some invisible force pressing at my spine. I stop, just at the table's edge where Skylar still fusses with Raelynn's tiny, restless fists.

"You don't have a Christmas tree—"

"We're getting one Christmas eve," she snips. She fights some silent battle, then softens her gaze. Another thick clump of hair has slipped from the messy pile, and she stuffs it behind her ear. "Shawn says they practically give them away if you wait long enough."

I shrug. "I guess. He doesn't work, though, so I'm not sure why he even gets a say."

"Sawyer—" she begins, her tone a warning. A threat.

"I'm gone." I lift my palms in surrender. "Relax. I got what I needed."

She shoots a puzzled look. Her affinity for gossip apparently stronger than her disdain for me. "What did you find? Who?"

I spin on my heels, yanking open the door fast. I call out over my shoulder as I step back onto the sagging porch. "Can't say anything yet, but I'll be here at least a few more days!"

"Sawyer—"

Rusted hinges *squeal* as the door slams shut behind me, a safety net between her world and mine. It isn't much, may be nothing at all, but something stirs from the pit of my stomach, like a parasite burrowing, feeding off everything I try not to feel.

Chapter Ten

I don't know what drags me back to Connersville, only that I can't sleep. Can't stay in that house where every memory coils itself tight and squeezes the air from my lungs.

The night is clear, the first since I came back to town. And out here, citrus and cattle country, the stars are endless. I suppose the back road has always been an escape for locals, particularly the younger crowd. A place to watch sparks of light burn holes in a midnight sky. To strip down and step into questionable water. To live without the chokehold of parental control.

The moon hangs low, a waning crescent spilling a faint glow over the open pasture. There's a back way to the lake, but the road is too narrow and choked with dirt thick as clay. I pull onto the shoulder and kill the engine. Crickets shrill. Bloated toads croak their midnight songs.

The car door slams behind me sharp as thunder cracking bone. I step over a sagging fence lying low to the dirt, just one of many paths worn out over the years. Sometimes a patrol car drifts through, spotlight sweeping over rowdy teens with cheap beer. Mostly though, the cops let the bonfire parties slide. Probably because they used to be out here, too. Once chased the same kind of wild. Hell, their parents probably did the same.

I was fifteen when Mason Brown first brought me out here. Mid-July. Humid air clinging like wet gauze you couldn't peel off. I practically lived in sundresses that summer, and Mason had roaming hands and hungry eyes. He was a grade above me, and drove an old beat-up truck that rattled to life only after the third try. He saved for years to buy that truck, and he drove it like a badge of honor—windows down, country songs blaring from the radio, always eager to give someone a lift.

Hallway glances. Hands that seemed to always find their way up my skirt. I was absolutely smitten with his charms. May have even scribbled his last name with mine. Just once. Maybe twice. We talked awhile, sharing secrets in his truck under a night sky. Right before giving in to teenage impulse. Fumbling, breathless, and not quite sure what we were doing but doing it anyway.

Mason was my first kiss, the first boy whose palms slid beneath my hemline. But fogged-up windows never stayed secret for long, and flashing blue sent us away before anything further could happen. I think some cops in this town are just bored, that they have nothing better to do than chase off teenagers and sip on burnt diner coffee all day.

Jay hated Mason. Hated that I ever gave him the time of day. He'd roll his eyes whenever I talked about my...sexual awakening. But, turned out he was right, a fact that he never let me forget. I was never special to Mason. His eyes wandered. And eventually, so did he.

The pasture is desolate. Empty. Once crowded with cattle and orange groves, now overgrown with dead grass and pairs of eyes glowing in the trees. Their gnarled branches like some creature from another world in the dark, enough to make the hair on the back of your neck stand at attention. I press on, following the narrow trail that leads to a thick patch of overgrown oak trees clinging to life. Spanish moss drapes from low-lying branches like spider webs. Fallen limbs and brown leaves *crunch* dead beneath my boots.

I don't see the tree root until my boot hooks under it. Just a jagged and gnarled thing that reaches for my ankles and yanks my feet out from under me. My balance goes, and my knees follow, hitting the dirt hard. A *thud* that knocks the air out of me. A *groan* rumbles as I push myself onto my elbows and straighten my spine again, brushing dirt from my hands and knees, jeans now stained on both legs and the *crunch* of grit in my mouth. I spit onto the ground, push out my tongue and brush it with my palm. Curse under my breath. Half from clumsiness and half irritated with myself.

Wind cuts through my sweater, cold seeping and burying in my bones, lips chapped and teeth chattering. I tuck my head low, ducking beneath a teetering branch hanging by a thread. Startle at something that slithers beneath a pile of dead earth, stirring up the leaves.

One last swat at the tangled threads of gray hanging from a limb and the path clears, opening to a field typically filled with messy beer kegs and an even messier crowd. Ahead, an ember glows bright, fire warning me of the shadowed figure fishing alone in the dark. I stop, my breath suddenly held hostage. I'm guessing it would take about ten seconds for someone to catch up to me, and out here, no one will hear my screams.

"Sawyer?" the shadow calls out.

I push forward. Careful. Cautious. A truck slowly paints the dark. Shining royal blue. Tires much too large and bulky. LED light bar fixed across the top.

"What the hell are you doing out here?" I mutter through gritted teeth.

"I could ask you the same."

Annoyance pushes past my lips, stolen breath settling back in my chest. My boots move faster now, curiosity and anger boiling beneath my ribs.

Colt sits perched on the tailgate, fishing rod in hand, the metal *clanging* faintly at his weight. That familiar, deadly smirk tugs at one corner of his mouth. I swallow hate like dirt. Fight the urge to spit it right in his smug face.

A fire roars behind him, a welcome relief from near-frozen hands and the chill that's latched on and won't let go. And as much as I came out here for solitude, to talk to Jay just one more time, the heat seeps in slow, sweet and thick as honey. Softens the sting of air that pricks like needles at my skin.

I fold my arms across my chest and head down the grassy embankment, now patched with brown, a dented cooler, and two fishing poles propped against its side.

"Catching anything?"

Amusement rumbles from his chest. "Not a damn thing."

"You come here often in the middle of the night to fish?" I unfold my arms, anxious fingers twitching at my sides. "I thought fish were more active at sundown and dusk anyways."

Another smirk, his sharp jaw and light stubble distracting. If one's into that sorta thing. Southern boys that trade dimly-lit nightclubs and pulsing bass for pretty girls, fishing poles, and quiet nights underneath the stars. And I'm not into that. *At all*. Watched Colt break too many hearts in high school, plus I guess I've always preferred being alone. My sister always said I wasn't trying to make friends, that I was *"off-putting"* and pushed everyone away, but I never saw it in that light. Besides, Jay was all I ever needed. And we spent most Saturday afternoons together, sharing music, secrets, and dreams that stretched long into the night.

"Spawning season," he offers.

My boots grind into dead earth as his smile suddenly fades.

"You never answered my question, Sawyer—"

Another breath pushes past my near-frozen lips, a *pfft* half-slipping in annoyance. Half sigh. Half scoff. "Couldn't sleep. I don't know...guess it just feels weird being back in this place. I mean, it's not even my home now I suppose." I shift my gaze to the tops of my boots, now caked in mud and God knows what else. I roll at a stick beneath my toes. "It just doesn't feel like I belong anymore."

Colt studies me, his gaze flicking to my mouth. Only for a second. One of those blink-and-you-miss-it kind of pauses. But it definitely didn't slip past me.

"Mama doesn't want me here," I spit out, immediate regret filling my chest.

He eases his stance, gesturing toward the flame. And though he's about the last person I want to spend the night with, I'll take the warmth. Maybe the company, too. At least for someone to talk to that doesn't flinch whenever I'm near.

Colt crouches, flannel pulling across his shoulders as he tosses another log onto the pile, flames leaping high as they cast shadows across his face.

"Ahh...good ol' Abilene. Folks don't see her around much anymore," he puzzles out, unfolding himself as he waves me closer. "Why do you think she doesn't want you here? That's your family, Sawyer."

My gaze lowers to the tops of my boots, mud-caked laces dangling in the dirt. I shift my weight, right then left, my head screaming at me to stop talking. To just shut my damn mouth. Every instinct urging me to turn around. To walk away.

"Our family died when Daddy left. Things were just—never the same after that," I reply, ignoring all warnings.

I lift my chin again, breath hitching as his eyes lock onto mine. Rich golden-brown like honey, flecked with green and gold, now soft with something like concern. They seem to shift. Or maybe that's just how I'm choosing to see him. A pull stirs beneath the surface. Just a flicker I slam down before it can grow. I tighten my jaw. Harden every part of me that might slip. There's no time for confusion or room for whatever this is. I swallow the feeling whole. Bury it deep. Gone.

"You ever fished before?" he asks.

"Well...obviously. Hasn't everyone in this town?" My jaw trembles as my teeth chatter wildly, and I claw at strands whipping across my cheeks, swiftly tucking them behind my ear. "Not really anything else to do except hang out at Wal-mart or day drink at the local bar."

His hand lifts, thumb grazing my cheek. His gaze follows the motion, softening as it traces my skin before finding its way to mine. Everything in me goes still—limbs, breath, pulse. His tongue skates across his bottom lip. The moment drags slow. Too long. I take a small step back, enough to put space between his mouth and mine.

"What are you staring at?" I snip.

"Easy now, tiger." The corner of his mouth curls into a deliberate grin that knows exactly what it's doing. "You had a little smudge of dirt on your face."

My hand flies to my cheek. First hiding whatever's left from my tumble earlier, then rubbing furiously to clean it off.

"Come on," he urges, fingers curling around my wrist before I can tell him no.

He leads us back to the water's edge, grabbing one of the fishing poles that rests against the open cooler. He turns and smiles. Big. Toothy. Crinkling at the corners of his gold-flecked eyes.

"Colt, I'm not—" rolls out then catches. My words hang lifeless in the air as he quickly gets to work, plunging his hand into a makeshift bathtub of Golden Shiner minnows, shoving a steel hook through the unlucky thing to use as bait. The pungent stench of fish punches at my nostrils.

"Come on now. You didn't get all soft on us, did 'ya? Big city squeeze the country out of you like moonshine from a mason jar?"

And though a part of me hates the slow, porch-sittin' country life, a part of me hates his disapproval more. "No," I snip, grabbing the line and pole from his hand, struggling minnow flipping through its last breaths.

I take a few steps forward, where murky water laps at brown earth. The reel struggles as it locks itself into place. I shove harder at it, frustration gnawing as I grit my teeth.

"Here—" he says, shifting himself directly behind as he wraps his arms tightly around me.

His breath whispers at my ear. Warm. Uninvited. Sending my pulse into a near sprint. I dig my heels in. Press my lips tight. Force the rush down before it gives me away.

Colt unlocks the spinner, placing his hands over mine as he gently casts out onto the water, a small *plop* slicing through the quiet. He stays there at my back, and I wonder if he can hear the slow and rattling breaths that echo loud in my ears.

My head snaps over my left shoulder. "Do you mind?" It's more of an order than a question, though.

Laughter spills from his chest like he actually thinks he's charming. And I hate it. Wish I had never come.

"Just trying to keep warm, Blue Eyes."

My face twists with disgust and my shoulders wiggle free from his grasp, disappointment sinking to my gut when he doesn't immediately pull me back in.

The bobber disappears beneath rippled water, excitement catching in my throat as something tugs on the line, deflating just as quickly as the buoy pops again to the surface. My shoulders sink, a *whoosh* of breath escaping as I quickly reel in the now-empty line.

"You're doing great," he soothes. "I mean, as good as anyone else foolish enough to fish out here in the middle of the night. They're just not bitin'."

I shove the pole forward, preparing to run the second he takes it from my hand.

"Take it easy, Sawyer." He rakes his fingers through dark hair, though each strand stays perfectly in place. "We're reopening the investigation."

My gaze locks, body pins with doubt, but clings to something fragile. "Really? Please don't toy with me, Colt. It's Christmas for fuck's sake."

"Sawyer, I'm not messin' with you. Promise."

The hint of a smile pulls at my cheeks, my chest just a little bit lighter as it rises with some kind of hope-filled air.

"You should probably thank Wes, though. He's been yammering non stop for days. You do have friends here, Sawyer. Seriously. You've got people on your side."

I lift my hands to my mouth, gently cupping them as I blow warm breaths into my palms.

"Cold?" he asks. He leans the rod and reel against the cooler's side once more. "Come on."

He slides onto the lowered tailgate, patting at his side for me to join. I decide to take him up on the offer, ice in my veins slowly thawing as I flatten my palms to metal and push myself up.

Silence hangs in the air, broken only by the chorus of frog croaks somewhere out in the dark. That's one thing I've always liked about home...folks don't feel the need to blabber on and on to shield their own discomfort. And long intervals of silence, with sweet tea on front porches, wrap like a warm quilt around a broken heart.

He shifts his leg closer to mine, eventually draping an arm across my shoulders and pulling me in close. The slight hint of woodsy-smelling cologne choked out by the scent of fish that now wafts through the air. I lean in, giving up the icy exterior, slowly warming up to him.

His eyes lift toward the stars. Mine follow.

"You can see Orion from here," he offers, lifting a finger toward the sky. "Do you see it? There's the belt...those three bright pinpricks. And there"—he adds, tracing the sky like an artist over an easel. "That's the hunter with his arms ready to strike."

"You're into astronomy?" I ask.

His eyes shift back to mine, sparks of something like desire flickering in his gaze. Or maybe it's just the light spilling from the crackling flames behind us. Yeah. Probably that. Most likely.

"My dad bought me a telescope for my birthday. I think I was turning ten. Maybe eleven. He worked long hours most days. Never made much time for us kids. But every Saturday night after that, he joined me in the backyard, showing me every constellation, rattling on and on. I didn't really see the importance of it then. Of course, most kids wouldn't. But I hold on tight to those memories. That's all I've got left."

My palm finds its way to *his* back now, rubbing in gentle circles, soothing in the helpless way everyone does to me. His words sting a bit in my chest, silent flickers of my own father playing like a movie reel in my head. But my father is still here. There is still time to make amends. Colt will never get that chance again. And no matter how I feel about him—the pain that drips from his words evident now—he doesn't deserve that.

"I'm sorry," I mutter.

There isn't much else I can think of to say. But Colt frees his arm from my shoulders and his palm finds its way to my thigh. I leave it there. It feels nice.

"Do you remember Mr. Abbott? We both somehow ended in his world history class." His other hand shifts behind his head, muscles flexing against his shirt as he stretches out his frame. "I don't know how or why because you were one of the smart kids. And I wasn't good for much anything other than throwing a football around a field."

"That's not true—"

"It is, Sawyer. And it's okay, I know I made bad choices back then. Wasn't the nicest. Threw away any dream of a professional sports career."

"You're a detective, Colt. That's impressive for someone your age."

"Pfft—only because of my father. I didn't do shit on my own. We both know that."

"I don't believe that," I soothe out. My palm continues in soft circles as he continues on.

"Do you remember how I would always cut up? Talk when I wasn't supposed to. Pass dumb notes around to get everyone worked up."

"I do. Unfortunately."

"I did it because the old man would move me to the front of the class every time. The front of the class...seated right next to you."

Silence hangs. Breaths still beneath my chest.

"You smelled like cotton candy. And you always had your hair pinned up off your shoulders, with these messy little tendrils falling out of place. Your hair was brown then, with these little hints of red that came out if you stared long enough."

I move my hand from his back and shift away, uncomfortable with the sudden shower of attention. My palms flatten at my sides as I push myself off, landing firm on soft dirt beneath.

"I need to get going," I stammer out. "It's getting late."

Colt hops down beside me without missing a beat. "Let me snuff out this fire real quick and toss the rods and cooler back in my truck. I'll take you back to your car."

"I can walk—"

"I know you can, Sawyer."

He kicks at the burning logs and ash, stomping the last of the embers into the earth, quickly grabbing the cooler by its sides and effortlessly tossing it into the bed of the truck. And I let out a slow breath, filled with exhaustion and defeat. His hand reaches for mine.

"Well, alright then."

Colt follows behind as I make my way up the steps, shining his flashlight beam toward the front porch so I don't miss a step and go flying onto my face. For the second time tonight. Admittedly, I've taken quite a few tumbles, mostly after late nights sipping terrible tasting liquor bought with a scribbled on license, birthdate clearly altered with blackened ink.

I reach the top of the steps and turn, his frame towering over me.

"You still have that paper?" he asks. He clicks off the flashlight's beam, searching my gaze as it falls to his lips. "The one with the names."

"Oh. Right," I say, quickly shoving a fist into my pocket and fishing out the crumpled note with trembling fingertips.

I leave it folded, pushing it toward him. He takes it, shoving it deep into the pocket of his shirt like he's afraid it's going to bite.

I consider spilling my suspicions toward Bryce Kincaid, though I really have nothing solid, just a last name and birth year that may resemble a stranger from the back alley of the digital world. It's the kind of reach that can make a girl sound like she's grasping at straws. I push away the thought, swallow it down, vow to continue digging. Alone. And now that I have something to hold onto, even if it's just a crumb, there's new life blooming beneath my skin.

"Are you going to track the names? You think you can find them?"

He lifts an empty palm, placing it between us as he gestures for me to take a breath. "I'll give it a look and pass it over to our digital forensics guy. He's the best in the state."

Satisfaction fills my chest, the urge to wrap my arms around his neck beating down my spine like a drum. But I won't. I'm not here for Colt. I'm here for Jay. And the only thing I want from Colt is his unwavering dedication to solving this case.

He struggles, fights some sort of inward battle with himself before placing two fingers beneath my chin, holding my eyes to his. "Alright, Blue Eyes, get some rest. We've got a lot of work ahead of us."

Chapter Eleven

Low hanging branches and sprawling oaks stretch across the narrow road, creating a canopy of dappled light that peeks through. My elbow rests, fingers dangling out of the window, welcoming the teasing sun. It won't last long, probably not more than a few warmth drenched minutes. But for now, I'll soak up every bit that I can.

I turned the radio off about a mile back. Can't think straight if the music is too loud. One time, Jay and I spent all day on the red sands of Ormond Beach, skin blistered and pink from the Florida afternoon sun. The drive home stretched long, so we filled it with karaoke of some of our favorite songs. One particular note got me so worked up that I swerved right, took out a trashcan and mailbox in one go. Finished the rest of the drive in silence real quick after that. And Jay...well, he never let me drive again. Can't blame him for that.

On the outskirts of town, out where Highway 17 meets 91 Mine Road, out where another quick turn right through a narrow dirt patch leads to tucked-away folks who don't want to be found, is Gaskins Road. Foot pressed to the brake, I make the turn where Spanish Moss drapes over the trees and ground like the webbing of something long dead. People pay good money for this look in October. Out here...it's a way of life, a veil from lurking eyes and mouths that carry stories too far.

A wooden post juts with weathered letters that warn strangers to keep on the main road. There are no holiday lights out here in this part of town, no inflatable snowglobes or reindeer in tidy rows. Just the warnings. Just the quiet.

Got the same mix of half-answers and rumors, all of them pointed here. Just a hop and a jump from Connersville Road, but far enough away that a good supply of canned beans and ammunition could help a person vanish for years.

I ignore the warning, tires rolling slow onto the soft earth. The back end slips, tires spinning, the engine humming loud as it tries to catch. A path made for big tires and even bigger trucks, making a fool of me for even trying.

What was it that Jay told me to do when this happens? Turn the wheel. Rock forward. Turn the wheel again. Rock back.

I keep at it, heart pumping fast and anxious, until dirt finally releases its hold on me and my pulse returns to its normal beat. I drive faster now. Not fast enough to flee, but enough to outrun the invisible thing that tried to swallow me whole.

The sun slips behind a dull canvas of gray. More rain is coming. You can smell it in the air. I roll up the window again as the path leads through low reaching limbs that scratch at the car's paint like the sharp claws of a beast.

A rusted out truck slowly emerges as the trees thin, revealing dead patches of earth and a worn trailer on wheels. Brown grass clings to life as it reaches up the tire's rims, a sign it hasn't moved for quite sometime.

The engine quiets as my spine presses into the seat. God, I hope the folks in town were right. That they didn't send me on a dead-end chase that leads to nowhere but a barrel pointed straight at me by a man with nothing to lose.

The trailer door pushes open, its paint flaking white against a sun-faded blue exterior. Footsteps thunder down sagging, water-logged boards ready to split, the shiny barrel of a revolver swinging at his side. I step out fast, slamming the door shut behind me as leaves crunch beneath my feet.

Graying hair is clasped behind his neck. Slicked with oil, in need of a wash, a far cry from the neat, polished style that I'm used to. His face, worn raw from the sun, filled with a lifetime of stories that he never told. Black tobacco peeks from the corner of his mouth, nestled between his teeth like something he meant to spit but never did. His thin cheeks sag slightly, and a deadpanned blue pins to me now, angry and suspicious. Loose jeans, smeared with dirt, hang from his waist, spattered deep crimson blotches down each leg. Warm flannel buttons up his chest like a sack over a weakened frame. His footsteps slow, pinning ten feet ahead of me, slowly tucking the shining weapon into the waistband of his jeans.

"Hi Daddy."

"Your hair's black," he croaks out, expressionless, tobacco wad finally spit onto the ground at his side.

I reach for the tangled tresses of dyed black, new growth of auburn chasing, peeking from my scalp. I smooth it down. Not sure what else to say. Not sure why I came.

"That's good." He spits chewed up black at the ground again. "You used to be a spittin' image of your mama."

"I know, Daddy."

"She ain't here, is she? She hidin' in that car?" he snaps, the crease in his brow returning even angrier than before.

"No. She isn't here. It's just me."

His eyes fall to my boots, crawling their way back up to meet mine, flickering with something I can't quite put my finger on. Not warmth. Not recognition. Softer, but filled with suspicion, as if he can't quite trust what he sees.

"Well—come on then, I guess. You came all the way out here. Let's get 'ya warmed up." He turns, spits the last of his chew onto the steps as he makes his way up.

My boots free from the soft muck with a sucking sound, my strides long as I follow behind, each step a jolt as tired boards bend beneath my feet.

Inside—worn carpet threads in dark brown and patches of black that look something like old engine oil. Smoke, rot, and liquor are etched into the wood panels that line the walls. A thrifted couch in burnt orange sags, surrounded by tables covered in scattered old newspapers and bottles of liquor cleared of every drop. A bulky air conditioner is wedged into the only window frame. Silent and still. Light from a gray sky barely making it through. The air is filled with the stench of overfilled ashtrays as the biting chill nips through my jeans. No photos to warm the place. No trace of the family long left behind.

Daddy pulls the gun from his waistband, setting it down on scattered papers of black ink, headlines of politics from years long gone. The handle a smooth wood grain in a rich walnut tone. A patch of diamonds carved into its side. An emblem decorates the shiny black behind the cylinder, scratched out letters mar the paint that decorates the barrel's side.

"'Spose you want somethin' to drink," he mumbles, almost under his breath, the hint of irritation rattling low in his throat.

He grabs a bottle of amber brown that looks like something cowboys used to keep in their pockets, and slides it from an oddly-placed counter that separates the kitchen from the burnt orange couch. His hands tremble slightly. I notice it now. My body inches onto the couch's edge as I rub at my palms furiously to cut through the bite in the air.

"This oughta warm 'ya up," he says, pushing a short glass toward me, filled to the brim with the stinky stuff.

I reach for it with shaking hands. Hesitant. Not sure if I should drink it. Not sure if I should run. But it's not the liquor I'm worried about, it's the way he looks at me...like he's not looking at me at all. Like I'm not even here.

"Well—go on now."

I bring the glass to my lips, spilling a bit with shaking hands as I wash it down my tongue. My throat closes up, trying to keep the nasty stuff down. Warmth slowly spills through me, the tips of my ears growing hot, my cheeks flushing with red. I lick the remnants from my lips, grateful for the reeky, soothing stuff.

He settles into the old wooden dining chair, its legs straining as he shifts his weight. He drinks directly from the bottle, just a long and bitter swig, washing back something bad. Maybe memories of Mama. Maybe memories of me.

"How'd 'ya find me out here?" he asks, stuffing another big wad of tobacco up into his gums.

I wrap my arms tightly around my knees, fingers clasping as I struggle with words. "Asked around. Most didn't have a clue." I swallow down the rasp sticking to my throat. "But I ran into Charlie Watts and Donna Bell at the old diner out on South Holland. They suspected I might find you here."

He mutters something inaudible under his breath, pausing to take another long swig of the drink before he begins again. ""Ol Buck don't know when to shut up. Runs his mouth too damn much. I'll see how he likes a little target practice all damn night."

"Who's Buck?" I ask.

No answer. I'm not even sure he heard the question.

He slides the gun from the table like an old Western quickdraw, twirling it around his finger without an inch of fear. My chest seizes. Eyes grow wide. One. Two. Three spins of the barrel around his finger before he finally sets it back down. My shoulders fall with relief. Beats stir in my chest again.

"Ain't seen 'ya in years. You've grown tall as a weed."

A smile eases from the corner of his mouth, falling flat as quickly as it came. His eyes appear vacant. Hollow. And I wonder when was the last time someone sat across from him, asked him how he's been, wonder when he last left this hopeless place.

"What do 'ya need? Money? 'Cause I ain't got none. Got everything I need to get along just fine."

I sit up a little taller now, picking at a loose thread on my coat until it unravels too far, the marbled button popping and flinging onto the old, splotted brown carpet. I decide to leave it there. Still unsure what critters might emerge from the woodwork and scatter across the dirty floor.

"I don't need money, Daddy. Been working since I left home."

"Well—that's good, I guess." Silence hangs thick as he polishes off his liquor and slams it back onto newspaper, sliding it forward to clear a bit of space.

"I miss you, Daddy," I choke out, fighting against the burn behind my eyes.

"Mmm," he grumbles in reply.

I guess I have to take it. Probably all I'm going to get.

Daddy and I used to be thick as thieves, me riding on his lap, ducking behind the dash whenever we passed a cop with nothing better to do than sip old coffee and hand out traffic citations. He always called me Bug. Said it was because I used to chase lightning bugs on summer nights by the lake, keeping them in old mason jars to cast a glow by my bed, releasing them with Daddy before they died. Seems maybe he forgot. Maybe he's been away from society a bit too long.

"Anyone ever visit you out here?" I prod.

More mumbling under his breath before he starts again. "Got everything I need right here. What do I need somebody badgering me for?"

"You have to feed yourself. You look like you've gotten pretty thin, Daddy."

"I eat when I get hungry. Got a stash of jars to last 'til I die, I reckon. Lots of pickled beets. Pickled some cabbage, too."

"Skylar had another baby," I blurt, not sure if she wanted me to tell him. "Girl. Raelynn. Lots of chunky rolls. Head full of curly blonde hair."

"Yeah?"

"Mmhmm—and River is getting pretty big, too."

I don't have much else to say about my nephew. There isn't much else to tell, really. The time between his first steps and days spent at preschool a mystery to me.

"You have heat in here?" I ask, chill returning as it creeps up my spine.

"For what? Don't get much cold in Florida. Well, except for this year."

"Daddy, you're gonna freeze to death in here. Rain and cold are brutal this winter. And we still have months to go."

"Got plenty of blankets." He pulls a smooth metal flask from inside of his flannel jacket pocket, twisting the top and throwing another drink down the hatch. "And got a good stash of liquor in the kitchen over there."

"That stuff will kill you," I spit out before I can manage a blink.

"That stuff is the only thing keepin' me alive."

Silence hangs heavy, the kind that festers, cut only by the sound of a rooster crow from somewhere close outside.

"Well...I got chores to tend to. Pigs need a feedin'. Chickens probably laid some eggs." He stuffs the revolver back into his waistband, flattening shaking palms to the table and pushing up as he mutters something low again. His hand flies to the back of his neck, pinching and pulling at the skin like something is gnawing at him. He paces right, turns, paces left. Turns to me again. "I reckon you can help. Your arms strong, girl?"

"I guess so."

I twist at the ring on my left thumb, a gift from Jay for my seventeenth birthday. A token of friendship. A token I never took off.

"Well?" he bellows. "You comin'?"

I push up from the burnt orange sagging thing, straightening my spine and brushing at the wrinkles in my fading jeans.

Outside, the air stinks of rust and wet feathers, the cold biting a bit sharper now than when I first arrived.

Behind the trailer, two large pens hold animals inside a wire fence. A weathered and rotting chicken pen on the left, muddy dirt with several fat pigs to the right. Daddy grabs a dinged-up bucket filled with feed, swinging it by its thin metal handle at his side. He reaches in, tossing a handful of the grain over the wire as chickens scatter. It rains down like hail as they race each other for the first bite. A rooster muscles through, shoving its weight forward through the pack, a scuffle breaking out as feathers are ripped from an unlucky hen's back. The squawking is loud, with wings flapping so wildly that you can't tell where one hen ends and another one begins. Just a screeching blur of rage.

"Hey!" he yells.

It ricochets like a gunshot off my chest.

Daddy drops the bucket at his feet, swinging open the gate as its rusted hinges whine, jumping into the pen to break up the fight. Just a little too late, it seems. He grips at the rooster's neck, snatching it up quick as feathers flutter softly to the ground. The other hens peck at their meal, loud *clucks* ringing through the air. Daddy holds him like a football in the crook of his arm while the injured hen cowers low, squawking in pain at his feet. A few steps to the right is a smaller holding pen, some sort of chicken time-out corner, I guess. Daddy chucks the rooster inside, muttering something bad under his breath.

"Damn rooster. Now this hen probably ain't gonna lay no eggs."

His palm finds its way back to the nape of his neck again, fingers rubbing and pulling as he struggles with something I can't see. A quick shake of his head and he walks back to my side, closing the whining gate, sealing the injured hen inside.

A few steps right and another gate on rusted hinges. I follow behind, stepping into the pit of mud, reaching back to latch the gate shut.

"Want some help?" I ask, voice small. Feeling useless. Not quite sure what to do with my hands.

Daddy stops. He pulls a crushed box of cigarettes from his back pocket, sliding one out and clamping it between his teeth as he lights the tiny orange flame. Smoke curls into the damp air, its scent wrapping around my throat and practically suffocating me.

"See that barrel over there?" He points to the back corner of the pen where a bright blue barrel sits, coated in mud from the ground to about halfway up.

I nod.

"There's scraps in that. Fill that bucket up and throw 'em in that trough over there."

I swallow down unease, unnerved by the chorus of snorts, frantic for their next meal as they gather like greedy, hungry beasts at my sides. My heels sink in shallow mud with each step, the daily patter of rain creating a sloshing pit of filth, thick as cake batter, that tries its best to suck me in. I lift my chin and push forward, willing myself not to flinch, not to let them smell fear.

I slide the lid off the barrel. The stench of rotting vegetables that form some type of slop is strong in the air—shrunken, shriveled pumpkins, potato peels, and stale bread filled to the top. I plunge a bare hand inside, fisting a smooshed wad of scraps and tossing them into the bucket. Squeals grow sharper, the filthy things circling at my feet. I keep going until the bucket's almost too heavy to lift, then drop the lid back in place and haul it to the trough. Each step grinds slow and heavy. My pulse echoes in my skull. All I want to do is drop this bucket and run.

"Now go on—toss it on in," Daddy hollers.

I lift the bucket up high, arms straining with its weight, and toss its contents at the hungry pigs who push forward, eager to fill their bellies with the rotting meal. I drop the bucket into the mud at my side—but I don't run, just need a little more time with him.

One pig keeps his distance from the others. Walks in slow circles like its chasing its own tail. My eyes pin to the pitiful thing, spinning like he's lost, my head spinning now with him as I follow each and every turn. Daddy joins at my side. Features expressionless, carved from stone. Another *grumble* forms beneath his chest.

"What's wrong with it?" I ask.

"Sick. Ain't no use keeping them around when they get like that. Meat's tainted. Ain't good for nothin' no more."

A loud *boom* thunders through the pen as my heart lurches into my throat. My ears split with a ringing so sharp that it knocks the air from my lungs. The world shrinks in the sound. Tunnels. Everything goes white. My ear drums scream. Hands fly to my head. The pitch is unbearable. Sharp as glass.

The pig falls to its side with a sickening *thud*, legs shaking violently as the others pigs stare. And then—they move on. Another moment and the ringing fades, replaced by hungry grunts and wet chewing in the slop as the shaking pig finally stills, thick crimson oozing from the blast that was blown through the center of its skull. Daddy's hand extends, frozen in time. Something like blood and brain splatter cover his fingers and his gun.

"Sickness don't stay put, girl," he mutters. "It spreads. Festers under the flesh. That pig was dead the second it started walkin' in circles. I just pulled the trigger. Somethin' bad's been feedin' on it from the inside."

A moment passes and he tucks the splattered barrel back into the waistband of his jeans, wiping the pig's guts and bone fragments onto the front of his pants.

Bile rises up the back of my throat. I push it down. Fast and hard. My fingers tremble slightly at my sides. I curl them into fists. "Why did it shake like that?"

He brings the lit cigarette to his mouth again, holding the smoke in for what feels like minutes before finally letting it go. It curls into the air like something from a steam engine. Thick. A heavy thing that crawls down throats and drags the air away.

"Nerves. Just like a chicken runs after the head gets chopped off. They don't feel nothin'."

I shove my fists deep into my coat pockets. I don't want him to see me twitching with fear. "What do you with it now?" I ask. Curious. Not sure I really want the answer.

"Burn it in that barrel over there," he says, lifting a finger in the air toward a side yard filled with gun targets riddled with holes.

We stand here for a moment, like some quiet memorial for the sick pig now lying still at our feet. Then Daddy shrugs, turns, and walks back to the gate.

"Let 'em eat," he calls out over his shoulder. "They'll be alright."

I follow behind, boots dragging through sloshy earth as we round the corner of the trailer. Ivy creeps up its side. Thick. Twisted. Crawling.

Pulling tight as if it wants to choke the place into stillness. The ground reclaiming what it can. The house. Him. Maybe even me.

The sky opens above us. Pitters of rain land on soft earth, filling up mud puddles that can never quite dry. I pull the hoodie of my coat tight over my head, fingers stiff from cold. I suppose that's about all I'll get out of him. Suppose it has to be enough.

He battles with something, eyebrows twitching as he forms thoughts into words. Something's gnawing at him. I can see it working through his shoulders. "Welp—you carry anything for protection?"

I blink. The question catches in my throat.

"You got a gun, girl?" he continues on.

"No, Daddy."

The rain patters steady now. Somewhere, a hollow *clank* echoes off rusted metal. Daddy doesn't flinch. It's as if neither the wet nor the cold bother him at all. Like it's soaked so deep into him, it just lives there now. He takes one last puff of the cigarette dangling from his fingertips, then tosses it where it sinks into muddy ground.

"Here," he rasps. He reaches back into his waistband, pulling out the revolver and wiping its barrel onto the flannel of his shirt like it's nothing more than a pocket knife. "Reckon you can keep this one. Holds six rounds in the cylinder. Well—I 'spose there's only five now."

He looks to the ground, shifting his weight right and left like he's unsure of something now.

Right.

Left.

Right.

Left.

Then his head snaps like the light just returned to his eyes. "You know how to shoot, don't 'ya?"

I nod. At least I think I do. Poppy used to take me to the range once I turned fifteen. Not old enough to shoot with the men, but they let me in anyway.

"Alright. You tuck it in tight. Use it only when you need to."

He pushes it forward as my knees buckle with fear. I take the gun with an unsteady grasp and trembling fingers, stuffing it into my back pocket with unease.

"Guess I'll be gettin' back now," he says.

He shrugs as he fumbles with a proper goodbye. I guess he's never been too good at them. He'll stay out here. Swallowed by the canopy of trees, the silence, by whatever's unraveling inside of him.

"Alright, Daddy. You take care of yourself." I turn toward the car door, locking my shoulders so I don't fold. So I don't drop to my knees and cling to his ankles, sobbing like a child until he comes home. I turn back. "I'll come back to check on you soon."

He nods like he believes it. Like we both believe it. But I know. The woods will swallow him. The silence will keep him. This will be the last time I see him. This will be our last goodbye.

Chapter Twelve

Cicadas hide in the dark, red-eyes peeking through low hanging branches, draped in webbed moss as they sing their summer songs. Flashes of white illuminate the sky somewhere in the distance, creating a dazzling light show that might send most people running for cover. But in Florida, it's just a daily norm, a brief reprieve from the constant stickiness that clings to our necks and steam that curls from the pavement in its wake. Grass tickles at my toes, the urge to scratch overwhelming, my right sandal lost somewhere in the perfectly manicured lawn behind us.

My knees *pop* and *crack* loud as I crouch, fingers curled tightly around the bars of an iron gate. Sweat trickles down my back, a damp patch forming on my dress. I give in, finally letting my knees rest on the ground.

A light shines from inside, creating fractiles of light that bounce off over-bleached pool water as a security guard performs his final check of the night.

"I lost my shoe. Back there," I whisper, pulling on the gate as I begin to straighten trembling legs, now going numb from the crouched, awkward position.

Jay pushes down on my shoulder as the country club door flings open, the beam of light shining directly toward us now. I gasp, holding breath hostage in my chest as it bounces off the deck, slowly easing it out as the guard deems the property secured. I turn back to Jay, his smile growing wide until we explode in a fit of laughter.

"Wait here," he orders, scaling the fence like some sort of webbed superhero and dropping onto the other side. He turns back, lip curling as mischief sparks in his eyes. "You coming or what?"

"Jay, if you don't open this gate right now," I threaten, though he and I both know I won't do a damn thing.

The gate *clicks* its release, and within seconds, he wraps his arms tightly around my waist, lifting me up as he spins to toss me into the pool. My palms push onto his shoulders as I kick my feet in protest, all the while enjoying every second of our summer ritual.

On the east side of town, out where perfectly clipped lawns are adorned with freshly planted flower beds, out where golf carts parade every night like trophies, is the Bartow Country Club. I think it's the land of no personality. The land of no soul. A land of overfilled lips and middle-aged men that drive expensive convertible cars, doing anything they can to cling to their youth.

A few sprawling oaks remain, creating canopies of shade on rooftops, though most have been ripped out in favor of perfect green lines and rolling hills for men in polo shirts to play with their balls as they sip cold beers in the morning sun.

Another flash of light shoots across a darkened sky, the boom of thunder chasing on its heels. Still too far away for us to care.

"Jay, put me down!" My left sandal gives in, falling to the pool deck as a *squeal* bubbles to the surface and escapes from my throat. I wrap my legs tightly around him, locking in as I pull our bodies closer. If I go down, he goes down with me. He knows the drill. We play this game on repeat, time and time again.

He begins the ritual count. "Three—"

"Jay—I'm not letting go. I swear!"

"Two—"

Another squeal slices through the cicada song. My head falls back in another giggling fit.

"One and a half—"

I struggle for a breath, my words barely coherent as he steps closer to the edge, leaping into the pool as our bodies land with a tsunami-like splash. My feet scrape the bottom as he releases me. I push off, quickly bobbing back up. Jay's eyes pin to mine, his perfectly white smile beaming with twisted satisfaction.

"Oh, you're dead," I tease, pushing up to reach for the top of his head just as he ducks from my grasp.

I fling forward, chest first, flopping into the water like an archer fish hunting for its prey. Water fills my ears, Jay's words muffled at the water's surface. I push up again, gasping for a breath as I wipe the chlorine from my eyes.

Jay's grandparents have a pool in their backyard, but after Jeanne Scott caught us butt-naked in the water last summer, right after we raided her mahogany liquor cabinet, we've preferred to drive out here instead. For privacy. To escape her window-peeking, Bible-clutching surveillance.

Idlewood Avenue. The country club neighborhood that goes to sleep early. Even on summer nights. Even when the sky still burns with streaks of orange and gold. Here, the world feels quiet. Almost too quiet, as if it's waiting for us to do something reckless as teens normally do.

I peel the straps from my shoulders, wriggling free of the now-soaked butter-yellow cotton dress. It's Skylar's, but I sneak it from time to time. Mason Brown said it's his favorite on me. Last time, she was steaming for days, hid it somewhere in the house, but it eventually found its way back into the closet...and into my hands. I lift it high into the air, tossing it as it lands with a resounding *smack* onto the pool's deck. Jay follows, peeling his wet t-shirt up and over his head, tossing it into the breeze now cooling on our shoulders. Something flickers in his eyes as they quickly scan beneath the water's surface.

He looks at me differently now. Teenage urges clouding our heads, blurring the faint line drawn in the sand that defines who we are. What we mean to each other. It's a scrambled mess. Years of friendship, a closeness most won't find in their lifetime, a spark of desire and love that can't be denied. But no one has acted on the urge. Not yet anyway. And I'm just relieved I don't have to figure everything out today.

"What am I supposed to wear home now?" I glide forward, reaching my palms from the rippled surface as he locks his fingers into mine, gently spinning us in circles as the distant storm fades.

"I've got an extra shirt in the car," he teases. "Don't be such a baby,"

My lips pull, cheeks tightening as I struggle to hold back a smile. Our locked fingers release as we glide toward the pool's edge and rest our arms onto the smooth tiles. We stay here a moment, nothing but the serenade of the little red-eyed creatures filling the air. Like a concert meant only for us.

"We should get ice cream after this," I suggest.

Most everyone in town frequents Sandy's Igloo, the ice cream shop that still serves baskets of fresh hamburgers and greasy fries by car hops on roller skates until late in the night. A lot of kids from school make the drive to Sandy's, a short twenty minute drive to a nearby town, the only local hangout open past nine. The small restaurant opened in 1951, and remains like a monument to the small town charm that locals hold so dear.

"You're going to be late getting home. Your mother is going to kill you," he warns.

"Mama doesn't care anymore." I swallow down the hardened lump in my throat. "I mean—at least she tolerated me after Daddy left. But ever since Skylar left too, feels like nothing but pure hate when she looks at me."

He spins in the water, resting his elbows as he presses his back into the pool's edge. His gaze shifts, up toward the stars, carefully choosing the right words to say.

Mothers are a heated topic for us, but we've found something stronger in each other. A bond that feels unshakable. Built from all the things we've survived. Jay's grandparents stepped up as their daughter fought demons we'll never quite understand. But Jeanne Scott has welcomed me into their home. Like family. And on sticky summer nights, we spend most of our time scrounging for late night snacks in her kitchen, blaring music as we lay on his bedroom floor.

Jay quietly lets the moment pass, knowing I get much too worked up on the subject of Abilene Ellis, often spitting fire from the tip of my tongue.

"Are you planning to go to college?" he asks.

The crease between my brows deepens as I ponder a future never questioned before. "Why are you asking?" I turn my body, my gaze pinned directly on his now. His smile fades. He chews at his lip the way he does when something gnaws at him.

"Sawyer—you're smart. Way smarter than I am. Naturally, college is the next step for you."

"Not if I have to leave you," I say, my lips pressing together in defiance.

"You can't stay here." He turns to face me directly now, something in his eyes pleading with desperation, like he wants me to stay, but the words stick before they come out. "You and I both know you're better than this."

"Well—what if I don't want to leave? What if I'm happy here with you?"

A drowned dragonfly floats toward us, its wings shimmering in iridescent blue. Gently, I cup my hands together beneath it, lifting it from the water, placing it onto the deck to dry. As if life will return to its tiny body. As if it will magically take off in flight.

Something catches in my throat as I feel his eyes lock onto mine. His breaths quicken, heart pounding so loudly I can hear its muffled beat. My gut somersaults. Heat rises up the back of my neck. I reach with my toes, finding his warm skin and tightly locking my leg around his like we're one. A silent vow to never let him go. "I'm happy here with you," I whisper.

Our fingertips glide along the water's surface. Slowly. Making our way toward the comfort of each other's hand. He pushes closer to me, his eyes carefully tracing the outline of my lips. My pulse races. He wants to kiss me. I've known for a while. And it seems almost inevitable that our friendship has led us here. The thing is, I want to kiss him, too. With his glasses off, he appears much older. More a chiseled heartthrob that makes teenage girls fall to their knees than the boyish nerd with glasses I met that day after school. I push closer to him now, the warmth of his body slowing my racing pulse, our fingers still interlocked.

Tires *screech* on pavement somewhere off the main road, shrills of laughter carrying through the dark. The heavy air lifts, the moment passing as we both swallow it back down until it decides to resurface. Our hands release each other, and we both turn, pressing our spines into the pool's edge.

"What are you going to do?" I ask. I swat at another bug floating along the rippled surface. "After high school, I mean."

"I don't know—maybe I'll work at my grandfather's company. They've been on my case about it for years."

Jay's grandfather owns a successful construction business of some sort, though I don't really understand what they do. Women and men in yellow hard hats survey land for local contractors, though it seems like only swamp marsh is left. Everything else now a concrete maze of discount stores and new housing for snowbirds that flee during winter months.

"That actually sounds awful," I reply. "Soul killing."

"Sawyer, I can't stay under their roof forever. I was never their responsibility to take on."

I choke on my words, wishing I could take them back. Wetness pricks at the corners of my eyes. I splash at them with chlorine water, a fast attempt to hide the threatening flood "I know—" I drop my head back onto the tiled surface as water gently laps at my ears. The moon is a perfect crescent with the bright glow of Venus directly on its heels. "Maybe we can get a place together."

"Sawyer—" he begins, releasing a breath like a tire losing air. "You're going to live in a big city somewhere, writing editorials for some stuffy magazine that you're absolutely going to hate. But everyone will eat it up because you're undoubtedly the smartest person I know."

"Well—I'm not leaving you behind." I lift my chin, clearing at my throat. "So, I hope you like the city life. It's you and me. No matter what."

His smile pulls wider now, velvet-brown eyes crinkle at the corners.

"Deal?" I ask.

"Deal."

My curled fist lifts to the door, vapor curling from each and every breath. My shoulders rise and fall. Weight shifts right to left. Electric zaps buzz from above as something flies to its death in the glow of a porch light. A wooden sign swings from a post in the garden bed to my right, the name Scott etched into the grain.

Cold whispers up my spine as the front door swings open, heat spilling from the dimly lit foyer.

"Sawyer—" Her eyes widen in surprise.

Her cinnamon perfume invades the air around me, choking out the scent of rain on pavement behind.

"How did—" I begin.

She nods toward the newly installed cameras flanking each side of the door frame.

"Oh," I manage out. I stuff my hands deep into my coat pockets, not quite sure what to do with them. Not quite sure why I'm here. Feels like I'm chasing dead ends in circles, no closer to the truth than I was when I first arrived.

"Come on in," Jeanne offers, taking a step back as she waves me inside.

She tugs at her robe, wrapping it tightly around as she reties the belt at her waist. A simple grayish-blue cashmere, with matching slippers on her feet. Always the vision of perfection.

The house smells of pine-scented floors and tiny dishes of dried petals and spice. Our homes sit in the same neighborhood, one kept with care, the other gone to waste. She closes the door behind us, immediately jumping to offer me a drink.

"Can I get you something to drink, Sawyer?" She steps behind, gently tugging at the shoulders of my coat as I peel my arms from the waterlogged fabric. "Coffee? Sweet tea?"

"Just water is fine, thank you."

"Of course. Take your coat off. Make yourself comfortable. This is still your home, too, honey."

She quickly disappears around the corner, where a large, open kitchen sits. I know the layout well, spent more time at Jay's home than we ever did mine. I peel the coat from my arms, gently hanging it onto a hook fastened to the wall. I dig my toe into the heel of my left boot, kicking it off and repeating with the right. The Scotts never wear shoes inside of the house. Never have a single knick knack out of place.

The large flat screen television plays a football game from the living room. A Christmas tree, that has to be at least twelve feet tall, casts a glow of soft white across the room, each branch perfectly flocked and decorated with precision. It gnaws at me. It shouldn't...but it does. I hope it was decorated before Jay's death. I can't understand how the holiday just keeps growing closer. How there could be anything here to celebrate.

Jeanne reappears, sparkling glass of ice water, lemon wedge garnished on top, dangling in her hand.

"Have a seat, dear," she says, following close behind as I make my way toward the deafening sports game and drop down onto the couch. Plush velvet sinks and practically swallows me down.

She hands the glass to me and reaches for a remote, muting the volume as fans cheer on a touchdown victory. I don't follow the sport. Never really understood it. Never took to it at all. Jeanne drops down onto her recliner, its cushions like soft clouds that hug you tight.

I spent many summer nights in that chair, watching Jay strum on his guitar as some movie we were never going to actually watch played in the background. Jay was a musician. A *real* musician. He possessed a natural talent for instruments, and I'm sure that one day he could have played somewhere like Carnegie Hall.

"Sawyer, it's so wonderful to see you. I'm glad you decided to visit," she proclaims excitedly, smoothing imaginary wrinkles from the cashmere fabric. She crosses her legs at her ankles. Always prim. Always proper. "I didn't realize you would be staying past the service."

I blink. Blink again. My chest hurts, something twisting in it tight. It's like I can feel him in this house. In this room.

"Are you planning to move back into town?"

"No," I reply sharply. I ease my back into the cushions, softening my tone. My anger isn't toward Jeanne Scott. She took both Jay and I in like we were her own. "Maybe through the holiday. Then I have to go home."

A clock *ticks* loudly somewhere, spilling from the kitchen. A metronome. The only thing breaking our carefully worded pleasantries, wrapped in unspoken grief. Perfectly wrapped gifts in shimmering gold with red bows sit underneath the tree, flickering lights bouncing off the paper in fractiles that project like glitter across the room. Something out of a magazine.

"Catching up with Abilene?" she asks.

I lift my heels onto the edge of the couch, wrapping my arms tightly around my knees. "Not really. Not much."

Jeanne clears at her throat, sipping at a glass of white colored wine that sits at the table to her right. "Things not any better between you both?"

"Worse," I choke out.

Greedily, I throw back the ice water. My mouth feels like a desert at high noon, every word trapped behind a wall of dust. The Scotts tiny, beloved fluffball of a dog appears at my feet. Queenie. Hypoallergenic, of course. Always pampered. Always with some sort of bow around her neck in some nauseating shade of pink.

"Queenie!" Jeanne calls out, reaching her palm down to the floor and patting at it. "Come here. Leave Sawyer be."

Queenie obeys, her tiny body making a few circles before finally resting at Jeanne's feet. Jeanne lets out a sigh, barely audible. But loud enough for me to hear.

"Sawyer—I know you miss him. How have you been getting along?"

How have I been getting along? How has she been getting along? How could any of us move on from this?

"I've been okay," I lie.

"I'm actually glad that you stopped by. There's something I wanted to give you," she offers, pushing up from her chair and shuffling to the Christmas tree, slippers dragging across the floor. "Now, I don't have to mail it."

Jeanne leans down, reaching for a small box wrapped in shimmering gold, perfectly tied red ribbon around the paper. She turns, shuffling toward me again as I plant my feet back onto the floor. Her arm reaches out, gift in hand, waiting for me take it from her. Waiting for some sort of acknowledgement on my face.

"Well—go on," she insists.

I reach for her, gently grasping the gift in my hands and sliding it into my lap. Limbs frozen, like some sort of ticking time bomb is buried within the tiny box. Jeanne turns, dropping right back into place and sipping at her wine.

"Jay's Christmas gift," she says.

I shift uncomfortably. My heart lurches into my throat.

"You don't have to open it now."

I release the breath from my chest, shoulders dropping with relief. I simply can't. Not here. Not now.

Queenie shakes her fluffy coat, spinning in a circle before jumping into Jeanne's lap. She has to be the most spoiled, yet loved dog that I've ever seen. Absolutely smothered with affection.

"Sawyer, I can tell you're having trouble healing from this," she observes. "The absence of our loved ones is never easy."

Absence? Absence is my father walking out on our family. Absence is missing a day of school to enjoy the blistering sun. Jay isn't absent. He's never coming back.

I swallow down disgust. I've always adored Jeanne, but even the mention of healing from this tastes like bitter melon in my throat.

Her face pulls somber. "I lost a daughter and a grandchild," she says. She presses her spine into the back of her chair, her shoulders slump with defeat.

"Tanya was right there," I protest. "At Jay's funeral. Doesn't that make you angry?"

"No." She ponders a moment, her curious eyes flitting about the room. "It doesn't."

"Well, it would have made Jay mad. You know that's the truth."

"Sawyer, addiction can swallow a person whole. It isn't them anymore. They don't mean harm to others. Tanya fell sick long ago. She fought something we can never understand, but she's still my daughter...she did what she felt was best to give Jay a better life than she could ever give."

"Well, she made absolutely no effort to be a part of his life. And he died with that. He died with that pain," I choke out, recalling the many conversations we shared about our cold, detached mothers over the years.

"I believe Jay's at peace now, and once we cross over, the pain collected during our lives is replaced with warmth and love."

Well, I don't believe that for a second. Jay can't possibly have peace. Not until I track down who is responsible for ripping life from his grasp.

"Would you like to see his room?" she offers.

My heart pounds against my chest. A painful and gut-wrenching *thump, thump, thump.*

"You spent so much time in that bedroom, Sawyer. Maybe it will help you to see it once more."

"Okay," I say, the word tumbling out before I can blink. I straighten from the couch, legs trembling beneath as I take one more long drink of ice water. It twists in my chest like a tourniquet, squeezing the breath from my lungs.

"You can head back. I'll give you some time alone," she says.

I take another breath. Slowly in through my nose, holding it in my chest and finally pushing it out, jagged in my throat like shards of glass. I place the glass onto the coffee table, slowly making my way toward the back hall.

Photographs in simple frames lined in gold decorate the walls like a shrine. Feels more like a tomb, though. Like I'm being buried alive. Our graduation picture the most recent, as Jay hugs me tightly in royal blue robes with tassels hanging from our hats. Our smiles wide and bright, ready to take on the world, still hopeful in spite of the scars only we could understand.

The television blares again in the background, causing my heart to practically leap into my throat. Another slow breath and I continue down the hall toward the framed door of heavy pine. A lifetime of memories behind its silent weight, thick with everything he left behind. I wrap trembling fingers around its knob, turning as I open to the time capsule holding its breath.

Posters still cling to his walls—his favorite bands and some of mine. The sheets are tucked tightly beneath the mattress. Each book spine on his shelf aligned. Jeanne must have tidied everything up, though his shoes still sit at the foot of his bed, laces still tied. As if he might swing his feet down at any moment. As if everything that's happened has been a lie.

The scent of his cologne wraps around me, its scent buried into old carpet where we used to lay on lazy afternoons after long days at school.

My feet pin beneath me, knees lock into place. It's as if I can feel him behind me, feel his warm breath on the back of my neck.

A shadow casts along the wall. My head spins over my shoulder and toward the open door, but no one, nothing, is there. The *whooshing* hum of heat that spills from the ceiling vent quiets, a cold chill racing up my spine in its wake. A cold that feels like something dark pressing onto my shoulders, holding me hostage as goosebumps rise over my flesh.

"Jeanne?"

I turn, taking careful steps to the door frame, peeking my head down the hall where Jeanne still sits with Queenie on her lap, sipping down the last of her nightly wine. I swallow hard, unable to wash it away. My gut wrenches tight as I close myself inside of the shrine. Locked with his memories. Locked with my grief.

I make my way to the neatly-made bed and perch myself onto the side. Papers and pictures lay scattered across the surface of the bedside table. I flick on the lamp and gently sort through the messy pile of memories—notes scribbled with phone numbers, bills he never got around to paying, and printed photographs he never put away. I shuffle through them, pain filling my chest as I face each one. Another shadow creeps across the bedroom window. Probably branches from the winter-bare magnolia tree in the backyard, loosely blowing in the night's breeze.

I tug at the bedding, yanking at its neatly tucked edges and wrapping it around my shoulders, inhaling the scent of him just one last time. As if I can keep him alive in my chest. A photograph buried beneath the scattered pile catches my eye, Jay and I poised at the side of his backyard pool, sun dusting our shoulders a faint shade of pink, eyes sparkling with something long gone. I peel it from the table, my lips curl at the corners, forming some semblance of a smile.

Something grips its claws around me, stealing the breath straight from my lungs. Staring back at me, another photograph, Jay surrounded by three faces I recognize from school. Two of the guys in the photograph a hazy memory, the other clear as day as it slices like a knife at my throat. His dirty blond hair a tousled mess, something wicked peering through the lens like a warning, a promise to destroy me the second I get too close.

Bryce Kincaid.

I rush to my feet, hands trembling as I brush through the pile that remains, knocking the lamp over as it lands with a loud *thump* onto the floor. My breaths quicken and my pulse races as Jeanne's slippers shuffle toward the door.

"Sawyer?" she calls out. "Everything okay?"

I tuck Jay's neatly wrapped Christmas gift into the safety of my elbow and rush to her, fighting to unearth every word buried in my throat. "Do you know them?" I ask, anxiously tapping my finger onto the glossy surface of the photograph.

She pulls the glasses from the top of her head down onto the bridge of her nose. "Ahh...yes. I saw them a few times. They came to the house. Nice boys. I was glad Jay started to make friends."

My brow creases. I gnaw at a mangled cuticle on my left hand.

"Besides you, of course. It was just hard on him with you being so far away."

"Can I have this?" I ask, tucking it into the inner pocket of my coat, not even waiting for a reply.

"Of course, Sawyer. Take anything you'd like."

I release a heavy breath, rushing past her shoulders and toward the fresh air outside before I choke to death in here, buried with his weight pressed into my spine.

My fingers reach for the heavy coat and swing open the front door, icy air slapping me across the face as I pull it shut behind me and sink into its frame. I pull the photograph from my coat pocket, fingers brushing across their faces as panic sluices my throat. I need to find Colt and

Wes. Now. Time is bleeding out faster than I can catch it, every second tightening the noose around my neck.

Chapter Thirteen

A sharp *crack* slices through the crowd of patrons, followed by a skittering *clatter* over thin felt. Music thumps from speakers, and voices battle to carve out space in the noise. Their feet grind tossed peanut shells into the floor as they drone on and on about holiday plans, as if any of it matters, as if there's anything left here to celebrate. I shift on the metal, hard seat, sliding the half empty glass of foamy golden ale in tiny circles on top of the bar. The liquid rocks and splashes against the sides like tiny waves lapping at a shore.

Penny pours carefully measured shots into a shiny metal cocktail shaker, her yellow hair slipping from an elastic band and cascading over her shoulders as shimmering silver chases on its heels. The mirror behind the bar catches the glow of holiday lights, drawing my attention like a crack of lightning in the sky or the flash of a camera snapped in your face. I lift my fingers, tucking wet hair behind my ears, smoothing palms over the top of my head. It isn't much. And it doesn't really help my appearance...shadows beneath my eyes, ashen and pale skin.

I peel the photograph from the inside of my coat, laying it down onto the lacquered grain to study just a little closer. My skin crawls like tiny bugs that make me want to scratch, and my chest tightens like a steel cable twisting mercilessly until I snap. Four faces stare back at me. Bryce drapes his arm across Jay's shoulders, pulling him close as if they're brothers, as if they share some unspoken bond. His tousled blond hair grown out from the photo in Skylar's yearbook, his frame filled out and shoulders broad. His lips curl up, pulling at his cheeks as he smiles through a lit cigarette that sits, dangling from between his teeth. A white cloud billows, partially obstructing one eye from view. But the other, dark, cold, pupil and iris made of the same color, something evil that chases up my spine.

The other two in the photograph are vaguely familiar. Skylar could most likely confirm. They always hung at Bryce's side, though, like cowards that took orders and nipped like chihuahuas at his heels. One has tightly curled dark hair. A tattoo in black ink peeks from the collar of his shirt, climbing up the side of his neck. I squint, only able to make out a faded cross and some sort of bible verse beneath a stubbled chin. His eyes, also dark, lids drooping as if he struggles to stay on his feet. The third stands at Jay's other side, fingers clasped together in front of his waist, stance wide as he pushes his jaw forward. Clearly a tactic of intimidation, though if Jay is six feet two, then this guy can't be more than five three. The corner of my mouth twitches. A silent laugh pushes from my nose. Fast. Then my eyes focus back to Jay's vacant eyes, suddenly pulling me back into the grave.

"You ready for another, honey?" a voice rattles from behind the bar.

Penny stares back at me, pouring beers from taps without even looking, leaving the perfect amount of foam at each glass top. Irritation drags behind each word as her tired eyes flit with impatience at my lack of response. She's a seasoned bartender with a no-nonsense vibe. I can respect that.

"Oh—" I sit up straighter now on the cold metal, shifting right and left with no relief. "I'll just take the check. I think I'm actually going to head out."

Her eyes roll back, strictly a performance for me as she turns to deliver two carefully crafted cocktails to men in suits at the end of the bar.

Someone decides to take up karaoke, practically screaming into a muffled microphone as they stand center stage before the rowdy crowd. Tinsel garland drapes around their neck as they shout slurred and drunken lyrics to the praise of cheers and clapping hands. I tap my fingers against the lacquer, carefully deciding my next steps. I came to Blackwood Social with the hope I would run into Colt again, but of course, he's nowhere to be found. Sounds about right. Cops never seen to be around when you actually need them. Too busy writing traffic citations or harassing the homeless for loitering.

Penny returns, holding out a slip of receipt paper and a pen.

"Can I ask you something?" I blurt out.

She lowers the paper and sets it down onto the bartop. I carefully slide the now-creased photograph across to her. Her expression puzzles, brows dancing as she drags her tired eyes across the four men captured and sealed onto glossy paper.

"Penny, have you seen these guys around here before?" My voice rattles—a mix of hope and nerves. I figure everyone who lives in town must visit Blackwood Social from time to time, even children who probably lick hamburger grease from their fingers as their parents drink overpriced craft beer. Penny places reading glasses onto the bridge of her nose, leaning for a closer look as the glow of light reflects off their faces. Her eyes widen, seemingly in recognition. She taps at the photo.

"These boys—I remember them." She lifts the reading glasses and perches them back onto the top of her head. "That's the Kincaid boy. Comes in here every so often flashing his money around, barking orders at me behind the bar. Probably hasn't been told no a day in his life."

"And the others?" I ask.

"Hmm...don't know their names. But they were in here maybe two weeks ago," she replies, her voice rising as if she's asking a question more than making a statement. "Something like that. The Kincaid boy and those two on the ends were just hootin' and hollerin' in my bar, got into a fight over something. I figured some girl, but it was pretty bad. They were drinkin' hard. Probably overserved by my other bartender. She's new, lacks common sense sometimes. Hard to find good help."

"No idea what they were fighting about?"

"Nope, but it got physical. One slammed his fist on the table and made the drinks spill everywhere. Then fists just started flailing and they were at each other's throats. Couple of other folks tried to pull one off the other, while their friend just watched it all go down. I had a couple of my regulars toss 'em out. Told 'em they aren't welcome in here anymore. This ain't that kinda bar, you know."

My pulse quickens, a mix of vindication and dread. Two weeks ago would have been right around Jay's death, and the three of them at each other's throats right around the same time leaves suspicion and implications that are nothing but dark.

The drunken karaoke turns into some incoherent medley of every swear word imaginable.

"Excuse me a minute, honey," Penny says, reaching underneath the bar, pressing some invisible button that immediately cuts power to the music and the microphone, leading to a drunken temper tantrum on the tiny stage. "Now y'all know better!" she yells out. "Can't control yourselves, then you know where the door is. You can see yourselves out."

Penny stands on business, running the bar like the commander of a tight ship. Intimidating, but probably the person you'd feel safest with the second trouble stirs.

"Did the police ever talk to you about that night?" I ask. "Did anyone report them?"

She slides the photograph back across the bar. "Well, I did mention it to that detective a few days later, the one who always comes in here on his lunch break. Told him about them causin' a ruckus, but he didn't seem too interested in any of it. Said he'd look into it, but I never followed up. I guess he didn't either."

An impatient customer at the other end of the bar shouts Penny's name. She holds up a finger, shooting a daggered gaze across the bar. "Now, I've got eyes all over this bar. I know you're there," she scolds. "Give me a damn minute,"

She turns back to me, eyes warming again, filling me with nostalgia of better days in this town. Days that weren't filled with Jay's absence and something awful chasing on my heels.

I reach across the bar, cupping my palms over her hand. "Thank you, Penny. I owe you one."

"Now, you don't owe me anything...'cept that check in front of you right there," she says, nodding toward the counter.

"Right," I reply, embarrassingly digging my hands into each coat pocket until I find the wadded pile of cash and toss a crinkled bill onto the counter.

"You need change?" she asks.

I slide down from the stool, boots planting firmly with determination. "Nope!"

I make my way through the bar, trading air thick with peanuts and bitter hops for the sharp cold outside. A heavy silence fills Main Street. The chatter of drunk patrons now a muffled, distant cry. My boots pin to the worn, cracked sidewalk, my spine presses against a brick wall.

A week has passed. Christmas is almost here. Feels like time is just slipping through my fingers like sand, but I still have to find Wes and Colt. No time to waste.

I pull the keys from my pocket and push forward. This'll be another sleepless night, but who can sleep when everything they have in this world either flinches, leaves or dies?

Still, there's something different in the air, something that crawls across my flesh like death itself, dragging its teeth over every inch of me.

I slam the door behind me. A line of cars, mostly pickup trucks, tuck along the shoulder of the road. I follow the all-too-familiar path, through the darkened tree line, the throb of music and murmurs of voices growing louder with each step. Finally....the clearing, with the same rambunctious crowd gathered around with cans of cheap beer and weed, as the fire's flames paint a flicker of orange across faces in the dark. I always felt like an outsider at these things during high school. Now, years later, everything and nothing has changed.

I push forward, swallowing like I'm drowning in open air, forcing a polite smile at a few familiar faces.

The bonfire roars, flames reaching high. My gaze sweeps over the crowd, searching for Colt's tall frame, but the darkness swallows everything beyond the circle of light. Dozens mill about, their silhouettes laughing, passing around red cups and tiny papers rolled tight with weed. The treeline looms like a ring of silent onlookers, just beyond the reach of the fire's glow.

Somewhere, bass thrums through the ground, pulsing at my chest. The heat of flames burns at my cheeks, then...a sharp *crack* from deep in the woods. I flinch, heart jolting against my ribs.

A hand rises high into the air waving frantically. Birdie bounds toward me, red plastic cup sloshing in her hand. She wraps her free arm tightly around my neck.

"You're still here!" she exclaims loudly. She pulls back, cheeks flushed from firelight and alcohol. "Have you been holding up okay? I heard you've been asking around...you know, like looking into things?"

Now, how in the hell Birdie got this information is a mystery to me. I don't ask. But if there's gossip to be had, she's always the first to eat it up. Well intentioned, but doesn't know when to quit. I remain guarded. She's already halfway to spinning a story for the whole damn town.

"Not really. Just dredging up old memories, I guess," I say.

A lie. Bold-faced and brazen. But I can't risk anything getting to Bryce or his lackeys before I can get to Wes or Colt. That might give them too much time to cover their tracks. To switch up their stories. To bury the truth six feet underground and erase everything that's left of Jay. I gnaw at a cuticle on my left hand, hoping she's satisfied enough to let it go.

"Oh Sawyer, I know it has to be so hard," Birdie offers, gently circling my back with her palm. "Especially this close to Christmas. Are you going back home to spend the holiday with someone special?"

Someone special. How do I tell her I spent the last year in almost complete solitude? Other than co-workers who all disappear into fluorescent lit cubicles anyway. Shutting out the real world and everyone in it. How do I explain that Jay has been my only lifeline in this world? My gaze falls, gently nudging at a pebble beneath my right boot. "No one special. But I hope to be home soon."

"Well—this is always your home, Sawyer. A lot of people in town still care about you," she says, trying her best to reassure me.

But...no one actually cares. Other than the occasional "Happy Birthday," I haven't stayed in touch with anyone in town aside from

Jay. Though surprisingly...it's been nice to catch up with Wes and Colt, words I never thought I'd say. "Thanks, B."

A *squeal* of laughter slices through the air, sharp and jolting. Our heads snap toward the water's edge where someone has Elizabeth Ryan's feet kicking into the air, her body slung over their shoulder like a flour sack, the unrecognizable culprit threatening to toss her into murky water in some strange mating ritual that simple guys do for pretty girls.

"Ugh—they're so cute, don't ya think?" Birdie swoons.

"Who is that with her?" I ask.

"Josh Searcy. Isn't he a drink of water? Apparently, they've been talking for awhile, but Josh seems to be getting more serious about her. He goes to Florida State, but came here just to spend the holiday with her. I think it's so romantic," she replies.

I admire Birdie's ability to romanticize literally everything in life. It has to be better than seeing everything through a dirty lens.

"It's too bad you can't hang out during warmer months. Last summer, Dane Whitlock got too drunk and fell into the swimming pit fully dressed. Came out looking like some sort of swamp monster!" she cackles, forcing me to break into a genuine smile.

"Whitlock?" I ask. I've never heard the name. Not in this town. Not from our time in school.

"Yeah—Dane's family moved here like...few years ago, I think. Most everyone calls him Zeph, but I'm not real sure why. Guess it just stuck."

"Zeph?" I choke out, the name like razor wire curling deep with every breath.

"Yeah. He hangs around Bryce a lot. I think they both come from money, 'ya know? Think they're the Kings of town just because their families are loaded," Birdie says, rolling her eyes.

"Listen—" I begin with urgency. "Have you seen either of them here tonight?"

"Oh! I know I saw Bryce earlier. Causing a scene as usual. Probably doing something stronger than beer, if you ask me."

Her carefully pinned hair now falls in messy tendrils, framing her face. Loose. Not looser than her lips, though. My eyes scan the crowd, desperately searching for Colt or Wes. Feels like the clock is ticking, every moment standing here a colossal waste.

"You looking for someone?" she asks.

"Birdie, have you seen Colt or Wes here?"

"Oh, you definitely missed Colt. He was here earlier, but not in any official capacity, know what I mean?" she winks.

Of course. Colt seems to be everywhere and nowhere all at once. I wonder what he was doing out here, though, or if he has any possible leads on the case.

"Oh!" She reaches for my wrist, clasping her fingers as she drags me toward the rambunctious crowd. "You need a drink. And I know *everyone* wants to see you before you head out of town."

A chorus of my name stirs through the sharp air as I force a cautious, but polite smile. Birdie, always the perfect host, excitedly reaches for a cup, grabbing the nozzle of the steel barrel and quickly filling it to the top. It sloshes as she pushes it toward me, but I take it from her graciously, sipping the cheap stuff and forcing it down my throat. Birdie's attention flits to new arrivals breaking through the treeline.

"You okay if I go mingle for a bit?" she asks.

"Of course, B."

The words fly out, too sharp and too eager, driven by a burning need to break free and steal a glimpse at Bryce and Dane, if that's what they call him. I call him a monster. They're both monsters and I blame them for everything.

"Great," she says, pulling me for another quick embrace. "Come find me before you leave, okay?"

"Yeah. Sure."

Birdie flits off as I toss the beer onto the ground and scan over the the crowd one more time, until I spot the familiar thinning blond hair, buttons ready to burst at the seams. I push forward, brushing shoulders with shadowed faces as I beeline straight for Wes' large frame.

"Wes!" I call out, frantically waving my hand in the dark until he turns, confusion washing over his features, shoulders dropping with ease as he finally recognizes my face.

"Sawyer—hey," he beams. "I didn't know you were still in town."

"Yeah," I rattle out, vapor curling from my mouth.

He lifts a paper coffee cup to his lips, steam rising from its lid.

"Coffee?" I ask, eyes wide with surprise. "You working tonight? About to haul us all in?"

His eyes crinkle at the corners, a muffled laugh escaping through his nose. "Just here unofficially. You know, making sure things don't get out of control."

"Got time to talk?" I ask.

"For you? Always," he assures, placing a hand behind my shoulder and guiding me toward a pickup truck backed up to the water's edge. Just far enough away from prying ears and curious eyes.

I slide onto the tailgate. Wes grunts slightly as he lifts his large frame and joins at my side. My fingers reach within my coat pocket, fishing for the creased photograph as I wrestle with what to say. What—I have a hunch? A strong instinct? Their names sound the same? I push it toward him, clasping my hands in my lap as my shoulders drop with doubt and defeat. "Wes?"

A moment of silence catches between us, short and quick as he waits patiently for what it is I need to say.

"Yes?" he replies.

"Every time I come out here, I swear...I can still see us all as kids. It's like no time has passed us by." My feet swing carelessly as they dangle off the tailgate's edge. "Same stupid jokes. Same small town drama. Like a time capsule that we can't escape."

Nothing. Just more *squeals* of laughter from somewhere behind us as we sit with our memories in the dark. He pats my hand lightly, like a quiet promise that I'm not alone.

"Something tells me that's not why you pulled me aside," he finally replies. "You alright?"

"Not really." I sigh. Loud and exhausted as I lower my gaze. Roughly, I rub at my fingers, as if I'm trying to rub the skin away. "Can you tell me anything about that night? Did you respond to the—" I choke back tears. Unable to spit the rest of it out.

He shifts uncomfortably, a small *groan* rumbling low in his chest. My gaze pins to his again, not sure if I'm ready to hear the details, but needing the answers anyway.

"All I can say, Sawyer, is that it was quick. Ambulance got there as fast as they could. He didn't suffer long, I promise."

My eyes well with tears, and my chin trembles as I fight to keep them in.

"Come here," he says, pulling me close as I rest my head onto his shoulder.

"I just keep thinking—maybe if I hadn't left town, if I had kept in touch more, he might still be here. I should've seen the signs. I can't help but feel this is all my fault," I say, stunned at my own confession. The tears come rolling now, racing down my cheeks as my eyes sting in the biting cold.

"You can't blame yourself. We've got our own paths. Jay made his choices. Sometimes there's nothing anyone can do."

He wipes at a tear trickling down my cheek, another rolling down right behind it. "I became a cop to save people. Thought it might give me purpose, maybe make up for stupid antics in the past," he says, glancing up at the blanket of stars above. "But I've learned I just can't always save them. Doesn't matter how much I do."

And suddenly, I realize that Wes carries burdens, too. Probably a weight unimaginable, stuffed down, hidden by his tough cop demeanor.

"Sawyer—did you find something? Did you come here looking for me and Colt?"

I sniffle, lifting my head and wiping my cheeks dry. Again, I reach into the coat pocket, this time pulling out the photo and urging him to take it into his hands. "I found that in Jay's bedroom," I say, my words now determined and clear. "Recognize their faces?"

Wes reaches into his back waistband, pulling out a flashlight and shining it onto the gloss as goosebumps prick across my flesh.

"I showed this to a woman who works at Blackwood Social. Penny. She remembers them, Wes. Said they were in there right around the time Jay died. Two weeks ago. *Two*. Got into a heated argument that got out of hand. She threw them out, it got so bad."

Wes' tongue presses into his cheek as his gaze flits over the faces staring back at him. "Bryce Kincaid," he responds flatly. He shines the light directly toward Jay's other side. "That looks like Grayson Black. David Black's son. You remember David Black?" he asks. "Grayson's our age, but he went to the old vocational tech school on the west side of town. The family owns a shitload of property." He waits. Waits for a sign of recognition in my eyes. But I don't really remember. "Anyways, they have money and no regard for the law. That's all I'll say."

I nod, pulse quickening its steady, thumping beat. My finger taps at the gloss paper now. "Whitlock," I blurt. "Dane, I think Birdie said. People call him Zeph, Wes. Sound familiar?"

His tongue shoves into his cheek again. Head twisting left to right.

"The names on the paper I showed you guys, Wes. Cade10699? DarkZephyr? And I would bet money that Grayson is the third."

My words hang in the air with desperation. Waiting for him to jump to his feet.

"Well?" I ask.

"I mean—it definitely sounds like something worth looking into," he finally concedes. He shifts again. "Can I keep this?"

"You'll give it to Colt?" I ask.

"First thing in the morning," he promises.

My lips pull tight, curling into my cheeks as I sling my arm across his wide-shouldered frame. "Thank you. You guys are my only hope," I say, knowing good and well that I plan to investigate them myself.

"Sawyer, don't worry too much. If there's something here, we'll find it. Not much we could do with a body and no witnesses, but this we can work with. You just might be onto something."

I pull back, flattening my palms and pushing off the tailgate, landing on soft ground. I wipe at the back of my jeans, cleaning off dirt, fish guts, and whatever else lives in these backwoods trucks. He steps down beside me, reaching back to grab the paper cup holding his daily caffeine.

"I'm going to head out and get some rest back at the house." I gently rub at the dark, puffy skin beneath my eye. The white parts probably bleeding red now after my emotional display. "I haven't slept much, I guess."

"Sawyer, go home. We've got this, okay?"

I nod, waving the invisible white flag between us. As much as I like Wes, he's still a cop. And I won't forget they're the ones who closed the case and walked away. I desperately need their connections and help, but there's no way I'm just going to sit back and wait.

"Alright, Wes. Here—give me your phone." I reach out, palm up as he gently places it into my hand. Quickly, I save my number to his contacts before pushing it back his way. "Call me as soon as you find out anything. Okay? I mean it. *Anything.*"

I turn, bounding back toward the fire, now raging out of control. It looks like someone threw a damn couch in it to burn, and honestly, the whole forest looks one spark away from going with it. Birdie stands in a gathered circle, eagerly swallowing every word being tossed around. I should tell her goodbye, just in case its our last. But something bad feeds like a parasite beneath my flesh, twisting around and around like a sickness waiting to strike. I bury my fists into my coat pockets, decidedly trading small talk for home.

I head toward the inky treeline as something evil catches in the corner of my eye. I narrow onto them, desperate to make out the figures in the dark. One face—clear as day. The other—back turned. The flickering glow of orange dangling at his side. A cigarette. He inhales deep, exhales slow, smoke curling upward as something passes between their hands.

My boots press in, dirt practically swallowing me whole as bile slowly rises up the back of my throat. Something like fear wraps like a noose around my neck, coiling as it slowly cuts the air supply to my chest. Bryce looks up, his eyes pinned in my direction. The other figure snaps his head over his shoulder to see what caught his friend's gaze. Friend. Accomplice. Business partner, maybe. Complicit in something sinister, something they clearly want to hide. I pull the hood of my coat over my head as I fight desperately to move my feet. I crouch, but catch *just* enough of the mystery figure's face to pin him to the photograph from Jay's room. Just enough to catch his familiar, small frame.

Don't stop, Sawyer. Move.

I pick up the pace now, desperate to put as much space between us before they recognize my face. Finally, I push into the trees, through the webbed moss that hangs from low-hanging branches, a makeshift wall that seals me just out of reach. My shoulder brushes bark, and my palms scrape against wood as I toss myself behind an oak, each ragged breath stabbing at my ribs.

Something *snaps*. Behind me. Close. Leaves crunch as something hunts with slow, deliberate steps. My lips press tight. I shake my head left to right, denying the dread clawing its way through me. These woods are filled with wildlife that stir in the dark. That's all it is. All that it could be.

Chapter Fourteen

Sweet Tea Junction sits at the bend of Highway 98 and Old Eagle Lake Road. Bustling, chaotic and absolutely drenched in southern charm. It's been here for decades. A relic of brick and rusted signage faded by years in the Florida sun. They boast the best flapjacks in town. I don't really see how you can mess up pancakes, though, seems pretty standard breakfast fare. But most everyone in town packs the place every Sunday morning. Even Mama and Daddy used to drag me and Skylar here when we were young.

Every table is filled. Waitresses in mismatched aprons glide through the crowd with ease, a delicate balance of hot plates, drink refills, and forced smiles. The tables *clatter* with half-finished plates. And church-goers fight against the blaring holiday music, their syrup-drenched laughs slicing through the sound. Cheap gold tinsel drapes from the window panes, and blinking lights dance to the music, lazily taped to the glass covered in spray-on snow that came straight from a can. A plastic tree flashes red and green in the corner, one strand flickering like it's gasping for air. The scent of maple syrup, scorched coffee and butter-drenched grits fills the diner. Children pound their sticky fists onto tables. And their parents pass out napkins like ammunition in some sort of sugar-fueled war. Old men hunch over their plates, giving the occasional side eye at the growing noise. A baby wails. And someone in the family of fifteen sitting crowded around the center tables laughs much too loud. The gold bell that hangs from the front door chimes once again. Wet rubber soles squeak past the bright yellow warning sign, across the tiled, mud-streaked floor. And rain slams the window in steady sheets with droplets slipping down the pane like they're trying to escape.

A palmetto bug seeks refuge on the sill. Fat. Dark. Its shell gleaming slick under the fluorescent lights. A dark, leathery ugly thing with a long antenna that twitches like it's sniffing me out. Its legs jitter as its beady little eyes seem to meet with mine. We stare at each other for a moment. Me, starved and mouth watering for a greasy plate of pancakes, country potatoes and eggs. Him, seeking shelter from the wet pavement outside. I blink. My head snaps. Startled by a drink somewhere crashing to the floor. I turn back. It's gone. Not skittering across the table. Not running around my feet. Leaving only the rain battered window at my side. I rest my chin in my cupped hand, elbow narrowly avoiding the coffee ring left behind.

Thunder rolls, shaking at the booth's metal base. I should leave. I think about it. Just for a moment, until my stomach growls loud enough for the next table to hear. I haven't eaten much in days, and I couldn't take another minute of Mama's rattling through the house, hacking between bad-smelling cigarettes, making it clear I'm not welcome to stay.

"You ready to order, honey?" a voice croaks with impatience above.

A waitress slaps a menu onto the table. I quickly flip it over. And over again. My fingers sticky with syrup that lingers on its laminated page. I quickly wipe them onto the front of my jeans.

"Can I get the Sunday special? Scrambled eggs. Sausage. And cheese grits."

"Coffee? Tea? Coke?"

My words catch, coming out in more of a stammer as I slink into the booth. "Just a coffee please. Sugar. Cream. You know—the fancy, vanilla kind."

Now I've gone too far. Pushed her to the brink. She sighs loudly, tapping her pen hard against the order book in her other hand. "We have half and half, honey." She pulls a dirty rag from her apron pocket, quickly wiping at the leftover coffee ring.

"Okay. That'll do," I reply. Half embarassed. Half too exhausted to care.

"Alright. Be back shortly," she says, turning curtly and rushing back through the crowd.

I fold my arms across my chest, spine sinking into the ripped vinyl booth. A Christmas song hums through speakers. And the *hiss pop* of pancake batter kisses a griddle from somewhere loud. It's much too noisy. Much too bright. But here, I sit invisible, just how I want to be. Lost in the excitement of hash browns and greasy bacon. Far away from *her*.

The bell rings loudly again, and a man steps inside and removes his wet brown crumpled hat.

"Have a seat anywhere!" a voice yells, slicing sharply through the grease-filled air.

One cup of bitter, black coffee and one pitcher of sad, flavorless cream are slid in front of me, the waitress gone again before I can even blink.

The man scans the crowd, but every seat seems to be filled. Though many sit, visiting with loved ones as the grease settles in their stomachs, table left with nothing but crumbs. I wave my hand high into the air, trying to grab his attention. Our eyes finally meet, and the corners of his mouth pull upward into his cheeks as I point at the empty booth seat.

He heads toward me, delicately shifting his frame through inattentive eyes.

"Brown!" I say excitedly, tapping at empty formica as he slides onto the seat straight across.

The noise in the diner dulls. Christmas music at the end of its playlist and the rolls of thunder now long gone. Water droplets now silent and still on the glass pane. Someone's spray can art display now a muddled, clouded thing. Brown sets his splotched, damp hat down beside him, the vinyl groaning beneath him as he shifts his weight.

"Well, kid—I gotta be honest. You look like hell."

"I feel even worse," I answer, tapping a spoon against the side of my mug.

I pour a splash of tasteless cream into the cup, gently swirling but not actually taking a drink. Brown taps his callused fingers on the edge of the table.

"Place is sure busy on Sundays after church. Almost turned around and went home," he says. "You doin' alright? I've been saving a hot dog for you at night. Hope to see you again before you skip town."

"I know, Brown. Things have just gotten so—" I run my fingers through damp strands of hair. "Complicated I guess."

"Well, your body needs fuel to keep going, kid. Food and sleep do wonders for a tired soul, you know," he offers.

"I know *what* I'm supposed to do. It's just that I can't. Food feels heavy and the nights way too long."

A different waitress brushes up against the table. Rushed. Quickly sliding one Sunday special in front of me—pancakes stacked five tall on the scalding plate. My eyes grow wide. And my tongue skates across my bottom lip as the scent of sausage, crisp and slightly burnt, punches at the air. Beside me, a tightly rolled napkin swaddles freshly shined silverware. I reach for it, greedily unwinding it as my mouth salivates in wait. I stab my fork into the fluffy cloud of yellow eggs, gulping down a bite much too big for my mouth. Brown stares back at me, lips slightly parted, a small chuckle bubbling from his chest.

"Aren't you going to eat?" I ask, quickly shoveling my fork into the congealed, lumpy grits, one square slice of yellow cheese half-melted across the top.

"Sure am. I know they're busy. I'll catch the waitress next time she comes around."

I push at a burnt sausage link, rolling it around the plate.

"Now, don't you feel you need to wait for me," he says. "You dig in and put some weight on those bones."

I oblige. Shoving the sausage into my mouth, greedily sucking on grease until I bite into something hard that chews like a rock between my teeth. I toss the fork onto the plate and lean into the table, voice hushed as I whisper secrets to my only friend in town.

"You know, I found something in Jay's old bedroom."

Brown's eyes widen as he waits patiently, hanging on my every word.

"A photo. Three guys—locals who went to school with Skylar, apparently. Well, men now, I suppose. I know one of them—"

"Yeah?"

"Yeah. Bryce Kincaid. You know the Kincaid's? Live on this side of town. House bigger than most know what to do with." I take a breath, pausing to gulp down another swig of bitter, burnt coffee as Brown waits patiently for the story to begin again. "The others—I think I know them, too. And Penny...Penny recognized them."

"Now, who is Penny again?" he asks, left eyebrow lifting as he struggles to place the name.

"Penny. The bartender at Blackwood Social," I reply, irritation dripping as Brown focuses on all the wrong things. "She said they got kicked out of the bar the night Jay died. Well—" I wiggle my fingers in the air as I count backward two weeks to the day. "It was definitely close to the same time. Got into a *very* heated fight. Fists flying. At each other's throats. Penny had them booted before they tore the place apart."

"That certainly sounds suspicious," he adds. "You tell the chief? Or that detective who works cases like this?"

On cue, my eyes roll into the back of my head as they often do with any mention of Colt Landry. "Chief hasn't been in, apparently. I've been dealing directly with Colt."

Brown sits quietly, wheels turning in his head.

"Detective Landry?" I ask, not sure how many locals actually know him as just "Colt."

"Oh right. Of course. Seems mighty young to be heading up Bartow's crime division. It used to be one of the best in the state."

My eyes flicker with impatience. "I haven't been able to tell him the latest. About the picture and—" My voice fades out as last night's moment of panic sluices down my throat.

"The picture and what, Sawyer?" Brown asks, drumming the pads of his fingers once again.

My voice hushes to a barely audible whisper now. "I saw them last night. Out on Connersville road. Well, I know I saw Bryce. Or...he saw me. Anyways, I think the guy he was with could be David Black's kid, Grayson." I turn my fork onto its side, eagerly slicing through the pancake pile and forcing another bite into my mouth. Steam rolls out of the flapjack's middle, spilling out like breath in winter air. "I can't say for certain, of course, but they were definitely passing something between their hands. Maybe drugs, you think?" I pause a moment, waiting patiently to field any questions that Brown might have. "Maybe secrets that can't be said out loud."

Somewhere across the diner, a fork drags across a plate, a grating sound that slowly drills into your skull, lingering far longer than it should. I stop talking. Stop blabbering incessantly, waiting for Brown to catch his breath.

"You think I'm crazy, don't you?" I ask.

"No," he replies. Short. Sharp. "You're not crazy, Sawyer." He leans in close, chest hovering over syrup that dripped from my plate. "You're closer to the truth. That's probably what makes it feel that way."

A perfect coffee ring sits on the table between us. I press my fingertip in, swirling in lazy circles before wiping it away with the shredded napkin across my thighs.

"I gave the picture to another cop last night. He promised to share with Landry. I'm still cautious, though. Can't forget they're the ones who decided to close the case."

He taps again at the table. Slow and steady. Like a metronome that no one else can hear. His gaze far away. Somewhere I can't follow.

"Smart to keep your guard up," he says, eyes drifting toward the other diners like they might be listening in. "But have you wondered how far that guard will take you before you're just standing there alone?"

I force another bite of lumpy, tasteless grits and rubbery cheese into my mouth. From the kitchen, a loud, rasping cough follows a clatter of metal onto the floor. No one reacts. Just part of the classic diner ambiance, I guess. Along with the smell of burnt toast and fryer grease.

"I know that boy loved you. Deeper than most men know how. Same look I used to get whenever my wife walked into the room." Brown leans in. Closer. Elbows on the table. Voice pitched so low that I almost can't hear it. "You ever think about jumping off that bridge?"

A pause stretches between us. The booth feels smaller. Tighter. The words land wrong. Heavy. Like cracks forming across a frozen pond, seconds before pulling you under until every last breath is squeezed from your chest.

"Sometimes you've gotta go where it happened. Jump headfirst. Might be the only way to feel him again."

I blink, fingers pulling at strips of the tattered paper napkin as my body settles with the weight.

"What did you say?" I ask, breath catching in my throat. I swallow hard, wishing I'd opted for a glass of cold water instead of the bitter dirt in my cup.

"I said maybe you oughta visit the bridge," he repeats gently. "It just might help you find some peace."

No trace of what I heard before. No suggestion of what I thought he said. I nod slowly. Not sure whether to believe him. Or if I can even believe myself.

"Sawyer, some things don't stay buried just because the town wants them to be. Some rot stays close to the surface."

I drop the fork onto the plate one last time, gently pushing at the lifeless, lukewarm food left sitting on my plate. The waitress reappears above me again, ready to top off the mug as she reaches for my plate. I place my palm over the rim. "I'm good here. Do I get the check from you?" I ask.

She releases a sigh of disapproval. And I sink again into the booth. She sets down my plate again to fish a black folded book from her apron pocket, slapping down a faded ink receipt. She grabs the dirty plate once more and quickly turns her back to top off anyone with a half filled mug. I glance across at Brown, now reaching for his crumpled hat and tucking it beneath his arm. He slides toward the booth's edge, groaning slightly as he plants onto the floor again and slowly straightens his legs. He perches the hat back onto his head, adjusting the brim on the old, crumpled thing.

"You're leaving already?" I ask, eyes flitting with curiosity. "But you didn't even—"

"Don't wait too long, Sawyer," he warns. His eyes pin with an urgency. "Rot travels fast."

And with that, he walks out. No goodbye. No glance back. Just a damp imprint left on the booth cushion, the only sign he was ever here.

I glance down at the tattered napkin on my lap. A palmetto bug watches as he lands with a tiny *thump* onto my jeans, it's papery wings folded tight, legs splayed in rigid paralysis. His beady eyes seem to meet mine. Maybe the same as before. We share a moment. Him watching me. Me watching him. His mandibles flex. And I bring my hand close, curling together my thumb and middle finger, sending the bug flying with one tiny flick.

Chapter Fifteen

The door cracks open as Jeanne suspiciously eyes the room, two glasses of freshly brewed sweet tea sloshing in her hands.

"I made tea for you both," she offers, eyes flitting about as she makes her final check of the night.

She never made checks before. Never seemed to feel the slightest concern about Jay and I spending time alone in this house. That was until she came home unannounced one summer afternoon and found us breaking every rule of decency in her pool. She seems to be a bit of a prude, never sharing in any displays of affection with Jay's grandfather. But she did crack a smile as she turned and walked away. I saw it. Only for a moment. Maybe for a second, it reminded her of days long gone. Days filled with secrets she holds tight. Jay and I have never done anything aside from swim anyway.

I rush toward the door, water droplets from my swimsuit spilling to the carpet below. "Thanks, Jeanne," I say, reaching to take each glass from her hands.

She gives me one last disapproving look, her narrowed eyes cutting directly to my swimsuit top and back up. Quick. But long enough.

Ice cubes clink against the glasses. I press a shoulder into the door, shutting it again as Jeanne shuffles off to bed. "She hates me."

Jay laughs through pursed lips. "She loves *you*. She just hates that you're corrupting her grandson."

"Corrupting you?" I push forward, straightening my spine as I make my way across the room, placing the sweating glasses down onto Jay's bedside table. "Right. How could I take advantage of her poor, innocent and defenseless baby boy?"

Jay snaps back his pool towel, winding it up good and hard before letting it fly straight at my right ass cheek. It stings. Lighting my skin on fire as I silently vow to get him back.

"Something wrong?" he taunts.

"Jay! You better sleep with one eye open, that's all I'll say."

"Are you going to change or just stand there and drip on the carpet all night?" he asks.

"Shirt—" I order.

"Grab whatever you want from the closet," he offers.

I turn my back to him and slide open the closet door, letting my fingertips trace the top shelf until they settle on Jay's favorite shirt, a memento of his first concert with his favorite band. The shirt he bought two summers ago. A shirt I know I'm pushing my luck by slipping it into my hands.

In the bathroom, the wet bottoms cling and suck against my legs as I tug them down, flinging them over the shower door. I unclasp the top and toss it next, throwing the oversized shirt over my damp skin.

A chill races up my spine. There's a heat wave this year. Temperatures reaching up to one hundred and five degrees by mid-afternoon each day. But Jeanne keeps the house ice-cold, always set to a brisk sixty-eight. I stuff my wet hair up into a dry towel and lean into the sink, carefully picking apart the girl staring back at me.

I hate that Mason Brown got under my skin. That every time I look in the mirror, I'm left questioning everything I didn't before. My body has changed. Lines that were straight and thin, now curved and full. I think my face is plain. Hair like my mother's. Probably another reason my reflection makes me groan. All that I see is her. And all that I want is to escape.

I flip off the bathroom light and make my way back to him, now sprawled on the carpet, spine resting against the bed frame. His ear buds pump music as he sings loudly, voice carrying beyond the door like he's got no care at all. And like he's got no clue how off-key he actually is.

He glances up, pulling one tiny speaker from his ear. His eyes slowly trace down my body, carefully inspecting the shirt I chose, but continuing past, below the hem.

"Out of all the shirts—"

"Consider it payback," I tease. I rub at my ass cheek. "That actually hurt, Jay."

His hand flies to cover his heart. His brown eyes sparkling with something devious. "More than the pain I feel with my favorite shirt ripped from my hands?"

"Well—it was in the closet. Plus, you haven't even worn it in over a year."

I drop down onto the floor beside him, stretching my legs long as he offers me the music pinched between his fingers. I take it from him, stuffing it into my ear as we listen together without a word. None need to be spoken.

Jay has always been some sort of music prodigy. Definitely nothing he got from Tanya, his mother. But I do know, from Sundays spent at church, that Jeanne can play a beautiful score on the piano. It's a religious experience whether you subscribe to that sort of thing or not. Recently, he began dabbling in creating his own electronic music, a mishmash of odd *beeps* and *boops* that seems to fit together in perfect rhythmic melody. I let my head fall, resting it onto the mattress as I feel his eyes steadily watching for every flinch. Every twitch. Any sign of my approval. I make him wait it out, squeezing my eyes tight enough to see sparks for the entire two and a half minutes of the song. Finally, I pull the ear piece and place it into my lap, peeling the towel from my damp hair and tossing it beside me.

"Well?" he asks, wide-eyed and anxious.

I turn toward him, a slow smile growing as it gently pulls at my cheeks. His dark eyes seem lighter than usual, maybe bleached from our afternoon in the sun. His fade tight—kept short and fresh every summer to help ward off the sticky heat.

"Sawyer, if you don't say something right now—" he warns, unable to fight the nervous laugh rising to the surface.

"Stop worrying so much," I say. I curl my knees, shifting to my left hip and resting my legs onto his now. "It's great. Really great. You'll be producing for big players before you know it."

"You think so? I know I have a long way to go—"

"Stop doing that. Stop doubting yourself. I think you're going to be huge one day. Big name in the game," I say.

He does something odd. Doesn't reply this time. Just pins his gaze to mine.

"What are you doing?" I ask.

The corners of his mouth pull slightly. Barely enough to notice. But it's there.

"I have something for you—" he says, climbing to his feet and scooping a tiny box from the bedside table drawer.

He grasps it tightly into his left hand, slams the drawer shut with the other, the contents rattling like the aftershocks of an earthquake. His free hand flies to the back of his neck, pinching and pulling the way he does when he's nervous about something. He pushes the box toward me.

"Here. Just a little something that made me think of you, that's all."

I take the neatly wrapped gift from him, placing it into my lap as he drops down onto the carpet beside me. "It's not my birthday—"

"I know. Would you just open it?" he urges.

"Alright," I concede, pulling at the small white ribbon wrapped tightly around the light blue paper. "You wrapped this?"

A small chuckle rises from his chest. He pushes his glasses back up his nose. "They offered gift wrapping for like ten dollars or something. I happily paid it."

Inside—a white box. Inside that box—a smooth felt hinged box made for a ring. I swallow hard.

"Can you hand me that glass of tea?" I rattle out, voice shaking from nerves.

Jay reaches left, sliding the glass from the table and holding it out for me. Outside the rim, water droplets race each other to the finish line. Greedily, I chug the sugar-filled tea, but it's not enough to wash down the knot in my throat. My hand trembles as I place it onto the carpet at my side, shakily flipping back the hinged top of the mystery gift. Inside, as expected, is a ring. No diamonds or anything like that. Not even a gemstone. I breathe a sigh of relief. I pull it out, a peculiar silver thing with a spinning layer on top.

"I know you like to mutilate your fingers," he shrugs. "I thought maybe that could help give your hands something else to do," he offers.

I turn the outer layer like a gear, spinning it right. Then left. Flipping the ring to find an inscription beneath the band.

"I had it engraved. See here?" he reaches over, placing his hand over mine as we look together. "It says 'meet me at the deep end.' You know—a nod to us and swimming."

My cheeks pull as I slide it onto my right ring finger. Not the left. Don't want him getting any ideas. Don't want to cross that bridge. Not now. The ring is a perfect fit. Filled with memories of afternoons soaking up sun in the backyard and evenings spent sneaking into country club pools.

"It's perfect, Jay."

His features wash solemn again. He leans in closer. So close I can smell the lingering pool bleach on his skin. So close I can see the tiny fleck of brown in the left corner of his eye. So close I can breathe him in. My heart stops beating. Air stops coming. My gut steels as I wait for whatever comes next.

"Sawyer—" he begins.

No. No. No. We can't do this. Don't do it, Sawyer. Don't ruin the only thing good that you have.

But his lips are full. Breath warm and sweet. And his muscular frame developed over the last year distracts my thoughts way too often to ignore. His eyes trace my lips. Then his finger. Then his beautiful, perfect lips meet with mine. And for a second, heat spills through me. A love that can't be denied. But still, a love that I push away.

"Jay—" I whisper, pulling away. Just a little. But enough. "We can't. I can't."

He peels the glasses from his nose and puts them onto the bedside table, the look of defeat washing over his face.

"It's not that I don't want to. Because I do. I just don't want to be those people that end up hating each other after the *everything* falls apart. And it will, Jay. It will because we're young. But we aren't that. I won't ever let us be."

"I know, Sawyer. It's okay," he says.

He shifts to face me, placing his hand back over mine. "But can we at least make a deal? You're single at thirty and I'm single at thirty—it's me and you. All in. Will that work?" he asks.

My cheeks pull more. I adore him. When other guys are afraid of commitment, Jay goes all in. When he loves, he loves hard. And I'm the luckiest girl in the world to be on the receiving end of what he has to give.

"You've got a deal."

At the end of James Point Drive, tucked into a cul-de-sac lined with sprawling Florida style homes and lawns still a bright shade of green in spite of the lingering cold, sits the home of Bryce Kincaid. Hedges trimmed to a perfect row and grass clipped into perfect lines. The outside, a boring HOA beige, grand double doors greeting visitors in a shade of robin egg blue. Lights flank each side, casting an illuminated glow like theater lights down the walkway paved with bricks. Low-lying flowers line the path, colored so bright, blooms so perfect, that they almost don't seem real. A perfect white fence with solid panels holds in their secrets tight, surrounding the home like a fortress hidden from curious eyes. Here, money buys silence. Even the wind and rain seem to tread lightly on this street, with its carefully erected palaces of stucco, every one bleached and bland.

The neighborhood is strung up in cheer. Woven reindeer in soft white lights stand frozen mid-prance, and inflatable Christmas scenes light up front lawns, each decoration perfectly placed, tethered to the ground with ropes and clips that fight against the wind. One inflatable snowman twitches slightly, deflates, then puffs back to life with a mechanical gasp. One week away from Christmas. Tacky decorations stretched tight across homes, as if they might keep something dark from slipping through the cracks.

I flick at pieces of fuzz clinging to the black leggings. Zip the hoodie up tight to my neck. Sink into the seat, fingers still gripped tightly around the wheel. The engine now cut, the street is an eerie quiet. Too quiet. Like this place is tucked away from the rest of the world. Across the street, eyes peer through window blinds, searching for my car, until finally a light goes dim and they slink back inside.

The car sits pressed against the curb, beneath the twisted shadow of an old oak with Spanish moss that brushes lightly onto the windshield. I tuck low into the seat, barely breathing as if I might give myself away.

Something moves across the dash. Long and thread-thin. No bigger than a nickel. Wiggling across a crack formed from years of blistering sun. A silverfish, twitching in spastic rhythm, like it's been trapped for too long and is desperate for an escape. I watch him for a long while as he slowly creeps, inching his way closer and closer. Filled with hope. Hungry for his next meal. Unaware that he sealed his fate the moment he crawled inside. The silence grows loud, humming in my ears as something tight coils around my chest. Slowly, our eyes still locked, I uncurl my fingers from the wheel and slam down onto the helpless thing. I lift my hand, searching my palm for bits of him, but it seems the smear of smooshed legs and wet pulp remains pressed into the dashboard grooves. Some things don't get to crawl out. Sometimes we're just trapped, and then we die.

The air is stale, and each breath fogs the windows more, sealing me inside, hidden from sight. I reach for the hood of my jacket, pulling it over my head like I'm some sort of cat burglar casing a joint before going in for the kill.

Headlights slice across the wet pavement, the quiet hum of an electric engine faintly breaking through the air until it quietly disappears in the rear-view mirror. Carefully. Quietly. I open the car door and swing my feet out, boots landing below with barely a sound. I ease the door closed behind me and crouch, pulse racing as I carefully rush toward the Kincaid home.

I know what I'm looking for. Know what I need. Know that Colt and Wes would kill me if they knew that I came. A light flickers by the side of the house. There's movement. Shapes hidden behind slatted blinds. I suck in a deep breath and hold it, slamming my spine into a brick pillar until the grass becomes dark. My heart thrums in my ears. Pulse racing in a maniacal beat. Slowly, I let the breath out as my knees buckle beneath me.

The scent of wet mulch turns my stomach. I flatten my palms against the brick at my sides, pushing myself straight and carefully tiptoeing toward the gate. I hold my breath as my fingertips reach for the latch, hoping they feel just safe enough within their HOA walls to leave it unlocked for criminals in the night. I push down. Miraculously, it *clicks* as the latch is released.

A dog comes rushing toward me. Big. Sunset golden fur. Maybe a lab-retriever mix. Panting and curious with eyes that glow a yellow-green. He barks. At least its not a growl. I dig a fist into the pocket of my hoodie, fishing out the leftover strips of bacon that Mama fried.

"Shhh," I whisper.

The dog pants more, saliva dripping from its tongue as it lets out a whimper. I crouch, resting my ass onto the heels of my boots, breaking up a strip, pushing it toward him as he gently takes the bite. A peace offering. You tend to your business and let me tend to mine sort of thing. Mutual understanding. I push the other half of the bacon strip at him and he greedily laps it up as I gently pat at the top of his head.

"Good boy," I say. The *hoot* of an owl breaks through the air as if he is watching us. Approving of our friendly exchange. "Keep quiet, okay? I won't be long."

I rock back onto my heels, slowly straightening my legs and watching the world spin around me until it all settles back into place. Softly, I close the gate behind, careful to not let out their beloved family guard. Blades of grass *crunch* quiet beneath each step as I make my way toward the back of the home.

The sky above is a blanket canvas of starless gray. No moon. Just the smothering hush of dark. But there's comfort in the nothingness. No faces, no voices...just me and the bloated toad sitting in a bird bathtub to my right. He just sits. Doesn't flinch. Doesn't even blink. Just white eyes, like pearls, staring me down in curious wait. I slink toward a large framed window that overlooks the swimming pool and sprawling lawn. Like a one way mirror. Nothing visible behind.

My breaths echo in my skull. Much too loud. Rattling me as the cold tears through my skin. I inch closer. Close enough to the glass that my nose is almost touching it. Eyes close enough to see every fleck of dirt on the glass.

Inside—a lamp flickers on.

His face glows in the sudden light, and he quickly ashes the butt of a cigarette into a beer can on the bedside table. He tosses a flannel shirt over his bare chest and rushes toward the front of the house.

I gasp, breath catching in my throat as my palm flies to my mouth and my shoulders pin hard again to brick. An engine hums with restraint, growing louder as gravel *crunches* beneath tires, light spilling over the lawn until the engine quiets with a final *click*. I push off the wall, sprinting silently around the corner and rushing toward the gate. I reach again for the handle, easing it down and gently cracking open the view as I toss the last of the bacon down at my side. My new friend laps it up, swallowing it whole in one large gulp before wagging his tail and trotting away.

The truck door softly opens, and boots land with a *thud* onto the brick paver drive. Bryce steps out from the front doors, tossing a knitted hat over his messy hair and pulling it low to warm his ears. The mysterious driver of the truck emerges, closing the truck door, but leaving it barely cracked. His face. Unmistakable. Bryce meets him halfway down the drive.

There's no light bar this time. No shade of royal blue. No gleaming badge. No holster. No radio clipped to his belt. Dressed head to toe in casual clothes. Jeans and a dark jacket. Mud splatter lining the dented metal side.

The two men meet at the front of the truck. Casually. Like old friends catching up. I strain to listen, their whispers barely audible over the rustling of branches that dangle from above. Bryce leans in when Colt speaks. Slaps a hand onto Colt's shoulder as they share a comfortable laugh. Wes must have given him the photo this morning. Tipped him off. I didn't expect him to jump to action so quickly, but grateful he's finally doing something. Anything.

A bark slices through the dark beside me, panting as something from his tongue drips onto the toe of my boot. Their heads cut toward me now, narrowing their eyes as I crouch low. Fast and hard. I lift a finger to my mouth, a gentle "shhh" leaving my lips. Quiet. Though it sounds more like a hissing tea kettle as it rattles through my head. My boot *crunches* over the edging that lines a garden bed manicured so perfectly that it's hard to believe its flowers are real. I steady myself. Holding the breath in my chest as the dog slips through the gate and joins at Bryce's side. Their voices clear as a bell now.

"Duke!" Bryce calls out, snapping his fingers to still the dog at his feet. "How'd you get out, buddy? Push through the gate?"

Colt pulls a flashlight from inside of his belt, quickly cutting light toward me as I shove myself into the garden bed, my back snugged into the wall of bricks doing my best to disappear. I hold breath again. Counting. Waiting. Half expecting to hear footsteps as they stomp straight toward me. But they don't come. The flashlight *clicks* off, and the beam of light disappears as their exchange picks up again.

I push myself from the wall, carefully tiptoeing through the newly planted foliage so I don't leave a single trace I was ever here. I peek through the cracked gate again, catching the tail end of some envelope being passed between the two, Bryce smacking his palm behind Colt's shoulder before turning away. Bryce disappears back inside of the house as Colt quickly climbs back into his weathered, old truck and drives away.

I push the breath from my chest, placing a hand over my heart, as if I can slow its frantic beat. A door *creaks* loudly from across the street as an older man wheels a garbage can to the road, then slowly disappears back inside. Just in time for me to make an escape.

My boots rush toward the car. Quickly. Almost a jog as my heartbeat thrums in my ears. Inside, I'm safe again, alone with my thoughts and tucked away from the world.

My eyes flit to the passenger seat beside me, pinning to the shimmering gold paper, red bow tied perfectly around the box. The ticking time bomb that was never meant for me but somehow ended up in my hands anyway. I place it into my lap, hesitating, my gut wrenching as tiny shimmering flecks dust the fleece keeping me warm.

A tag with Jeanne's writing is still attached. I trace my fingers over the ink as if I can erase it. As if I can make it anything else. I should put it back. Throw it out. Pretend I never saw it. Pretend I'm not holding something that was meant for only him.

"Merry Christmas, Jay," I whisper.

I pull at the ribbon's edge, unraveling Jeanne's perfectly wrapped surprise. The foil crinkles like dead leaves covered in frost. Inside, a strap for his guitar, initials pressed into leather, a gift she had custom made. Beneath is a photograph in a simple black frame. Jeanne and Jay at the piano, side by side, a beautiful memory of the love they both shared. I can swear it smells just like Jeanne's home. Cedar chests. Freshly mopped floors. Cinnamon perfume that lingers in every room.

Wetness pulls at my eyes. Silence presses in. Somewhere outside, an inflatable holiday something collapses. He never saw this. Never got the joy of opening it. Never had the chance to hold it in his hands. The ringing returns. Slow and steady. High-pitched, but bearable. Building like a siren. A sob stutters up my throat, my head falls to the steering wheel as tears stream down my cheeks. They pool at the corners of my mouth, finally falling to my thighs below.

I startle as the mechanical whir of that damn inflatable hums back to life, like a firecracker exploding in my chest.

Even that fucking thing gets to come back.

For a while there's nothing. Just the sound of that stupid thing outside. The rising pitch in my ears. Every inhale scraping against my ribs. The neighborhood outside like a silent stage where everyone knows their parts. And I'm the only idiot who doesn't know their lines.

Chapter Sixteen

The sky is colored ash. Thick and silent, not a single star in sight. The bridge's concrete spine stretches wide, like a bandaid on a festering wound that refuses to heal. Centuries-old tree branches reach in the dark, twisting and ominous. No grand arches. No sign welcoming you to town. Just poured stone, rusted bolts and a cold, metal rail that hums when the wind curls through its ribs.

The road is tired, stretched with worn pavement and faded paint. Below, a retention pond about to burst from weeks of relentless rain. The soil around it, soft and black, ready to cave at any moment with the pond's swelling weight. Tossed beer cans litter the surrounding pockets, tucked into trees and scattered over twisted roots. The only sign of life.

Somewhere in the distance, tires hum on wet asphalt and a radio thumps against windows like a pulse. The cold wraps around my throat, slithering beneath my collar and coiling into the hollow at the base of my neck. Stealth. Venomous. My breaths fog the air and hover silently, waiting for *something* to happen before finally breaking apart. My fingers twitch at my sides, but not from fear. It's memories. Memories racing against time through my veins.

The pole lights that line the bridge cast halos onto the pavement, forming segments quietly set like a stage.

Spotlight.

Blackout.

Spotlight.

Blackout.

A theater set for only me.

The soles of my boots scuff against the damp road, each step an echo that bounces off concrete and steel. My fingertips drift across metal, scraping up bits of flaking rust until I reach the stone steps that lead below. A streak of light illuminates the trees. Only for a moment until the night whispers dark again. One more deep breath like it's my final one, and I step down onto the narrow path curled beneath like the entrance to a catacomb. Hidden. Overgrown. Slick with moss and algae, coated in dark green, thick layers of sludge.

Below, leaves stick to everything—the pillars of the bridge, the concrete curbs and now the tops of my boots. Leaves are tossed in lazy spirals as rain *plinks* into pothole puddles worn over time. Leaves flutter as they fall to their death below. And leaves scatter across pavement in frantic bursts, rolling to their final resting place as the wind gets its final say. Leaves crunch beneath each step. Leaves collapse into gutters, disappearing as the rain claims each water-logged, brown and dead piece. And leaves dance in a tiny cyclone, spinning carelessly with the wind until dropping lifeless into the mud.

Just ahead, wet bleeding into dry...where the overlap of the bridge saved him from being completely washed away. Where the overlap of the bridge holds secrets I would give anything to know. I keep moving. Breath in my ears. Louder and louder.

There are no candles. No flowers. No signs that this is where he took his final breath. I crouch. My knees ache where they press into damp pavement. Ache where pieces of him are soaked into the cracks.

Water drips from above in a slow, rhythmic tap. Wet asphalt laces with iron. I swear that I can almost taste it in my mouth, like copper pennies, rusted metal left to rot in the rain or battery acid swallowed down your throat. My fingers drag across the stain, catching on grit and filth that the rain couldn't quite reach. Deep crimson. So deep that it's almost black. I grind my flesh into the cold until my fingers throb. The wind and rain couldn't quite get here no matter how hard they tried. Couldn't quite wash away the blood stain so thick it now fills each tiny crack like motor oil. I dip my flattened palms into the pothole puddle at my side. A puddle that holds rain clotted with leaves and dirt. Holds the ghost of everything good that I lost. Shock crawls up my arm. Something like electricity. Or maybe the fear that I keep running from. I leave my palms here and make myself feel it. I deserve every painful shard.

Footsteps *crunch* just over my shoulder. I jerk, quickly flattening wet palms to my jeans and rising to my feet. I inhale sharply as his hands lift in protest.

"Sawyer, it's me," he spits out. Colt slides the dark hood of his jacket off his head. "I didn't mean to scare you."

I blink. Pitters of rain fall again, landing with gentle *plops* into the puddles at our feet. I blink again.

"I was driving by. Just happened to see your car and thought I'd check on you," he says. "Promise."

Rain falls softly around us. Me, standing where Jay took his last breath. Colt, now close enough for me to inhale the bergamot lingering on his neck.

"Do you ever wonder what it feels like?" I ask. I claw at the damp strands of hair clinging to my skin. "That last second before someone lets go."

Colt folds his arms across his chest, now rising and falling with each thoughtful breath.

"No." His stance widens, like a protective shield between me and something bad. "I see way too much death. If I made it personal, you know...let my emotions get the best of me, then I could never see the crime for what it is. I gotta keep a clear head about it."

Rain pours in sheets now as we step beneath the belly of the bridge. I stuff my curled fists into my pockets, knuckles stiff from the cold.

"You're human," he softens. "Grief gets in your bones sometimes, Sawyer. Like you still carry them with you. But that's not a weight you need to be carrying alone."

"Mama thinks I'm broken," I interrupt. "Says I scare her. That I need help."

I shift my gaze to the tops of my boots, where brown leaves are stuck with a paste made of dirt and rain. Leaves that swirl aimlessly in tiny pothole bathtubs, around and around with no hope of escape. Leaves that scamper across cracked asphalt like something horrible is chasing them. Maybe the howling wind. Maybe the neverending rain that pours from the sky. Maybe the whisper of death that lingers in this place.

"And my sister—" I meet his gaze head on again, begging him to listen, a silent plea for a friend. "—she'll barely talk to me anymore. Thinks I've lost it. While I'm over here wondering how in the hell everyone else can just move on."

More *plops* of rain. Louder and louder as it falls in sheets around us. There are no signs that any other life exists here. Not tonight. No squirrels scampering across the road. No opossums or fat raccoons flattening blades of grass as they hunt for their next meal. No glowing yellow eyes watching us from the safety of the trees. Just him. Just me. Just boots cemented to the pavement and a shattered heart that can't let go.

"Well—you don't scare me," he simply states.

I reach beneath my coat, gently ensuring my father's gun is still safely tucked into the waistband of my pants. It makes me nervous—carrying around a weapon that I barely know how to use. Five bullets in the chamber. Only one needed to take a life. Ruin a life. Instill the fear of

God in a life. Instill the fear of God in me. It's still there. Tucked tightly. Barrel stretched and long. I should ask him how to use it. I don't believe Colt is a great person. I'm not even sure he's a *good* person. But he does know how to handle a gun.

Plop. Plop. Plop.

Rain—steady and cold. So much the earth has had its fill. But out here, Christmas is long forgotten. It doesn't chase me like some deranged holiday cloaked in silver tinsel and forced cheer. There is only quiet here. The occasional hum of tires on wet asphalt. Dead branches that slap at water-logged leaves in the trees. The steady drops of rain that lull an aching heart to sleep. Pain stops. Stops because I know he's here. Because I know *here* is where he took his final breath.

The rain spills harder now. A night so wet the gutters at the 3800 block of Highway 98 will certainly overflow. So wet the banks of Peace River will disappear as water chases after the residents in nearby homes. So wet that it will be impossible to pass through Lakeland's Cherry Lane and Dunn Road.

"At least come get in the truck, Ellis," he pleads.

Colt swings his arm up and over my shoulder. It lands gently onto my back, guiding me toward the slime-ridden steps that lead to the silent bridge above. Nothing but wind howling through its ribs. Nothing but spotlights that shine on an empty stage.

It's cold. Everything around me is cold. The fabric wrapped around my skin is cold. And my coat has grown heavy and water-logged. I'm tired. Exhausted. Drained to nothing. Sopping, frozen and tapped out. There's no energy left to put up a fight. I go where he leads. I walk up first. In case I fall, in case I lose my footing, Colt will be there to catch me.

I'm grateful for the tread on the soles of my boots as each step sends my heart lurching. Slide, then stop. Slide, then stop. Once. Twice. And almost a third. All while rain pelts like hail into my eyes. At the top, I pause as he grabs my hand, leading us toward the dented truck, caked-on mud still clinging stubbornly to its side.

Colt swings open the passenger door, placing his palms onto my waist to help lift me up. He shuts me safely inside and makes his way around to slide in beside me.

"Whew!" He runs his fingers through soaked hair and wriggles his arms free of the damp flannel, revealing a tightly fitted shirt beneath. Too tight. A man who loves himself too much kind of tight. Warmth spills through the cabin as he turns on the heat. He turns to me now as I shiver beneath my coat. "You going to get out of those wet clothes?"

"And put on what exactly?"

He smirks. And part of me wants to smack his smug face. But another part of me, very small, wants him to move closer. To feel his warmth brush against my skin.

Colt reaches behind the seat, hand fishing in the dark until he pulls a dry, clean flannel shirt from the abyss. He waves it in front of me.

"What kind of man do you think I am exactly?" he teases, feigned shock on his face.

I snatch the dry shirt from his grip.

"Jury is still out—"

The smirk is glued, his eyes pinned to mine.

"Can a girl get a little privacy?" I snark.

Colt's grin widens as he shifts in his seat, turning his gaze to the raindrops that race down the truck window's glass. I quickly peel the wet coat from my arms and rip off the black sweater beneath, wool weighted and water soaked. I toss it at my feet and slide Colt's flannel on, hastily fumbling with buttons as I fight with shaking hands.

"Alright. You can look now," I say.

He turns, gaze slowly lowering to the warm, checkered fabric before returning to mine. A huff. Smirk returns.

"What?" I ask.

"You, uh—" He reaches for the shirt, fingers playfully toying with a button on the front, "—I think you missed a hole here."

I look down, face flushing as I realize—one collar higher than the other, and every button out of place.

Rain pelts onto the roof with a clatter of thunder as warmth finally settles into my bones. His gaze still pinned, he brushes loose, wet tendrils, gently tucking them behind my ear. Fingers gently tracing the flesh behind. My pulse quickens. Heart flutters out of beat. I swallow it down. Not him. Not now. I shut the thoughts away.

Colt works the buttons on his shirt loose, each movement slow. Deliberate. His breath brushes my skin, cool at first, then warm, laced with the sharp bite of wintergreen on his tongue. A bead of water slides from his temple, carving a path down his cheek before slipping beneath his collar. It takes my focus with it.

He presses back into the seat as his attention shifts to something outside. Or maybe nothing outside. His expression falls flat. Like some big secret is pulling on his mind.

A half-worn sticker peels from the glove compartment. Some sports team. Maybe some fandom long gone. I reach for it, gently rubbing with my fingertips back and forth over the faded paper and glue. Steam begins to curl at the windows. Slow at first, like it's holding its breath. Now, it spreads. Crawling across the glass like vines. It shields us from the bridge outside. Swallows the night. Leaving only this truck. This seat. This moment. I watch the fog breathe. Don't move. Just watch. Matching my own breaths with its slow rhythm.

"You okay?" he whispers softly.

Our gazes pin straight ahead. Barely a movement. Barely a breath.

"I always hated rain like this," I admit, shifting in the seat as I rub at my thighs for warmth. "But now...it's the only thing that reminds me I'm still here. Still alive."

Colt turns up the heat. The scent of dust and motor oil drifts from the vents. His palms finds its way to my thigh, gently resting there.

"You're still shivering," he says.

I pin my gaze to the glass as the steam-filled windows begin to clear again. A reminder of the looming storm. Of a town I can't seem to escape. A reminder that death is silently coming for us all. "I'm not sure it's the cold anymore," I choke out.

His palm rubs at my thigh in gentle circles. Not the kind that Wes or Birdie make when they want to comfort me. The kind that send warmth flooding through your body and make you want nothing but to be held in their arms. But I can't be held right now. By anyone. I'm too far gone for that.

"Why are you being so nice to me?" I ask.

His gaze turns to me. I don't meet it. But I can feel it. Pinned to me as I hold my breath.

"Because you need someone to be, Sawyer."

"No...I mean, really," I say. I finally meet his gaze dead-on. "What's in this for you?"

"Well, for starters, I blow another case wide open—become even more of a hometown hero than I already am—and, of course, impress the girl," he says.

I blink, holding his gaze with nothing but the hum of heat spilling from the truck's vents. The rain stopped. Nothing but tiny droplets of water sliding down the glass. Nothing but damp everything and leaves swirling aimlessly in puddles outside. Leaves that flutter like confetti to their death. Leaves that stick to the tops of boots, rails with flaking rust, and slime-ridden steps just outside.

"You think I need a reason to care?" he asks.

His palm stops spinning in tiny circles, and it settles in my gut like sour milk.

"I think people like you *pretend* to care," I say. I lace my fingers together in my lap. My gaze follows. I go for whatever cuticle I can mangle first.

I feel his eyes pinned to me. Not intense. Not hungry. Just pinned. Watching.

"I wish I had gone with him, you know. Wish it had been me instead. Wish that I had packed my shit up in the car and visited him the second I heard in his voice that something was off."

"So why'd you choose to stay?" he asks, softly. Not pushing. Gentle. But we both know what he means.

"Because someone has to remember him right. I have to do that, Colt. I have to fix things." I pick at some white, fuzzy thing stuck to the fabric on my thighs. "Did you get anything out of Bryce?"

His breath seizes. "How did you know about that?" The leather strains beneath him.

"I went to his house earlier," I confess. "I wasn't going to confront him, I swear. I just wanted to look for answers, but then I saw you pull up and figured Wes showed you the photograph I found in Jay's bedroom."

I lift my gaze. His mouth parts slightly, widened eyes slowly narrowing on mine.

"Ellis, goddamnit..." he bellows. "You're going to get yourself killed if you don't stop this shit right now. I told you already...if you have information, come to us. We will follow up on every lead. *We*...not you."

"I know," I confess. I bring the mangled cuticle on my left thumb to my mouth, biting it between my teeth. "Listen...I know it was stupid, but something is off Colt. I feel it. That photograph was recent, and Penny at the bar says they were in there the night Jay died. Or...at least close to it."

"Let me take care of it," he soothes. Gentle again. Soft. "Jay needs you here. Alive. Understand?"

I nod. All I can give. But it's a lie. And it's a big one.

"You're stronger than you think," he offers.

My heart beats louder, picking up speed as it thrums in my ears. That line. That line—it *should* have sounded cheap. But the way he said it, the quiet tone, made it feel real. The tips of his hair are still wet. His jaw tense. But his eyes are soft. Almost like he understands. Like he's felt storms like this before. I hate how much I like his eyes, a warm espresso with flecks of gold throughout. I hate how his lightly-stubbled jaw is lined perfectly. I hate how the weight of his palm rests, like it belongs on my thigh. I hate how I can smell the scent of bergamot lingering on his shirt. But mostly, I hate that I can hear his heart thrash against his ribs, too. Just like mine. I draw a shaky breath. But I don't stop it. And I don't want to.

"This probably isn't a good idea," I choke out.

"The best ones usually aren't."

"Do you want me to ask you to stop?" I ask.

"Do you want me to?"

He slides his arm across the back of the seat. I rest my head onto the warmth of his skin. Fog blankets the glass now, sealing us from the outside world. Creating a sort of confessional out of the truck's cabin. Only him. Only me. Only our deepest secrets shared.

"No," I reply.

The pad of his thumb gently traces at the base of my neck. My skin burns beneath his touch. Every hair on my arms, raised, every breath stolen as its caught in his hand.

"Do you want me to pretend I don't like this?" I ask.

"Only if it makes you feel safer," he says.

"Okay. I hate it."

He shifts his body toward mine, gently lifting his finger to slowly trace the outline of my lips. With care. With ease. With something I've never felt before in my life.

"Sawyer..." he whispers. "You know you're allowed to stop running for a minute, right?"

My name drips from his tongue like a secret. Something you whisper into the dark when you're not sure you'll be heard.

"I'm not here for this," I falter. The words feel like pencil on thin paper. Weak. Easily washed away by the storms and rain.

"But you are...still here, Sawyer" he softly reminds me. "Do you want to go?"

"No."

The fabric of his shirt rises and falls as it clings to his chest. He waits patiently for my reply, like he's already decided this moment is for us. But the calm scares me. Scares me more than anything like hunger or disease ever could. I peel his fingers from my skin. Peel away the arm casually slung around my neck.

"Then we don't have to do anything. Take as much time as you need," he says.

I shift my knees toward the passenger door, leaning onto the glass as fog slowly recedes. The faint reflection of Colt remains...half-formed and soft at the edges. More a feeling than a man. Closer...a reflection barely visible. An illusion that disappears with a puff of smoke. Like some cheap magician's trick. Here she is. And now she's not. I try to lock in on her. To hold this moment in time. But I can't hold her. Keep slipping through time and space. Leaving only the cold. Leaving only the dark.

Wetness pools at the corners of my eyes...I didn't even notice. Like a criminal on the run suddenly caught. I blink. A single tear streaks hot down my cheek.

"Need a lift home?" he offers, voice like a rich velvet that surrounds you. "Wes and I can get your car back by morning."

"Okay," I choke out.

"Come on, Ellis," he soothes, reaching again with his arm and gently pulling me toward him again.

I follow his lead. Rest my head onto his shoulder. Let the tear roll *hot* down my cheek and fall to his flannel shirt. I let him hold me. No one has bothered to for a long time. I rest here. *Here* is where time can pass as slowly as it wants.

His fingers find the edge of my sleeve, slipping beneath and brushing against my wrist. The skin there still cold. His hand pulsing and warm. My breath hitches in my throat. Not pain. Something I need more. Shock. Connection. Warmth.

I pry my eyes open, lifting my head and meeting his gaze again. His face is close. Closer than I've let anyone get in months. And his breaths ease closer, fanning across my cold skin with euphoric heat—the scent of rain and dust and bergamot mixing like some sort of magic spell. One of his hands rests gently on my jaw, and his thumb brushes the corner of my mouth, soft and feather lite.

He whispers my name like he's afraid to break it. "Sawyer—"

I close my eyes as his breath fans across my face, and our lips finally meet with a quiet, gentle press. Nothing forceful. Nothing hungry. He begins to pull away, but I close in for more. Our lips meet again, slower this time. My fingers curl into the fabric of his shirt. Just holding. Making sure I don't disappear or float away.

We pull back. Neither of us speak for a long moment, letting the kiss suspend in time. The heat between us still coiled like smoke, but it doesn't push. It waits. Patiently.

"This doesn't mean I'm okay," I remind him.

"I know," he says. His lip curls again with the faint return of a smirk...like he knows a secret that I don't. "It just means you're still here."

Chapter Seventeen

Salem purrs on my chest like a finely tuned engine. I stretch my legs beneath the blankets. My bed back home is fine, but this one...this one feels like years of myself buried into the springs. Years of jumping on the mattress with Skylar while Mama pleaded for us to stop. Years of crying over ridiculous crushes that would never amount to anything. Years of Jay and I sharing secrets after school. And years of crying over Daddy, heart aching over his absence. Salem's weight seems to steady a fractured heartbeat. Gives me a moment to quiet the panic, quiet the fear, so that I can think with a clear head. Wes and Colt are right...I'm no use to anyone if I don't get rest myself.

Bryce Kincaid. I didn't know him well, but maybe Skylar did. I'll need to drive out to see her again. Maybe she can tell me something. Anything. Maybe she's seen Bryce around over the last few weeks. Noticed something odd. I just can't leave any room for doubt.

His face haunted me all night. Hair—unkempt. Careless. Like someone who knows he doesn't have to try, and that's what makes it worse. That ember dangling from between his teeth. And those eyes—dark, lifeless, with no spark behind them. Pupil and iris made of the same. Like the North Sea. Cold. Violent. Unforgiving. A stretch of water with a history of wreckage, swallowing whole anyone foolish enough to test it. Looking into them feels like stepping too close to something that only knows how to consume. The other faces in the photograph a bit hazy now. But Bryce—something about him sends something cold crawling beneath my skin. Something about him makes my entire body seize up with fear.

"Colt," I gasp, placing Salem onto the blanket beside me and shooting up on the bed.

Light streams through the window—breaking through missing slats never repaired. I rub at the corners of my eyes as a groan rumbles from my chest. How could I be so stupid? How could I even sit with him in that truck? Christmas is almost here, time's slipping through my fingers, and Mama—well, she's about to lose her patience with me once and for all. Problem for another day. It has to be. Right now, I need Skylar. More than ever. Then, I pay another visit to Colt and Wes down at the station.

I peel the blanket from my legs, swinging them around and landing with a *thud* onto cold, tiled floor. I shuffle across the linoleum, each chilled step coiling with pain. The simple overnight bag packed for a short stay, now overflowing with wrinkled, dirty things. I fold myself in half, quickly piling the crumpled clothing into my arms and heading for the washing machine with a quiet tip toe down the hall. I peek my head around the corner, a ridiculous thing. A habit from years of walking on eggshells through this house. There's no sign of her, but something else catches my eye. A tiny Christmas tree, barely two feet tall, sits perched atop the old coffee table, base wrapped in wrinkled gold foil.

Morning light filters gray and dull through the kitchen windows and the sliding glass door. A sparse string of lights blinks lazily in red, blue and green. The needles sprout in defiant tufts with only a few ornaments dangling from the plastic branches—the star that Grams crocheted a million years ago, Skylar's handprint glued to green paper with a gold ribbon laced through the top, and a handful of candy canes that I know damn well survived at least five holidays past. The whole thing looks like it came from a thrift store clearance bin. It's crooked, missing branches, and a few lights flicker at the top as they slowly die. It should make me laugh. It should be a ridiculous sight. But it doesn't. And it isn't. In fact, it stops me dead in my tracks.

My fingers tighten on the door frame as pressure builds within my chest. We always had a Christmas tree when we were little, but that stopped when Daddy left. Not even when I begged for one. Not when I was sixteen and bought the fancy icicle lights and a Tiffany star with money I made from bussing tables all summer long, only for Mama to tell me to "take that shit back." Not last year. Not the year before. And not as much as a simple snowman or candy cane since Skylar and I left. And now—here it sits. Fragile. Pathetic. *Sacred*.

I release my grip on the frame, slowly shuffling my way across the floor and toward the tiny relic of Christmas cheer. Perhaps some sort of peace offering. Perhaps it's nothing at all. I don't touch it. Don't dare risk breaking a bulb. I just take in the sight. Like it belongs in a museum somewhere. Like something unreal.

I turn on my heels, quickly making my way through the dim-lit house toward the washing machine that sits in the cold garage. Mama strung a line across to hang clothes to dry. Didn't believe in "wasting power," but the truth is we never really had the extra money to spend. Skylar and I had everything we ever needed of course, we just had to make due with what we had. When other kids at school spent their summers on lavish vacations to theme parks with thrill rides, I spent summers with Grams and Poppy, where thrill rides were replaced with backyard hunts for bugs and dandelions, picking sticky burrs off my clothes after rolling down a grassy hill, and sleepy afternoon naps as thunderstorms rolled through the sky. In my eyes, there wasn't much better than that. I lift the washer lid, toss in the pile with a little cleaning detergent, and release the lid as it slams shut again.

Back inside, tucked safely into warmth and the slowness of morning, I reach for a mug from the cabinet and pour the burnt-smelling coffee in, steam rising and curling from the top. I add a splash of flavored cream for taste and swirl it with a dirty spoon from the sink. On the kitchen table, sits a roll of shiny paper adorned with cats in tiny Santa hats, a single pair of cutting shears, and several rolls of tape, each one about halfway gone. Salem winds in and out of my feet, her soft head butting into my shins, her tiny cries for attention fading in her throat.

I head toward the front porch—a quiet place to sit and watch the neighbors scramble for last minute gifts, turkeys and honey-flavored hams for Christmas eve meals, and clean eaves, driveways and polish windows for out-of-town guests. The door gently *creaks* open as Salem runs to hide beneath my bed. Then I hear it. That cough. Rattling. Sharp. Worrisome. Cold fingertips wrap around the mug for warmth. For comfort. For safety. The only thing I can put between us.

Her tired eyes cut sharply toward mine as she flicks an ash into an old jelly jar at her side. And the porch *creaks* with every movement as I inch my way out of the threshold and slide onto the old, weathered chair with the flaking white paint.

Her flannel robe is pulled tightly around her waist, with a familiar, old patchwork quilt draped over her legs—cigarette pinched between her fingers and one slipper dangling off her foot. She doesn't turn. Doesn't even seem to notice me perched on the edge of my seat. Afraid to breathe. Afraid to make a sound. Afraid to take up space in the one place that should bring me peace. She just stares into the frost-dusted yard as if I'm some sort of ghost lingering just out of reach.

"Didn't know you were up," she says. Flat. Gaze never breaking from the frosted blades of patchy grass.

I sip at the coffee in my hands, already lukewarm after just moments in the morning's sharp air. "Thanks for making coffee," I offer.

Her gaze finally shifts as her eyes, filled with exhausted disappointment, lock onto mine. "Don't see no one else in this house doin' it," she rattles.

I feel a smirk pull at my cheek. I don't even know why or where it comes from, but I know it irritates her more. The silence settles thick over us, like dust in some abandoned, old room. I sink into the rocking chair, porch boards creaking beneath my weight. Mama puffs at that damn cigarette, at least what's left of it, and blows it straight in my direction. Not rudely, but not gently either.

"I saw the tree," I blurt out. I swallow at the morning rasp in my throat and curl into myself, wind gusts slicing right through the thin, cotton pajamas slept in last night.

Mama groans beneath her breath as she grabs the patchwork quilt and tosses it into my lap. Greedily, I pull it tight over my legs as I push out a sigh.

"Thanks," I tell her, though her gaze already broke away.

"Hmmph."

I fix my gaze onto a little golden-brown dog spinning in anxious circles across the street. "Didn't expect it, that's all," I say.

"Didn't expect you to still be here," she rattles back.

I throw back another swig of now-cold coffee and settle it into my lap. The mug is chipped. Right next to the handle. I run my finger gently over the rough ceramic before pressing down hard and jamming it into my skin. It feels good. Feels like proof that I'm still in this body, whether I want to be or not.

Dead leaves scatter across the porch as another gust blows through. Leaves tumble and roll, then take flight across the yard. Leaves crinkle like tiny, dead, papery things. And leaves settle again as the air stills and silence settles again.

"Why'd you do it?" I ask.

"Do what?"

"Put the tree up..."

Mama shrugs, flicks ash off the edge of the porch now. "Just felt like it."

"Well—you never 'felt like it' before," I snap.

"How long are 'ya gonna harp on that goddamn tree, Sawyer? I felt different this year. That's all."

The flannel hangs off her frame now. Loose. Draping. Her cheekbones more sharp. Pronounced. The slight tinge of gray beneath her sunken eyes. The cigarette trembles slightly as she sets it free into the jelly jar, not missing a beat as she reaches for another from the pack.

"You sick or something?" I ask.

Mama doesn't answer. Looks out at something. Or nothing. I'm not even sure she's looking at anything possible *to* see. She lights the fresh cancer stick, taking a long drag without missing a beat.

"You always were a sharp one," she says.

"What does that mean?" I ask.

My jaw tenses as she locks her gaze onto mine. Something is off. Tone has shifted. She exhales. Smoke trails from her lips like a steam train.

"Started in my lungs," she says, voice like gravel. "I figured it would. I earned that much, I guess."

I don't breathe. Don't blink. Don't dare say a word.

"Doctor told me over a year ago. Said it was movin' fast. Took root in my bones. Hurts like hell most days—spine mostly, I guess. They say I've got a few months left. Well..." Something cracks beneath her voice. "That was a few months ago."

"You're joking—"

"I haven't laughed in years, Sawyer."

She says it like she's bored. Like we're just talking about how to fix the plumbing underneath the bathroom sink. But I can see through it.

The way her throat bobs when she swallows. Not from pain. But from fear. Fear she stuffs deep, so no one else has to carry it.

"You knew—this whole time. And you never said anything."

"There's no point," she says flatly.

"I'm your daughter—"

"And you made it pretty damn clear that didn't mean much to you," she snaps.

I flinch. That was a slap. Hurts more than the other kind.

"That's not fair," I say.

"Neither is dying at fifty-two."

Car tires crunch on gravel, and a dog barks somewhere in the distance. Just once before the morning goes silent again.

"So you're just—not going to fight it? Just going to give up?"

"For what? To buy myself a few more months just so I can puke my guts out here in this house alone? I'm tired, Sawyer. I've buried Jay. Might as well have buried your daddy. And I damn sure buried my own damn pride. I've earned the right to die in peace."

I rake at strands of black, piling them on top of my head as I watch. The wind tugs at a screen door across the street, rattling it against its frame. Steam curls from the neighbor's car, drifting across the cracked sidewalk. A small dog yaps furiously at nothing. Holiday lights blink weakly on a porch. Some bulbs dead. Some still stubbornly bright. A newspaper flutters past, snagging briefly on a fence before skittering into the gutter. And a windchime clinks violently as it's shoved in endless loops. Everything moves. Everything is alive, except for us. And I want to scream at her for stopping herself, for letting this happen, for leaving me here staring at the world like it doesn't even matter.

"Does Skylar know?" I whisper through trembling lips.

"No. And don't you bother her. Your sister's got enough on her plate."

I press my spine into the back of the chair and slowly rock, letting the heavy air settle just a bit. Stare out where the sky meets rooftops, like it might offer some way out.

"So what happens now?"

"There ain't much left, Sawyer. Christ, you don't think I still hear your Daddy's boots echoing down the hallway almost every day? Still sit down to eat and stare at the place Jay used to sit? I cared for him, too, Sawyer. He was like a son to me."

I blink fast and hard. I don't want tears. Not here and not now.

I push up from the chair. Ready to run. Anywhere.

"I didn't come back for this."

"No. You came back for justice and blood. Right? Maybe a little comfort you'll never admit to wanting anyway. But you damn sure didn't come back for me."

"What do you want me to do with this?" I ask, voice cracking on that last breath.

"I'm not askin' for anything, Sawyer. I don't need you to hold my hand or cry about it. Hell, I don't even want you to stay," she snaps.

I don't know if she really means it or if it's the pain taking her away from me. But it hurts. Cuts deep and rips like the teeth of a knife, jagged and sharp.

"Then why tell me at all?"

"Because—when I'm gone, you'll think back and wonder why if I didn't. And I don't want you carryin' that around. Not on top of everything else."

I pull my bottom lip into my teeth, biting down hard. I consider telling her about Daddy. She might want to know that he's okay before she's gone.

But I'm lying to myself if I say that he's alright. Truth is, he's farther gone than any of us. And she'll spend the last of her days searching for him and end up with a heart broken worse than before.

"I don't hate you, you know—"

"I know," I say. "You just don't like me much, but that's okay."

Mama stands. Slow. Stiff. A low *groan* rumbling somewhere deep in her chest as she shakes away the pain. She pulls the patchwork quilt from my lap and gently shakes it out, wrapping it around my shoulders like I'm a porcelain doll she was never allowed to play with. Or the lacy handkerchief she always kept tucked in her Bible, pulled out strictly for funerals and more solemn days. I don't say thank you. And she doesn't ask. Just returns inside the house as if the clock isn't ticking by. As if time isn't chasing right behind.

Plastic candy canes now line both sides of the steps, and the chaos of children's toys, slightly faded from the sun, are piled into one corner now. The doorbell still hangs from its box, dangling from cords never repaired. My curled fist pounds on the door as porch boards sag beneath me, ready to give at any moment. Baby cries burst from the other side of the door. And a dog's bark thunders through the walls. Impatiently, I wait, bringing my cupped fists to my mouth and blowing into them for warmth.

"Go away!" her voice yells from just beyond the door. "We're not interested!"

"Skylar, it's Sawyer. Open the door," I urge.

The door swings open as she bounces Raelynn on her hip. Her eyes narrow into thin slits as she huffs, then bounces Raelynn some more.

"What the hell do you need, Sawyer?"

"Would you let me in? Fuck, I've been in morgues that are warmer than this—"

Her eyes roll into the back of her head. Raelynn smiles. Followed by a tiny giggle that, if caught in a jar, I'm sure could light up a dark room. I lift my fingers into the air, wiggling them at her. Her eyes sparkle with something like joy. At least amusement. I can do the cool aunt thing. I think kids like me enough. Except for River, of course. But that kid definitely takes after Shawn. Skylar slaps my hand back. Fast and hard.

"Last time you're coming in. Got it?" she bites.

Skylar steps back, and a massive dog with jet-black fur barrels straight toward the door. Straight toward me. The dog stretches onto its hind legs, pushing its paws against my chest and violently licking at my face like I'm some sort of frosty dog treat. Skylar closes the door behind me and walks to the dining table.

"Can you get your dog, please?" I yell out.

"Trig!" Skylar calls out, causing all of us to jump out of our skin—me, the baby, the hundred pound furry beast that seems to like the way I taste.

I brush the loose fur from my coat before slipping it from my shoulders and draping it over a chair by the door.

I follow behind her, pulling out a seat and settling across from her at the dining table. I don't think they eat here much. Not sure they eat here at all. Not sure where food would even go with the piled-high stacks of mail and half burnt candles scattered about.

"You got a dog—" I say, sinking back into the chair as if I'm here to stay awhile.

"And you're getting a little too comfortable in my house," she counters.

I decide to ignore her, to let the shit from the past go. She sighs, then shifts, slowly letting down her wall.

"Shawn found the dog abandoned behind the bar last week. Thought it'd make a nice Christmas gift for us," she says, carefully placing Raelynn into some sort of chair that vibrates and rocks babies to sleep. And Raelynn is no exception. Takes all of five seconds for her eyes to snap shut as her head falls back into the seat. "Sawyer, what are you still doing here?" She pops a pacifier between Raelynn's lips and turns her focus toward me now. "I don't mean here. My house. I mean this town. Daddy's gone. Mama might as well be. What's left for you? What is it that you just can't leave behind?"

I came to talk about Bryce. To find out anything she might know about him. But only one thing sits on my mind.

"Mama's sick," I blurt out. Words just roll off my tongue as if consequence doesn't tumble right behind.

"What are you talking about?" she huffs.

"Cancer, Skylar. I'm talking about cancer. Stage Four. In her bones now."

"And how do *you* know this?" she asks.

"Because she told me. This morning."

Skylar lets out a nervous laugh. "Yeah, right. Like she'd ever confide in you before me."

"Damn it, Skylar. Would you just let go of whatever scorecard it is that you're keeping? This isn't about you *or* me. Our mother is dying. Doctors say she has months left to live...and that was months ago. Do you understand it now?"

Skylar sinks back into her seat, lips pulling tight as her eyes search something beyond the walls. Her fingers wrap tight around a mug half-filled with coffee that no longer steams from the top. Silence surrounds us. A quiet, heavy weight that sticks in your lungs like smoke.

"Well—" she begins, gulping for air like a fish out of water before beginning again. "What am I supposed to do about it? Apparently, she doesn't even want me to know."

"What do I want you to do? How about look after her? Jesus, she's all alone in that house."

"Sawyer, she's your mother, too. And last I checked, you don't have a husband, a kid, and a new baby to care for. Hell, now I've got Shawn's overgrown mutt to feed while he's gone all day."

"Where is he, anyway?" I ask, clawing at a loose strand of hair. "And can I get some of that coffee?"

She shakes her head, and tiny flecks of gold shimmer at the corners of each eye. Stage makeup left from last night, I assume. A part of me hates that she has to do that because Shawn refuses to work. Another part sure that she'd do it anyway, whether Shawn has a job or not.

"He picked up some work delivering food orders. It isn't much, but the tips are helping us get by," she says. Her words ring hopeful, though her eyes tell a much different story.

"Well—it's a Christmas miracle," I snark.

"Would you lay off him just once?" she asks, but it lands more like a slap.

She rolls her eyes back, straightening her legs and spine and grabbing a clean cup from a cabinet door that hangs off its hinges. The sink is still piled with dishes stacked tall. I'm not sure a single one has been washed since I sat here the week prior. Skylar slams the cabinet shut, seemingly not worried that it's about to crash to the counter below, and pours the last of the coffee. She makes her way back toward me, forcefully setting the mug down as it splashes against the sides like tiny tsunamis. Fitting, as that's the perfect way to describe our relationship. Wounds pulled from the deep. Quiet and calm before violently clearing everything from its path—roots, foundations, and lives. Each surging wave leaving things more broken than the last.

"You want cream? Or are you still drinking it like battery acid?" she asks.

I wrap my fingers around the top, sliding stacks of unopened envelopes and sale flyers to the side and placing it in front of me. "Battery acid is fine. Thanks."

She slides back into her seat directly across, folding her arms over her chest as a shield between us both. "So...is she," Skylar begins, twisting in her seat, "in pain?"

Raelynn fusses momentarily before letting out a quiet sigh and drifting back to sleep.

"Yeah. She is," I say. I clear at the rasp in my throat as my finger trails the mug's lip in circles. "She won't accept treatment. Says she doesn't want to spend her last days puking alone."

Our eyes meet. And something dark rests on her shoulders. A flash of the sister that I used to know bubbles to the surface. Short and fast before it locks itself away again.

"Are you—upset?" I ask.

Her shoulders rise and fall. Her arms uncross and settle into her lap. "Not really. I guess I've never expected anything more from her. I don't mean it in a cruel way. Just that she never did want anyone fussing over her."

I lean forward, resting my elbows onto the table and my head into my hands. "I guess—"

"Mama's always had limits. I just stopped expecting what she couldn't give, while you couldn't let it go," she rattles on.

"I just don't know what to do," I say.

"Nothing *to* do. Just be there if you can, *if* she'll let you. But that's a boundary you have to respect, whether she's our mom or not. Daddy leaving broke her. Bad. She couldn't recover from that and we need to understand. I know you were always Daddy's favorite, but you tend to forget how much she was hurt."

The television sits quiet in the next room. Sunlight slowly filters through curtains, revealing tiny diamonds made of dust that dance in the air.

"Where's River?" I ask, forcing the right expression. The one that says I care.

"Shawn's parents are keeping him until tomorrow night. Wish they'd take the baby, too, but I'm trying to get her off the breastmilk and she's just giving me the hardest damn time. Guess she cries all night with Shawn since she won't take the formula bottles."

I shift awkwardly in my seat. I don't know much about babies, but can't imagine my body pushing out a ten pound demon, then letting it bleed me dry.

"Sawyer, I swear, you need to get over yourself. You're going to have kids too someday, you know."

"Well, I assure you that won't be happening, so—"

"There's something else bothering you," she interrupts.

Her words jolt me back into reality, eyes landing squarely on the high school yearbook still lying face-up, surrounded by this past week's mail.

"Bryce Kincaid—" I begin, the words tumbling from my throat with desperation.

She rolls her eyes again. "Not this shit again, I swear Sawyer—"

I reach for the yearbook, ripping open the cover and flipping pages until I reach the senior class. His eyes stare menacingly. The words "Shout out to the janitor who never asked questions" beneath his photo in a black and white tux. I assume it's about the multitude of rumors that Bryce broke into the school to infiltrate student files and left markings in spray paint in his wake. I turn the book toward Skylar and the pad of my finger lands hard onto his face.

"He killed Jay, Skylar."

Her jaw hangs slightly, eyes widen in surprise. "How do you know that?" she asks.

"Jay told me that he was hanging out with some "old friends" from school. Smoking weed. Running around cow pastures searching for magic 'shrooms. It wasn't the Jay I knew. It was like he was trying to escape something. He always talked to me. About everything. But the last few months, something wild was eating him up." My chest heaves as I force a breath down. "I went to visit Jeanne. You know—Jeanne Scott?"

Skylar nods impatiently. "Of course I remember, Sawyer. Would you get on with it?"

"I found a picture of Bryce in Jay's room. In the photo, Jay's surrounded by Bryce and two other guys I saw out at Connersville. They watched me, Skylar."

"You're paranoid," she huffs. "They were probably just looking at everyone."

"No!" I slam the yearbook shut. "I'm so sick of no one listening. Of no one taking this seriously." I slow my words, pausing between each breath. "I was alone. They were hiding something—and then they froze and just stared at me like I was supposed to get it, Skylar. It's like they were warning me. Like they knew. Bryce has something to do with Jay's murder."

"Murder, Sawyer?" she replies. Gently now. Filled with pity. The same thing I get from everyone else. "He jumped. And the sooner you come to grips with it, the sooner we can all move on with our lives."

"Move on?" I shout, shoving back from the table as I rise to my feet. Raelynn's eyes jolt awake as tiny cries build within her chest. "None of us should be moving on until that piece of shit is behind bars!"

"Damn it Sawyer, you come to my house, unexpected, after none of us hear from you in years, upset the damn dog, wake my baby up—you've lost your damn mind! Now sit the fuck down or get out. Everyone is exhausted of your shit."

My arms tremble at my sides, and fire travels through my veins. I could spit flames from my tongue right now. Scream at the world from the top of that bridge. But I need answers. Can't let it all explode. I drop again into the seat, folding my arms protectively against a fractured chest.

Skylar reaches for Raelynn, lifting her top and latching the baby onto her breast.

"One of the bartenders at Blackwood Social saw Bryce the night Jay died. Or maybe a day later. A group with Bryce started fighting, yelling in the bar. Said it got real bad. Bad enough she had to kick them out. She said they matched the faces from the photo I found at Jay's."

Skylar softens again.

"Do you see now?" I ask.

"Everyone hated him," she begins. She manages to pile her hair high onto her head into an elastic, baby Raelynn never missing a drink. "I mean, they laughed with him. Pretended he was the most popular guy in school. But it was mostly out of fear. I mean, he threatened anyone who didn't do exactly as he said. Like he was rabid. Always seconds away from biting someone."

I pull at the mangled cuticle on my left thumb, ripping the skin as warm blood trickles in its place. Her words eat at my insides. Tear everything good that's left to shreds.

"You know—maybe there is something," she begins again.

I shift. Straighten my back with attention.

"Shawn and I went out to Connersville a few times the past few months. We ran into Jay. This had to be September. Wait. No. Maybe

October. As soon as the weather settled down a bit. Bryce was there. I mean, he kinda always is. Where else will addicts get their supply, you know?"

"He's dealing now?"

"That's the rumor, at least. But God, in this town, who the hell knows."

"What else did you see at Connersville?" I ask.

"Bryce watched him a lot. I thought maybe Jay did something to make Bryce mad. You know...same shit as always. But it was odd. I know Bryce started doing mechanic work on the side. And I guess I just figured Jay asked Bryce to fix up his motorcycle and they had some sort of falling out. I should've checked on Jay. At least for you. I'm sorry I didn't."

"So he just...watched?"

"Just leaned against his truck and watched, smoking cigarette after cigarette. Evan Shawn thought the guy was weird."

"Think he was obsessed with Jay or something? None of this makes sense," I say.

Skylar shrugs. "I really don't know anything else. Bryce isn't really liked, but he *is* protected, Sawyer. You need to remember that. If the town is getting their drug supply from him, they aren't going to let you get in the way of that. Not without a fight. And his parents come from money. They're not like us. Money like that holds power that you or I just don't have."

I push back from the table again, rising to my feet and walking back toward my coat. "Well, I have the cops on my side. Jay's side. And yours if you want to join. Or you can sit in this rotting house with Shawn and forget about Mama. Forget about *me*." I shove my arms into the coat, pulling it tightly around me.

"You're leaving already?" Skylar asks as she follows closely behind.

Silence settles thick again. The little bit of sun that filtered through replaced again by gray. Feels like another goodbye that's firm. Absolute. Buried six feet under, never to be unearthed again.

"Skylar—I'm running out of time. Mama is too. Are you going to help us or not?"

"Shawn isn't going to let me—" she begins.

"Then there's your answer, Skylar. You're more loyal to a man who views you as nothing more than a goddamn baby machine with a casserole dish. You sleep next to a coward every single night and call it love, all while Mama's dying and Jay's killer is on the loose. All you do is smile, bite your tongue, and ask for permission while I have to suffer for *your* mistakes."

"Get out, Sawyer. Now."

"Don't worry. This time I won't come back."

I swing open the door, stepping beneath a bleak gray sky.

Tsunami. That's me and Sky. One minute the swell is gone, the next we're tearing each other apart. And when it's done, neither of us even knows what the hell we were trying to save in the first place.

Chapter Eighteen

I glance down at the watch on my wrist. Approximately twenty seconds have passed since the last time I looked, and I still haven't managed to make it up a single step.

A car horn blares from somewhere...at me, at a car who mistakenly cut them off, at someone who sat at a green light for one second too long. Who knows. I pull my coat tight around my chest and continue my restless pacing, undoubtedly the consequences of an afternoon spent chasing caffeine.

Almost there. The toe of each boot stops just short of the bottom step, concrete chipped where it was repaired before. I release a breath, vapor curling high as I turn and pace some more.

The greenery that tops each city monument sign looks cheap now...tacky plastic on wire formed into a symbol of joy, tiny glittered cranberries and sparkling lights embedded into every branch. I stuff my hands into my coat pockets as Christmas chases right on my heels. Hell, practically stomps on my chest, squeezing out any bit of happiness that may have been left behind. I pull the hood of my coat over my head. The station closed over half an hour ago, yet their trucks sit in the parking garage behind, cold to the touch.

What the hell could be keeping them for so long?

The front doors barrel open wide...startling me as I spin on my heels, paralyzing me as my gaze locks with his. He stops just shy of the top step, reaches into his back pocket and pulls a cigarette from the pack. His eyes narrow onto mine as he flicks a lighter, igniting the orange ember that burns between us now. I swallow to keep from choking on bile. Stop breathing to keep the panic at bay. Those eyes...unmistakable. Something evil lingering just behind.

Slowly, deliberately, he makes his way down each step—chin held high as he takes another drag. Long and slow. Fear pins me to the pavement, but I don't dare blink. Don't dare to look away. His eyes devour me...like a golden-orb spider spinning silk, ready to liquify me from the inside out. A slow torture. Trapped. Terrified. And eaten alive from within.

The cold beats at my chest, Wears my patience down thin. He takes another step. And then another. Enough smoke barreling from that cigarette to rival a steam train. Enough evil behind those eyes to drag the dead from the earth, only to kill them once again. Closer and closer. The *crunch* of grit and gravel beneath each step interrupted by a police siren nearby. But I don't dare blink. Don't dare to look away. I refuse to let him win this fight. Refuse to let him see me break.

He stops. Five feet away. His boots facing mine. Mine facing his. A loose flannel draped over a simple white shirt is all that keeps him warm. And jeans, marked with stains, make me wonder if some of them are Jay's. He takes another drag, blows smoke directly at my face before reaching a fist deep into his pocket. I flinch as he pulls his fingers free. My heart lurches into my throat. But I don't dare blink. Don't dare to look away. He flings a key high into the air and spins it around his finger in loop after taunting loop. His lips pull at the corner into a half-smirk.

"You're Skylar's little sister, aren't ya?" he asks.

The blaring siren fades into the background. The gentle hum of tires on wet pavement quiets again. I choke. Choke on his words, choke on my own bile, and choke at my sister's name in his mouth. I widen my stance. Fold my arms tight to my chest. Lift my chin to match his. But I don't dare blink. Don't dare to look away.

A slight laugh escapes from his chest. Mocking. Provoking. "Yeah, you are..." he continues, smirk returning more sinister than before. "Jay's girl."

The air fills my chest again. Fast and hard. Like I've been starved for air, and life, much too long. I suck it in. Every last bit my lungs can hold.

The doors behind him swing open again as Wes raises his hand high into the air and gives a big wave. Bryce's head snaps left. And for the moment, he decides to let it go—giving me a slight nod as he pulls his hoodie over his head and makes his way down the sidewalk, toward the parking garage. I fold myself in half, placing my palms just above my knees for support.

The cold air hits hard, each breath tightening around my throat. A hand slides around my back, cupping at my side and gently lifting me back up.

"Sawyer, what are you doing here?" Wes asks, features washed in concern.

I take a long breath. And then another. "Why is he here, Wes? Are you guys charging him?"

"What?" he asks, taking a slight step back.

"Bryce Kincaid. Is he being charged?"

"Sawyer—" he begins.

"Don't do that. Do not treat me like this delicate thing. Not you, Wes."

"I wasn't involved this time, Sawyer. I swear. Bryce spoke with Colt in his office privately. I'm guessing Colt was likely asking questions about that night, but you gotta run that by the Chief."

"Wes...tomorrow is Christmas eve. I don't have a home here any longer. And I don't have time for the bullshit." The words tumble out like a dam finally giving way. "Bryce is still walking free and Jay died weeks ago now. You took an oath. You—"

"Breathe Sawyer, damn," he interrupts.

"You guys keep telling me to calm down, but we're no closer to solving this case than when I first arrived. I handed you a prime suspect. Do I have to get a confession, too?" I ask.

"Well, it could be helpful—"

"Where's Colt?" I blurt.

He eases his stance, steps toward me again. "You want a milkshake?" he asks.

I choke on everything. Blink away the confusion. "What are you talking about? It can't be more than thirty degrees out today," I argue.

Wes shrugs. "Milkshake will last longer."

My head shakes right to left, weight shifts left to right. "I—guess?"

He drapes an arm over my shoulders, steering me toward the crosswalk at the traffic light on Main.

The street looks just as it did before, with tiny window scenes that spring to life for passersby. The sky remains gray, our bodies starved for just a touch of sun. And wreaths glare from lamp posts and street signs. Tacky, sure. But maybe, for once, they do offer a kind of warmth in a town that's barely moved at all. Maybe, just sometimes, change isn't what we need. Isn't for the best. Here, it's like everything was locked into a time capsule, each place steeping with memories of a childhood that probably wasn't so bad.

The light turns green and Wes gently guides me across the street. We walk past Blackwood Social as patrons in stuffy ties and black suits begin to flood their doors. Most of them make space for us. At least the six-five man at my side dressed head to toe in a menacing shade of hunter green.

"Nothing has changed. Everything looks exactly the same," I say. Christmas music blares from a toy shop as the door swings wide, then quieting again as last-minute shoppers seal themselves inside. "How is that even possible?"

"Well, some folks don't like change, I suppose. They like what's comfortable. They like what they know."

"Maybe they've got it all figured out," I puzzle. "Maybe we're just destroying ourselves always chasing bigger and better things,"

"Now—you can't tell me you don't miss bonfires out at Connersville. Dips in swamp water pits in the middle of summer? Gossip fresh outta the Baptist Church every Sunday, always startin' right with Missy Robinson's big mouth?"

A laugh bubbles to the surface. "She still doing that?" I ask. I claw at strands of hair as the wind whips through, sending leaves tumbling across sidewalk cracks. "That woman can find gossip about anyone in town."

"See? It ain't all bad. I mean, I know it's nothing compared to the big city where you live—"

I stop. Brace against the blowing force that makes a cold day even colder.

"Actually, Wes...it can be pretty lonely."

He doesn't respond. Not with words anyway. His eyes widen with surprise as he ponders a moment, then shrugs slightly as we continue on our way. We stop just short of the ancient relic that welcomes patrons to Udderly Southern, a statue of Miss Tilly Moo herself.

Long before Bartow got its first traffic light or chain coffee shop, there was Tilly. Some wide-eyed holstein raised on John Maverick's dairy farm, a retired rodeo cowboy who swore Tilly could wink on command or cry when she was sad. Tilly stole the town's heart when she wandered into the annual Fourth of July parade. After that, she became a town fixture...marching in every parade with some sort of sash and flowers blooming around her neck. She did photo ops at every Harvest Festival, and birthday parties at the local parks. Now, her memory lives on as a permanent Main Street fixture where teens take selfies in front of her pink sunglasses and kids rub her nose for good luck.

Bells hang from rope on the top of the door, and they ring loudly as Wes steps inside. We're the only customers here, the only voices that carry across the walls.

Burnt sugar and peppermint cling to the air. Sweet. Almost too sweet. And the white tiled floors gleam with a fresh coat of wax beneath our boots. Rubber soles *squeak* loudly as we make our way inside.

Squeak.

Squeak.

Squeak.

Two girls stand behind the corner. One with her long blonde hair in a braid, the other with star earrings that blink red and green. Blondie whispers something into the other girl's ears, and both cup their hands to their lips as giggles erupt. It's the kind of laugh that seems harmless, but isn't really. My stomach clenches. As Wes approaches, both straighten at attention.

"Welcome to Udderly Southern, what can I get y'all?" the one with the braid asks.

Wes takes a small step back, placing a hand on the back of my shoulder. I don't really want ice cream. But I definitely don't want to be out there. With him.

"Can I get a peppermint mocha shake?" I ask.

I drum the pads of my fingers onto the laminate countertop that peels at one corner as a bulb overhead buzzes, then dies out for good. The girl with the star earrings doesn't seem bothered. She turns on her heels and heads to the back where she promptly gets to work scooping and mixing. The girl with the braid pops the gum in her mouth, then turns back to Wes.

"And one eggnog shake for me," he adds, digging into his too-tight pants pocket for his wallet.

"Coming right up. Y'all can have a seat and we'll bring these out," she says, popping her gum once more.

"What's the total?" he asks.

She smiles wide with a mouthful of perfect, white teeth. The kind that only come from appointments kept every six months. The kind that only come from years of turning and tightening metal brackets every painstaking visit. Mama said we didn't need braces. Said our teeth were perfectly fine, though I never did have the most confident smile. One canine juts slightly at an angle. Jay always said it gave me personality. That in today's world, where people want to be carbon copies of celebrities, it's "refreshing to see people with imperfections." And maybe he was right. He was definitely wise beyond his years.

"Cops don't pay," she smiles, smacking her gum some more. "Direct orders from the boss."

Wes puffs his chest out a bit more. Stuffs his wallet back into his pocket. Widens his stance. "Well, tell your boss thank you from the station. Nice to be recognized in the community."

She cups her hand to her mouth and giggles again as she turns and joins her friend at the back of the shop.

I make my way to a small table just near the front window, where Tilly Moo looks on with side-eyed annoyance. Wes slides into the booth across from me. I expect him to talk as we wait. He doesn't. Another bulb flickers. Much too fast. Like it's panicking that Christmas is almost here. Maybe we both are.

Both girls emerge again, each one with a milkshake in hand. They stand side by side as they place them onto the tabletop in front of us. "Anything else we can get for you?" Blondie asks.

Wes shifts in his seat, absolutely smitten with the attention. "These look great. I think we're all good here," he says.

She turns to me now.

"No thank you," I say.

Both girls take a long glance at each other, something knowing in their eyes, then disappear again. Greedily, I unwrap a straw and stab it into the milkshake, sucking and sucking and sucking until finally, a big, gloppy chunk of ice cream, flavored with peppermint, washes down my throat.

"I think I might get a hotel room," I blurt out. Haven't even really considered it until this moment. "That way I can stay here a little longer. Until the case gets solved, you know?"

Wes softens. Sinks into the booth. "Sawyer, won't that get expensive? Don't you need to get back home and back to work?"

"I have a little left in my savings account. And as far as work...doubt I'll have a job when I get back." I shrug like it's nothing because I'm not worried. Know that this is where I'm supposed to be. Know that anyone with half a brain can step in to write blog posts and social media captions at a junior copyright level marketing job. After all, the role is to churn out content. Creativity is rarely required. "I can take a quick trip home, throw some things in the car and turn over the keys."

His jaw drops slightly. V settles deep between his brows.

Behind him, the two girls stand still behind the counter. The one with the blonde braid peeking around the corner again. Just watching. She leans toward the other and whispers again. More laughter. This time, I hear it. Barely.

"She smells like wet dog. Probably wearing her dead friend's clothes."

I freeze.

Wes looks up and asks, "What?"

I shake my head quickly. "Nothing."

He presses the straw to his lips and sucks the eggnog milkshake down in what seems to be one long gulp. It's quite the astounding feat. I rub at my temple and wrap my hands around the cold glass, just to tether myself to something real. Something cold and absolute. I look down. The whipped cream is gone. Melted too fast.

"You ever thought about leaving town, Wes?"

"No," he answers, the words spilling out fast. "I mean, I hope to stay on the force and maybe make Chief someday. Or...maybe start a family one day soon."

"Of course. I forget being a cop is pretty big in your family, right?"

He nods, lips curling upward into a smile. "Big party every time one of us graduates the academy," he beams.

"And what local girl do you have your sights set on?"

Something mischievous sparkles in his eyes as his lips pull tight. Something he isn't being honest about.

"You're joking—"

He still refuses to answer. Just sucks on that damn straw though nothing but air is coming out.

"You know Shawn will kill you, right?"

"I'm not worried about him."

"She's got kids already, Wes. One is practically a newborn," I whisper, just a little too loud.

My words echo like sin off the walls as the girls in the back peek around the corner and giggle again.

"Hey, I like kids! I think I'd make a great dad," he beams.

I sigh, pushing the goopy, melted minty thing away from me. "Well, I don't understand it. At all. But—" I begin, clearing at the milky clots in my throat. "Shawn might be dealing drugs under Bryce. Do with it what you want."

He grins as if I just handed him a stack of crisp hundred dollar bills. And I can't stand another minute in this claustrophobic ice cream shop under the watchful eyes of Mean Thing One and Mean Thing Two.

"You ready?" I ask.

He nods, squeezing his frame out of the booth and making his way toward the front door. The bells chime loudly as Wes pushes his way through and onto the sidewalk again, Miss Tilly Moo at his side. I follow, but stop abruptly when a hand presses against my shoulder from behind. I turn, finding myself face to face with blinking red and green earrings and focused on wide, rich velvet-brown eyes. She leans in, voice breathy, meant only for me.

"He's still under there, you know," she whispers.

"Who—"

"He's really cold. All this rain is making him look just like a prune."

My body seizes. Heart misses a few beats. *Prune.* Her lips purse together so perfectly when she says it. Like it's this sweet, delicate thing to be spoken softly about.

"You need to get him, Sawyer. Hurry. Rot travels fast."

My fingers tremble at my sides. Heels pin to the lacquer below. Back dampens with sweat.

"Merry Christmas," she says, then turns and slips behind the counter, busying herself with cleaning the machines.

"You comin' girl?" Wes' voice booms from behind my shoulder.

I turn, rushing outside as the cold greets me like a slap on the face. I throw myself into Wes' side, burying my head deep.

"You okay?" he asks, wrapping his arm around my back.

I nod. A lie.

"Just wanted to thank you for the milkshake, that's all."

The sun sets early every evening, usually around six. The gray sky has turned black, and the shiny tinsel and tacky lights create a glow from above. My boots scrape across the cracked asphalt behind the station, the distant hum of a busted vending machine the background to a katydid song.

The wind cuts sharper now. Harder than before. Wes had a call come in on the radio, somewhere nearby, so I walked back alone. The alley behind the police station reeks of cigarette smoke and leaking motor oil. I round the corner. Reach deep into my coat pocket before stopping dead in my tracks.

Bryce Kincaid.

He leans against his truck like he owns the place. Like he owns the whole damn town. His boot is kicked up against the bumper. Cigarette balanced between his fingers, smoke rolling like poison through the air. I consider turning back, though my car is just behind him, about four spaces back. Still...if I turn now, just race right back toward the glow of Main, maybe I can escape the shadows that stretch long across the sky.

"You lost?" he asks, voice casual. Molasses-thick.

I try to swallow, but there's nothing there. Just dry desert left behind.

"Thought maybe you were looking for me," he continues.

I steady my breath. "I didn't know you worked here," I manage out.

He smiles, thin-lipped and evil. "Don't. Just visiting an old friend," he says. His eyes sweep me up and down as he flicks ash to the ground.

I pull the coat tighter around me. Knowing he can't see my skin through it, but hiding it anyway. I ease my way toward the passenger door.

"You think I did it, don't you?" he asks, eyes boring directly into mine.

I shake my head left to right. "No," I say, voice unsteady under rattling breaths.

"Yeah, you do," he smirks.

He pushes off the truck. Slow. Deliberate. The sound of his boots scuffing on pavement. "He always thought he was better than the rest of us. You remember that?" he asks.

I take a step forward, barely able to keep the fire on my tongue at bay. "I remember him being kind. I remember he would give the shirt off his back to anyone. I remember him being better than all of us combined."

Bryce smiles. The kind of smile you see in the woods...right before a trap shuts tight. "Funny. I remember him being a liar. About what he wanted. Who he was. Thought he was better than this place," he continues on.

He steps closer to me now, placing a finger beneath my chin as I fight to steady trembling lips.

"Pride like that comes with a price," he growls.

"That what you think happened, Bryce? Pride caught up to him?" I ask.

"You know...you got an awful lot of questions." He takes another drag. The cigarette tip glows like a slow heartbeat. He leans in. Places his lips close to my ear. "But you're not asking the right people, Sawyer."

I pull away. Smack his hand away from my face. "And who would that be?" I ask.

He chuckles. Takes a few steps back. "Not me."

Time to go, Sawyer. Now.

"You should head back home," he taunts. "It's getting dark."

"Are you afraid of the dark?" I ask him. "Scared of ghosts?"

He smiles with teeth. "Nah. But maybe you should be."

I spin on my heels. Walk straight to my car. Don't even look back. What's the point when I can feel him there, leaned up against his truck again? Watching. Sneering. Lip curled against his teeth. A gaunt coyote with ribs showing, circling a newborn fawn too weak to even stand.

Chapter Nineteen

Brown's store is mostly dark now, except for the neon sign that flickers "OPEN" like it can't decide if it really is or not. He stands behind the counter, stocking shelves filled with cigarettes and nicotine patches for those trying to quit. On the roller grill, one slightly burnt, wrinkled hot dog turns over and over and over again, grease bubbling along the skin so much that I swear I can smell it through the glass. My mouth waters. I curl my fingers into a fist and lift them to the streaked glass just as his head snaps in my direction. His lips tug at his cheeks as he drops the box in his hands and makes his way toward the front.

The door *clicks* its release, and his arm wraps around my shoulders before I can get a single word out.

"Come on in, Sawyer! I was hoping to see you again before you left town," he says, voice so jolly I could almost swear I'm standing in front of Santa himself.

Warmth spills from inside like summer trying to crawl its way back in, and I peel the coat from my arms, draping it onto the rack beside his old, brown crumpled hat.

"Are 'ya hungry? Kept this dog on the rollers for 'ya in case you stopped by," he offers, eyes wide with excitement.

"Smells good, Brown," I say, plopping myself right down onto the counter's edge like I own the place. "You got ketchup and mustard, too?"

Brown quickly scoops up a bun and places the sizzling, wrinkled old leathery thing inside, shoving it toward me with handfuls of wadded paper napkins and tiny condiment packets before I can take a breath. I watch him with a smile stretching wide. It's nice to see Brown staying active. To see him keeping the old store alive.

I watch him rustle behind the counter, toss a half-empty bag of stale chips into a trash bin caked in dust, tobacco, and grime. Then comes the sound.

Tick.

Tick.

Tick.

An old clock with a yellowed frame, coated in dust, hanging just above the soda machine on the far wall. The numbers are faded. Second hand moves in more of a twitch.

"Has that thing always been so loud?" I ask.

Brown doesn't look up, just keeps tossing old bits of trash aside as he asks, "What thing?"

"The clock, it's—" I begin. I glance back to the twitching hand. "Nevermind."

He follows my gaze.

"That old thing don't even work. Been dead since spring. Needs new batteries I suppose, but I'm gettin' too old to be climbing up on that ladder anymore."

I blink. But I heard it. I know that I did. A metronome on the verge of snapping.

Tickticktickticktickticktick.

Now, its hands are stilled. And the quiet hum of the coolers is the only soundtrack to a late night meal.

"Brown?"

"Yeah, kid?"

"How did you..." I falter, letting the words hang in the air, "...Move on after Patsy died?"

Brown presses into the floor. His feet. His gaze, too.

"I'm sorry, Brown. I didn't mean to upset you," I offer.

His gaze shifts back to me. Palm clings gently behind my shoulder. "Nah kid, you didn't upset me. Just always knocks me back a few steps when I hear her name, that's all. She was the love of my life, 'ya know?"

I place the hot dog and its little paper boat down onto the counter beside me, ripping open one packet of ketchup and applying with perfect precision. I bring the small plastic packet to my lips and squeeze the remainder in. Tart. Delicious.

"I know, Brown. Everyone could see how much you loved her. How much you loved *each other*," I say.

He scratches at his head, then pats loose strands down again. Brown's hair used to be dark, but these days it's silky strands of white just barely covering his head. He drops down onto a stool as he releases a long breath of air.

"Patsy was everything good in this world. That smell of citrus in an afternoon breeze. An azalea bush in spring. Or the way the lake water sparkles just before the sun drops off the horizon. I just couldn't ever get her to see it. And I knew Patsy most of her life—high school sweethearts, and all. It took me a lot longer to get past the loss than most folks around here realize," he says, voice cracking on that last word.

I shove the hot dog into my mouth, biting off what I can barely chew and fighting to get it down.

"Grief's a funny thing, Sawyer. We try to ignore it. Outrun it. Hell, might even try to kill it. But it ain't going nowhere. Not until you sit down with the ugly thing and face it head on. Only then can you carry the thing, instead of lettin' it carry you."

I manage to swallow the last of my greed-filled, greasy bite.

"Need some water?" he asks.

I nod, tears almost filling my eyes. Brown pops off his stool and grabs a bottle from a cooler with a door that hangs desperately from its hinge, then tosses it back to me. I twist off the cap, greedily chugging the water down as if my life depends on it.

"Better?"

"Better," I nod. "Thanks."

Brown nods.

"I mean, I know Patsy was your wife. The two of you were soulmates, everyone could see that."

"And Jay was *your* soulmate—" he says.

The words sting a bit. Like stepping barefoot onto shards of broken glass. Or ripping off a bandage that's stuck to the wound. Friends sounds better. Friends lets me off the hook for allowing this to happen and not being there for him like I should have. Soulmates, though—that comes with the uncomfortable truth that I should never have left him alone. Soulmates comes with the crushing grief that I'm truly the one to blame.

"I should have been there, Brown. I knew he was hanging out with them. I knew—"

"Now, you gotta stop that right there. You can't change the circumstances. That's out of anyone's control. You were never gonna stop what happened that night. But you can be the one who puts those boys away, you hear?" he says, more like an order than a kind request.

"I know exactly who did it. It was that Kincaid boy. You remember? I stood face to face with him tonight. Something about him—" I say, my skin crawling with unease.

A cockroach peeks from between hot dog rollers, antennae twitching as he sniffs out the place. His shell gleams slick under the fluorescent lights. Not clean. Greasy. Like he just crawled from months of hot dog drippings below. Its legs move in stiff jerks, each one tipped with tiny barbed spikes. And I swear I can hear it skitter across the rollers and down the side, like the old TVs going static at the same time every night, crackling through a silent room.

"It's like he's so smug. So damn sure he'll never get caught that he doesn't even care that I know," I continue on, sucking a big glob of ketchup from the side of my hand. "Practically laughs in my face about it."

"Folks with that kinda money tend to think they're untouchable," he mutters beneath his breath.

Brown gets it. He's one of *us*. Those of us who don't get to live on that side of the tracks in a brand new construction build. Those of us who work hard with blistered hands and calloused fingers for everything that we have.

A second cockroach peeks his head between metal rollers, antennae twitching as it speaks in some sort of insect code. Brown's voice tunnels, thin and far-off. Like background noise fed through a drain. Swallowed by the sound of tiny legs with barbed spikes on slick metal as it skitters to find its friend. The thing is fast. Faster than it has any right to be. Even when it stills, it pulses with breath, hunger, or maybe even nerves as it finds its tiny body face to face with me now. It watches me. At least I think it is. Maybe it wants the rest of the hot dog in my hands. Maybe we're both just wet, gutter-starved things.

I place the remaining hot dog down, lick the ketchup from the corner of my lips, and drum the pads of my fingertips against the counter's laminate until he skitters close. Close enough for me to bring my palm smashing down hard onto his slick back. The *crunch* is loud. Louder than it should be. Wet. Popping. A splatter of white pulp and exoskeleton oozing from beneath my palm like a rotten grape. I lift my hand and stare at the mess.

The sounds of the world return in layers—the hum of coolers, the buzz of fluorescent lights, and the soft rustle of Brown shifting his weight. My chin flicks to my left shoulder where Brown watches me. Not confused. Not disturbed. Only mildly curious. As if I just spilled a packet of mustard onto my pants. The muffled fog lifts, replaced by Brown's natural, low gravel tone.

"You want a napkin?" he asks.

I nod once. He passes one over to me. I wipe my hands. The thing shreds into about a million pieces. Tiny tattered strips that stick to cockroach guts and sugar-filled ketchup sauce. I do my best to scrub at the white pulp sticking to my skin. Do my best to get most of it before tossing the wadded shreds of napkin away.

"They're gettin' worse this year," he offers up. "Too much rain. Too many out-of-towners leavin' food wrappers around. It's just gettin' to be too much."

"Maybe you should hire more help, Brown. This is a lot to manage at your—"

"At my old age?" he interrupts.

"You aren't old. But we need help sometimes. Me and you both."

"Eh—I can't find anyone who wants the damn place. Hard to even find decent help nowadays," he mutters. "I'm sorry Sawyer. Don't mean to go on and on, but lookin' like I may have to close the place soon."

I place my palm flat behind me and lean back, reaching for a tacky pair of sunglasses complete with a cutout of Florida atop each mirrored lens.

"Afraid I can't let you do that, Brown. Where else can someone buy a ninety-nine cent can of beer, scratch-off lottery ticket and one-of-a-kind couture sunglass frames?"

A deep V forms between his brows. A deep V of concern. "Any gas station in the state—" he begins before I promptly cut him off again.

"Sorry, Brown, but the people have spoken. And I'm afraid it's your duty to answer the call."

"All jokes aside, Sawyer...what next?" he asks.

"I don't know," I say, sucking a truckload of air into my lungs before chasing it away. "I guess I was kind of hoping to just sit here until I figure that part out."

"Well, I'd say sit here as long as you like, but the town is practically shut down and it's almost time for me to head on home. Now, I've got a nice, warm little guest bedroom you're welcome to use. Patsy set it up just before—"

His gaze falls flat. The same way it does every time someone brings up Patsy Fisher's name. The same way you might expect for someone who had their entire life ripped from their hands.

"Brown?"

He startles a bit. Gives me his full attention.

"You know how to handle a gun?" I ask.

A low chuckle escapes his chest. "I'm from Polk County. That's like askin' if I ever saw a gator swimmin' in a kiddie pool," he says.

"Can you show me?" I ask.

Now I have his full attention. Eyes focused solely on me.

"What are we talkin' about here, kid?"

I reach behind me and pull it out. Lay the barrel flat against my thigh. The metal feels heavy and cold from riding at the small of my back.

"Jesus, kid," Brown says as he takes a few steps back.

"Daddy said it has five rounds left in it. I think."

He flattens a hand to the counter's surface and eases himself back onto the stool. "This your father's gun?"

"Mm-hmm. I went to see him last week."

He reaches for a pair of reading glasses beside the cash register and perches them onto the bridge of his nose. He taps his finger onto the laminate surface. "Here. Place that down here," he orders. His eyes never leave the gun's barrel. Not once. "Nice and slow."

I follow his order.

"Finger off the trigger," he says sharply.

I jerk my finger back, making sure to listen, to obey every word as I lay the thing down between us. He looks at it like a snake ready to strike. But he reaches for it with calm hands. Hands that know what they're doing. Hands that have probably done much, much worse.

He turns it over in his palms. Opens the cylinder and checks, just to be sure. "Five shots," he confirms.

He looks at me. Eyes soft. Obviously confused as to why I even have the damn thing. But he doesn't ask anymore questions. Doesn't pry into personal affairs. I stare at the wall behind him, where a water spot looks like some sort of broken crown. He lifts the revolver up, holds it with both hands and passes it slow as he guides me.

"Hands like this. You don't choke it. You respect it."

He shows me how to open the cylinder. How to load. How to check for misfire. How to aim.

"It kicks more than you think. Don't trust the weight. She'll buck."

"Like Mama," I mutter.

Surprised myself with that one.

"Yeah, just like that," he smirks.

We go over it, over it, and over it again until I can do it on my own. The one thing I can't do is shoot. Brown doesn't ask why I have it or what I plan to do. Doesn't even say I shouldn't. Just makes sure I know what the hell I'm holding in my hand and carrying tucked beneath my waistband.

He hands me another bottle of water without me having to ask.

"You okay, kid?"

"Not really. But I'm going to try really hard at pretending I am," I assure him.

"Sawyer," he whispers low, like he has a secret to spill. "If you aim that thing, you better mean it. No half-measures with a weapon like that. No second-guesses. And *no* trembling hands."

I nod and straighten my spine. Tighten my fingers around the grip. Blink away the wetness threatening to spill down my cheek.

"You only raise that thing if you're ready to live with what comes after. You understand?"

I slide my fingers over the smooth barrel as Daddy's tired, confused face flickers through my mind like some sort of film watched ages ago. "I understand."

He studies my face. Almost as if he's trying to see past the dark shadows formed beneath a set of tired eyes. "I mean it, kid. You steady yourself first. Because if your hand shakes, it could mean the difference between walking away and not."

I meet his gaze head-on now. Still my wildly beating chest. Slip the barrel beneath my waistband again. "I won't shake."

I hop from the counter and make my way around to the coat rack, shrugging it on slow, each motion heavier than the last. The revolver's weight presses at my spine, and my boots tap against the tiles as I push toward the front doors. But I can't open them. Not sure why. I turn back and watch as he pulls out a bucket of water and a mud-stained mop.

The store feels colder now than when I first arrived. Emptier.

"Thanks for the hot dog, Brown," I say, voice barely above a whisper. "And...for everything."

"Always happy to see you walk through that door. You tell your mama that I said she's got one hell of a girl."

My brows pinch. I should ask to stay. Ask to see him once more. But the words don't come. Only the wind that howls against the glass.

"Goodnight, Brown."

He nods once. "Goodnight, Sawyer."

His words sit heavy in the air. Feel so final. So cold. I push my way onto the sidewalk outside. Onto the curb. Onto the pavement. Dab the toe of my boot into an iridescent puddle, slick with rain and oil. I think about going home. About going back into the store. But by the time I turn and search the glass, the store lights are dim.

The neon "OPEN" sign has flickered its last breath, and somewhere down the block, a street lamp *buzzes* back to life. But behind me, the dark lays still. And the silence feels heavier than it ever was before.

Chapter Twenty

Christmas Eve. It's supposed to mean something. Magic. Sugar cookies. Twinkling lights. But for me, it's just another day of gray—a lifeless sky, water-logged everything and a kitchen void of human life.

The house is silent. Except for the *ticking* of the clock and the ragged coughs that echo down the hall. The rain has been steady all day, drizzling like a faucet left barely on. Cold seeps through the cracks and wraps around my ankles as I sit curled on the bed. I stare at a crack in the wall. Can almost swear that it moves, slithering like a snake over the room. I wiggle my toes. One sock dangles, barely clinging to my foot.

I should get up. Know that I can't hide here forever. It's just that I can't stomach another holiday, not when everything inside of me is fraying at the edges. Still, as long as I lay in this bed, Bryce Kincaid walks a free man.

I peel back the covers, jolt up on the bed and land hard on my feet. Salem *meows* and scurries underneath the bed. I reach my arms wide, spine *cracking* down its length like a snapped branch, then make my way into the bathroom that Skylar and I once shared.

Large tan tiles line the floor...several cracked so deep that they teeter underneath your feet. Mama did the remodeling herself. Oak everywhere. Oak cabinets, oak-framed mirror, and trim wrapping the window above the spacious garden bathtub. It's always been my favorite spot in the house. From here, you can still see the old rose bed Daddy planted when we first moved in. I peel back the lace curtains as dust floats through the air like confetti. The rose bed...now just overgrown, thick branches, many now without leaves. Like this house just sucked the soul from everything in it...Daddy, Mama, Skylar. And now me.

I fold myself in half and turn the faucet handle. Let the water fill the tub. Peel the sweatshirt over my head and toss it onto the floor. Flannel pants follow—tossed right behind as I lower myself down. I add a few drops of bubble bath that's been sitting in here since God knows when, and lean my head back into the warmth until the water almost overflows. Kick the faucet off and close my eyes.

Twelve days. Three suspects. And a town that moves too damn slow. Grayson Black. Dane Whitlock. Bryce Kincaid. Grayson and Dane are staying low, but Bryce is practically breathing down my neck. Already thinks he's gotten away with it. But if I can just get a confession, an admission that he was there that night, then this nightmare might just go away. I can get him to talk. I just have to find him now, the way that he found me. His arrogance will be his undoing, probably the one thing that puts him away.

I splash water onto my face. Dip my head lower into the water. Heat seeps through me now, all the way to the tips of my fingers, now pruned to the bone. The pad of my finger draws on the water's surface, creating tiny caves and hidden paths through bubble walls. Mama's cough spills through the house again, rattling like gravel through her chest. Slices through the silence like a razor on glass. I don't know what to do for her. Guess there's nothing that I can. She won't let me. Won't let anyone in.

I give myself a quick scrub down, wash my tangled hair twice, and let the water drain while I dry off and cocoon myself in a towel. I lift my curled fist to the mirror, rubbing in circles until the steam gives way. The reflection staring back at me isn't one that I know.

Wasted. Even in just two short weeks. Dark shadows beneath both eyes that look like bruises. Bones jutting too sharp beneath tired skin. But I'm close now. Almost got him. Just need to give it a couple more days. Still, if I sit in this house one minute longer, I'll lose what's left of my mind. So I'll drink. Find warmth at the bottom of a glass. Pretend everything is fine when it's not.

A fist pounds on the door, startling me like I've just been shot.

"You gonna be here tomorrow?" she yells.

I reach for the knob, gently turning to see her slightly folded frame. Shoulders hunched like a wilting tree, breaths labored and hard.

"Mama, I'll be out soon, I promise. I'll get a hotel or something. Still trying to figure it all out," I say.

She shakes her head left to right as her gaze meets the cracked tiles below. "No Sawyer. That's not why I'm askin'. Just didn't know if you might want to have coffee in the mornin'. Or maybe we could watch that old Christmas movie they play on repeat all day."

My jaw goes slack. Eyes widen. I don't answer. Wouldn't know what to say if I tried.

"You know...that one with Jimmy Stewart and that angel?"

I shift, uncomfortable on my feet, like the floor itself might give way under the weight of what she said.

"I just—," she begins, but stops like the words cause her to choke. Water pools in the corner of one eye. And her bottom lip trembles slightly when she's upset. Just like mine.

"I'll be here," I promise.

She swallows down something. Pride. Pain. The taste of the end. Bitter and familiar on her tongue.

Blackwood Social smells like cedar, a bit of cinnamon, and some dark, hoppy craft beer that I'm sure tastes terrible. The crowd is thick, and bodies continue to pile in from the cold. The colorful lights cast shadows along the walls as an eager group dons tinsel garland around their necks and take turns singing off-key. It's kind of nice, I suppose.

I shed my coat and slide onto the bar stool closest to the heater.

"Well, look who the cat dragged in," Penny says, already reaching for the whiskey. "How about a hot toddy tonight? Bartender's special."

"Sure. Sounds great," I reply.

Still hate whiskey. But Penny thinks that I don't, and so I'll chug the horrible stuff anyway. She gets to work—slicing oranges into tiny wedges and dripping honey all over the bar. And for a moment, I close my eyes and take in the place, let the noise drown everything out. The ridiculous Christmas donkey song that blares through speakers. The *crack* of pool balls that slice through the air. Someone laughing way too hard at a joke over my left shoulder. I suppose it's nice, though—the music, the laughter, the excitement as Christmas nears. But they all have someone to go home to. Probably all have gifts waiting beneath a tree.

Penny slings a bar towel over her shoulder as she slides the steaming drink my way. "That oughta get 'ya nice and cooked like a Sunday roast," she calls out.

I raise the glass high into the air as a thank you, though I don't know how I'll get the nasty thing down.

"Fancy seeing you here," a voice croons from over my shoulder, lips brushing at my ear.

My head snaps right. Colt stands at my side, still dressed in his work suit and tie, perfectly wrapped box with tiny sparkling snowflakes tucked tight beneath his arm.

"How did you—" I begin.

"There's only so many places someone can hide in this town. You're pretty easy to find." His lips curl into a dangerous smirk as he places the box on top of the bar and slips out of his blazer. He drapes it over a chair behind us, then slides onto the seat at my side. "Mind some company?"

"Little late to ask, isn't it? You're already here."

"Now Ellis, it's Christmas Eve. Where's your holiday spirit?" he taunts.

"Buried six feet underground with my best friend," I say, throwing back the whiskey drink fast. It burns like fire, but the honey chases behind like a heating pad on a bellyache. Instant relief, though the pain is still lingering there. "You talked to Bryce yesterday."

His smile fades fast. The V between his brows deepens. "How do you know about that?" he asks.

"I was waiting for you outside the station. Bryce walked out and saw me," I hurl. I throw back another drink of the warm whiskey. Goes down easier this time. "Did you get anything out of him?"

He clears at his throat and hunches over the bar. Penny returns.

"Handsome," she grins, happy as a pig in mud. "Merry Christmas. You want a hot toddy, too?"

"How about a beer. Whatever's your favorite," he says, lip curling again as he flirts shamelessly.

I'm beginning to wonder if Colt Landry takes anything seriously. He shifts on the stool and turns to me.

"Now, tell me again exactly why you were hanging out in front of the police station. Because Ellis, I simply cannot understand for the life of me why you think you're on the force. Why you keep putting yourself in danger."

"Did you get anything out of him, Colt? That's all I need to know."

"Ellis—"

"Landry, I'm not a cop. But, I *can* get a confession out of him. I know I can. He's slipping. Getting a little too comfortable with what he says."

Penny slides a tall glass of beer the color of molasses Colt's way. Smells awful. He throws it back quick, licking the foam from his lips.

"And just how are you going to get a confession exactly? We interrogated that man for an hour straight. His story never changed. Admitted the two hung out, but it was just because Jay asked him to fix something up," he confides.

"Well, at least I got something out of you," I reply, celebrating the small win. "But you know that's a bullshit story, right? He was cocky with me. Knows I'm onto him."

"Yeah? Listen Ellis—I'm worried about you. You're gonna get yourself in a situation you can't get out of. And I'm not always gonna be around to keep you safe."

Someone belts a high note over the microphone, startling us both. And apparently the entire bar as every head snaps right toward the small stage.

"Jack Waters," he says, as if I should know who that is. "Moved here with his wife and girls a few years ago. He'll climb in bed and pass out later. Wake up in a stupor tomorrow, nurse a hangover, whole time surprised by every gift his wife put under the tree."

"I take it he does this often?"

"Just about every damn night. We've had to practically drag him out of the bar a few times, but Penny says he's harmless. And he usually walks home."

"Mama's got cancer," I say, leaning my elbows onto the bar and resting my head in my palm.

The words come fast, like a knife slicing through fabric. Colt goes still. Probably waiting for me to speak. Maybe waiting for tears to follow.

But there aren't any to come. And it's not that I don't care. I just don't know how I should act, or what I'm supposed to say to a woman who flinches when I walk into a room.

"You serious?" he asks, finally breaking the silence that hangs between us.

"Stage four. Lungs. Spread to her bones. She didn't plan to tell anyone, not even me. Says she just wants to die quiet."

Colt reaches for my hand. It sends a shockwave that travels the length of my spine. I leave it there.

"I'm sorry, Ellis. Really."

"I just don't know what to say or do to comfort her. How do you comfort someone who doesn't even want it?"

We fall silent again. Like a record player spinning on a silent groove, needle scratching nothing but dust. His hand leaves mine.

"That's a tough one. Abilene knows just about everyone in town, too. She nursed everyone to health for decades 'round here. If she asked, I know folks would run to her side."

"I know. Just seems like something broke in her when Daddy took off. And I happened to shatter whatever was left simply because I was a constant reminder of him."

His hand finds its way to the small of my back. Eyes linger on mine. My pulse quickens.

"You gonna open your gift?" he asks, spark returning to his eyes, chestnut with flecks of gold that catch in the glow of Christmas lights.

"This is for me?" I ask, straightening my spine on the seat. "Why on earth would you get me a gift?"

He grins wide. A dimple appears on his left cheek. Never noticed it before.

"It's Christmas, Sawyer. That's just what people do."

A smile tugs at the corners of my lips. Feels foreign. Almost like I forgot how.

"Not for me," I whisper. I clasp my hands in my lap. Gaze drops. "Not that I need gifts anyway."

His fingertips gently wind at loose strands of hair as he tucks them behind my ear, and his thumb brushes my cheek like I'm something delicate he doesn't want to break. Normally, I hate the pity, but it feels different coming from him. It feels safe. It feels warm.

"You deserve to be happy. Now go on. Open your gift."

My fingers wrap around the box. White paper with glittery snowflakes tied with a perfect red ribbon. Almost too pretty to touch. I set the whiskey glass down with a *clink* and slide the gift toward my chest. Carefully pull at the perfect folds on each side.

"Oh just rip it, Ellis. It's not like you're gonna keep the damn paper," he teases.

"It just looks so pretty. Didn't realize you had hidden talents."

"I don't. Girl at the store wrapped it up for me."

I grin wide. "At least you admit to your shortcomings, Landry. That's progress."

I tear into it now, pulling off the ribbon and ripping it right down the middle.

A white box sits in front of me, thick with a lid on top. Carefully, I lift it, half preparing for something to jump outside. But there's nothing in it except a beautiful coat, stuffed thick with soft down. I remove it from the box and shake it out at my side.

"You're old one is looking a little beat up, that's all. Thought you could use a new one," he says.

He waits for a reply. Eyes eager and wide, though I pin to the seat, unable to move an inch. I don't recall Colt Landry ever doing nice things for people. Don't understand why he'd start with me.

"Check the pocket," he urges, mischief sparkling in his eyes.

I plunge my hand inside, fingers landing on something small and hard. I pull it out to reveal another box, the size you usually find jewelry inside, wrapped neatly in the same snowflake paper. Something tight fills my throat. I swallow it down hard. Place the coat across my lap. Slowly open the top. Inside—a chain holds a charm in the shape of a tiny gold key. I place my fingers beneath, lifting it from the box with care. I rest it in my palm, twisting right and left as the lights hit the gold in fractiles like sparkling dust. No one ever gifted me jewelry. Well, no one other than Jay.

"What's this?" My eyes narrow onto his. "Key to your heart or something?"

"You flirtin' with me, Ellis?"

"Never," I say.

He leans in close. "It's a key to the city," he says, the sarcasm that usually drips from his tongue fading. "So that you don't forget you still have a home."

My throat closes. Water threatens to spill from my eyes. "It's not my home any—"

His hands reach for the chain, unbuckling the clasp as he orders me to spin around. "It is, Sawyer. You have people that care about you here. Wes. Birdie." He clears at his throat as he reaches around my neck, clasping the chain secure. "Me."

My breath seizes as I pin my gaze to the garland that drapes the wall. I blink away the wetness and draw a slow breath in. "Why?" I ask, spinning back around to face him.

"Why did I choose the necklace or why do I care?"

"Both," I say.

"Hoping I might convince you to stay," he says, voice smooth as velvet. "I don't know. I thought maybe we could give this a real shot."

My lips slightly part, ready for words to tumble out. But they don't come. I grasp the key in my fingertips, clasping it tight to keep it safe.

"How about I whoop your ass in a game of pool?" he asks. He reaches for my hand, gently pulling me from the stool before I can answer. "Come on, girl. Let's go."

Only one pool table sits open in the back corner of the bar. I've never been particularly good at the game, but I do seem to get better the more that I drink. I guess I'll stick with that strategy.

Colt grabs a cue stick, digging it into the floor at my feet. "Well?" His eyes gleam devious. Dimple returns.

"Alright. Challenge accepted. But I'm gonna need another drink."

Colt lifts his arm high into the air, waving Penny down at the bar. "Another whiskey, Pen?" he shouts.

She nods, slinging the bar rag again and crafting drinks without missing a beat. Colt gets to work, racking pool balls and chalking up the cue stick. I never understood why people do that, but follow his lead anyway. He grins from across the pool table, and my stomach flips like a fish on a dock. Every word lost somewhere between my chest and my throat.

"Ladies first," he says.

Penny rushes over, sweat beads forming on each side of her temple, tendrils slipping from the elastic on top of her head. She slides another warm toddy onto the pool table's side and rushes away. I toss it back, a bit more eagerly this time. The whiskey glows like embers in my chest. Softens the edges just enough. I slam the glass down onto the edge again. Slowly make my way around to where he stands. But Colt doesn't move. Doubles down.

"Easy now, Tiger. Aren't you forgetting something important?" he asks.

That damn grin returns, sending my gut into another somersault. The smell of something familiar lingers on the collar of his shirt—bergamot, maybe. Or sandalwood. Something woodsy. Something intoxicating.

"Solids? Stripes?"

"Stripes," I decide.

I turn, spin the stick once in my hand for dramatic effect, then fold myself over green felt and let her *crack*. The balls scatter over the table, rolling gently until they stop.

His breath whispers at my neck, causing every hair to stand at attention. "Sloppy form, Ellis."

I straighten my spine as heat crawls up my back. "Let's see you do better," I hiss.

Colt's tongue drags over his bottom lip as he narrows his eyes at the table, carefully plotting his next move. He pulls at his tie, loosening it and his collar, before folding himself over the table's edge. His muscles flex against the fabric of his shirt. Colt is undoubtedly sculpted by the Gods. The problem, however, is that he knows this. And it's gotten him out of situations that others simply could not. But looks aren't all he's packing. Colt is sharp. Calculating. Maybe a little manipulative, if you ask me. After all, you don't become a lead detective straight out of college without being smarter than everyone expects.

A ball sinks in. Solid. Colt winks. I hate that I like it, but I do. I take another turn, sinking in a ball with a green stripe. I take my victory dance, wash back the remaining whiskey, and lean over the felt to sink some more.

Colt whistles low. "You always this competitive, Ellis? Or am I just special?"

I grin wide as a hint of joy bubbles to the surface. "You know, my Daddy used to say I have the eyes of a sniper."

"Oh yeah?"

"Of course he always had a beer dangling in his hand when he said it. But still—"

Laughter spills from his chest, and his eyes do this crinkling thing at the corners that about steals every last breath from my lungs. I line up the next shot as he circles the table slow, almost prowling, then stops. He leans against the table's edge. Folds his arms tightly to him. I lean in. Miss the shot.

"I think it might be the whiskey," he teases slow, southern drawl slipping through as the beer in his hand empties. "Messes with your aim."

"I'm taking it easy on you," I say.

"Sure," he grins. "You always this full of fire?"

I lean back against the edge, pressing myself into the wood. I prop the cue stick beside me. "You try living in this town with *my* history and see if you don't come out a little singed, too."

"Everyone liked you, Sawyer. You just never believed it. Never believed in yourself."

He pins in front of me now. I lift my gaze to meet his.

"They whispered about me. At lunch. In the halls. Jay was the only protection I had in this world."

A breath pushes past his lips as he raises fingertips to my face, slowly running his thumb delicately from my temple to my chin. Gently. Softly. Ensuring my gaze never leaves those eyes that hold everything he doesn't say. My knees buckle beneath. Breath catches in my throat.

His head lowers to mine, lips brush soft against my ear.

"You've got me now, Sawyer. And I swear to God, no one touches you without going through me first."

My knees threaten to give. I grab onto his arms to hold myself up. Maybe I want to touch him, want to feel his lips pressed against mine one more time.

"Come on. Dance with me," he orders softly.

He takes the pool stick from my grip, places it across the table as our fingers lace.

"I don't dance, Landry," I say, fear bubbling beneath my ribs.

"That wasn't a question, Ellis. It was an order. You see, the problem here is—you didn't get me anything for Christmas. So, I'm afraid you owe me this one."

My eyes roll back. Lips pull at my cheeks. I cave. "One song—"

He's already dragging me behind as he pulls us toward the makeshift dance floor, stage now clear of screeching voices that butcher every song. Bing Crosby and Rosemary Clooney croon over the speakers, soft and low. And he lifts our locked hands into the air, his other landing onto the small of my back.

"Just follow my lead," he orders.

This time, I don't fight it.

The bar grows golden and dim, like the dance floor was made for only us. Rain taps steady at the windows. I lean in, resting my head onto his chest, allowing my eyes to close for just a moment. His heartbeat thrums against my ears.

"I meant what I said earlier, Sawyer. You've always got a home here, whether you believe it or not."

"Doesn't feel like it. Kind of feels more like wearing clothes that don't fit anymore," I reply, head still in place against something steady, the flicker of something I'm much too afraid to name.

"Then you get new ones," he says softly. "Clothes that feel like home when you slip into them and not that armor you've been wearing."

I straighten my spine, lift my head from the safety of his chest. His eyes meet with mine as something silent passes through us both. The air grows thick. I search his expression. All of that golden boy charm, yet something sincere lingering beneath.

"If only I could have gotten your attention in high school. Maybe things would be different now. Maybe you would have never left home," he soothes.

He stills. Holds me steady as the bar quiets. Only murmured voices left as the rain pitters its last drops. His head lowers. His soft breaths whisper at my skin. I don't stop him. Don't even try. Just push up onto the balls of my feet eagerly, while heat rolls through me like thunder in a summer afternoon rain. His lips meet mine. Soft. But sure. Like he knows what I need before I do. His hand remains in place at the small of my back. The other gently caresses at my cheek. I let him guide. Let him lead me. As if I'm the only girl worth kissing in this entire town. He pulls back—my head left spinning, breaths stolen from my chest. I grip at his arms to hold myself upright.

"That's twice now, Landry," I whisper low.

"Three if I get my way," he says, voice soothing like liquor.

"Last call!" Penny yells from behind the bar.

"Where you headed now, Ellis?"

My shoulders rise then fall. I take a step back, missing the warmth of his chest.

"It's Christmas Eve," he urges gently. "I've got a little place over on Lake Mariam. We could have a few more drinks? Maybe talk a little more."

His fingertips brush loose strands behind my shoulder as his eyes search mine in wait. I can either stare at the ceiling in a house that doesn't want me anymore. Or I can let this feeling stretch just a little bit more. I lean into him. Let him hold a fractured heart.

"I'm all yours," I whisper.

Colt takes my hand as my feet land swift onto the pavement below. The truck door closes behind me and he leads us toward a wood-planked dock. At the end, a houseboat in a coat of bright white sits against an inky background with pickerelweed floating on a frosty shore. I tug at the coat, pulling it tight to my chest as I follow steadily behind. Colt gently squeezes my hand as we step on board and into the boat's cabin.

Inside, all the modern amenities one person could need. There's a small kitchen across from the captain's wheel, equipped with just a sink and a stove. Only a coffeemaker that sits on the countertop appears to ever have been used. A simple blue couch and old antenna television sit at the rear, a bedroom with minimal decor at the other end. Simple. Small. No sign of Christmas. Just peace and quiet against a backdrop of rippled waves.

"What made you move out here?" I ask.

Colt opens cabinets, searching for something as I remove my coat and drop down onto plush blue.

"Why wouldn't I?" he asks, slamming cabinets shut as two glasses *clink* onto the countertop. "Some of the best fishing around, quiet so you can hear yourself think, and the women seem to love it."

And there it is. That smug attitude I remember walking down the halls at school each day. That hint of performative charm meant for whoever happens to be watching. I sink into the plush cushions. Defeated. Wondering why I even came. Colt lowers a glass in front of me. My shoulders tighten as I take it from his hand, whiskey bottle still dangling from his other. He drops beside me, breath escaping like he just finished a grueling twelve hour shift.

"Right. Wouldn't want to interrupt your little fan club," I say, words tumbling faster than gossip spreads at the First Baptist Church.

He freezes, hand still gripping the bottle's neck. A soft exhale escapes as he turns to face me fully now. "Sawyer, come on," he says, voice lower now. Careful. "That's not what I meant."

"You seemed pretty sure a moment ago," I pout, bottom lip shaking with disappointment I can't seem to control.

I lift the glass to my lips, but don't drink. His eyes search mine for the switch to bring us back to life.

"I was just talking. Trying to impress you. I wasn't thinking." His eyes plead, searching mine. "Come on, you know I don't see you that way."

I raise an eyebrow, but swallow words down. Unsure how I even let it get this far. I let him keep going. Let him bury himself even more.

"Look, the truth is..." He drags a hand through his hair, settling it neatly back into place. "I haven't brought anyone out here since I moved into the place. Not one person. You're the first one who's stepped inside besides me...and the guy who came to fix the air compressor."

He smiles again. A big toothy grin of perfect white that eases the hurt. My fingers grow slack. I set the glass down onto the floor at my feet. His words land soft. Softer than any apology could.

"Why is that?" I ask, trying to disguise that I even care.

He throws back another shot of whiskey, gulping for air like a fish on land. "Because they weren't you," he confesses.

"Oh come on—" I interrupt.

"They weren't the girl who made me nervous at every pep rally the school forced on us. They weren't the girl who broke every curve and gave a hundred speeches in school. They weren't the girl who always smelled like cotton candy and sun."

The room tilts just slightly. I reach for the whiskey glass, throwing it back to soothe my shaking hands.

"You think I'm full of it. I know," he says, clearing the rasp from his throat. "But I was hoping you would stay because I wanted to do this right. And I know I keep screwin' it up because I'm still that idiot kid who doesn't know the right thing to say."

"You're not an idiot, Colt," I say, hand reaching for his. "Well...maybe you used to be. But not anymore."

He smiles at that, something vulnerable seeping through.

"First name basis now, huh?" he teases. "At least you're starting to let me in, Ellis. You need someone to talk to. To sort out all the mess you're hiding behind those built-up walls."

"I have people to talk to," I stammer out.

"Oh yeah? Like who?"

"Brown. We actually talk all the time."

Just a little white lie. Nothing big. I mean, I do plan on visiting Brown more often. He probably needs the company as much as I do. His spine straightens a bit as his tongue skates across his bottom lip. Colt studies me for a beat longer than I'm ready for.

"Brown?" he asks.

"You know...Brown," I repeat. "William Fisher? Owns the old shop on the east side...the one we all scraped change together for every day after school."

"Ahh yes," he smiles. "I remember him."

"Well, he's been like a father to me these past few weeks. I see him all the time."

He places a hand onto my thigh. Takes my glass with the other.

"That's good, Ellis. We all need someone," he soothes.

"Well—" I begin. I place my hand over the top of his now. "You need someone, too. It can't be easy to hold it together with all of the things you have to see."

He takes in my face like he's trying to memorize it. Freckles. Worry lines. All of it. He leans back just slightly, grazing his thumb softly against the fabric on my thigh, sending something warm racing toward my ribs.

"You always look out for other people like that?" he asks.

I shrug. Press my spine into the couch. "Maybe. I don't know. Guess I'm just not used to someone looking out for me. Other than Jay, of course. But, I don't have—"

His fingers wrap around mine, holding me securely in his palm. "You shouldn't have to get used to being alone, Sawyer."

I don't answer. My gaze drops to my lap. His hand holding mine. The scent of bergamot slowly softening whatever edge is left. He lifts his hand again, fingers slowly tracing every curve of my face. His thumb grazes my bottom lip, gently soothing any trace of fear.

You're good at this," I whisper softly.

His fingers pause, leaving me aching for more. "Good at what?"

"Listening. Being kind. Making me feel like I'm not just trying to survive."

"I didn't used to be. Not with girls like you."

"Girls like me?" I ask, shifting away from the hands that just held every broken piece.

"Girls who feel everything. Carry other people's pain along with their own. Probably scared they'd see right through me and that act I used to put on."

My throat tightens as I struggle with words buried somewhere deep. "That's a hell of a thing to say."

"It's true, Ellis. You think nobody sees it, but I do."

He lifts his hand again, thumb falling right back into place as it brushes against my lips. And I'm suddenly aware of every inhale. Mouth too dry to even form a defense. I'm gone. Melted down to nothing but desire and want.

His gaze lingers where his finger slowly traces, and for one suspended moment, neither of us breathes. The space between us thick and electric as he holds me tight with only a touch. Suddenly he inches close, lips brushing mine with purpose. The taste of him blooming in my chest like a lit match.

I pull back.

"That's three," I whisper.

Fingers wrap gently around my neck as his lips meet mine again, kissing me like I'm something fragile and holy. Like he's been waiting years for this moment. Like it's something worth holding onto. And maybe it is. At least for tonight.

FALLING

Chapter Twenty-One

Night pins to the window, with droplets of rain speckled across the glass. I pull the blanket beneath my chin, curling myself into a ball on the worn springs of the thrifted couch. Reruns play muted on the television as I press the phone closer to my ear.

"So...next weekend? Feels like I haven't seen you in forever," he says.

"It *has* been forever, Jay. But we can't let Christmas get away from us," I reply. "We already missed the parade last year."

He chuckles low. "Of course not. Can't miss the Dollar Store plastic baby Jesus or Santa playing Christmas songs on a bass boat."

My lips pull at my cheeks. Bartow's Christmas parade is typical small town, but it's tradition. Jay and I sit at Wilson and Main, just a few short blocks from the First Baptist Church because they always pass out hot cocoa as everyone bundles up on the curb. Honestly, it's the best in town—rich, steaming, probably made with real milk.

"Oh come on," I giggle out. "It's not that bad. I'm especially partial to having candy canes chucked at our heads. And the soap snow that gave us some sort of skin fungus that year."

"You had blotches for days," he says, drawing out the last word. "Looked like a swarm of mosquitoes decided to attack."

Laughter bubbles in my chest. I flop onto my back, resting my heels onto the arm of the couch. A Publix holiday commercial flashes onto the television screen. The ones that always make you cry.

"I miss you a lot," he confesses, tone dropping like a stone in a well. Deep and distant.

My stomach falls. Lands hard as I swallow down something in my throat. I've tried to get him to come. Tried to convince him to move into the spare room. But he just won't budge. Something, or someone, has a hold of him in that town and I just can't reach him anymore. Like there's some unspoken tragedy lingering just beyond our words.

"You know I want you here, Jay. I just want to make sure you're okay. That you have someone to talk to besides Jeanne."

"Sawyer, you don't need to worry. Plus, we're barely two short hours away. I'm making friends. Been spending time with some guys from school," he consoles.

Jay and I really only had each other in school. Of course, he knew people from the high school band and got along with almost everyone, but I don't recall either of us really having outside connections.

"Who from school? Anyone I know?" I ask.

Silence passes between before he replies, "Probably not. They weren't in our class. They're cool. Different. Just live a little wilder than I'm used to. Late nights. Dumb shit. You'd hate it."

"Guy shit? You're probably right," I say. I clear at my throat and shut off the television, chucking the remote onto the floor.

"Yeah...guy shit. Dropped us all off in some pasture. They were digging around cow patties for magic mushrooms. I didn't, of course. Just watched them run around in the dark, like idiots."

"That doesn't sound like you, Jay. Not the you that I know, anyways."

"I guess I'm trying something new. That's all. Trying not to be so predictable all the time."

"You're not predictable. You're just solid. You're...*Jay*. You've always had a good head on your shoulders. Do you trust these guys?"

"Not really. I mean, I don't exactly trust anyone besides you. But they're kind of nice. I mean, we get along okay," he says, though not very convincingly.

"I just need to know you have someone to talk to when I can't be there. Someone to give a damn."

"You give a damn," he says.

"That's not even a question."

Silence stretches long again. The only sound the *click* of a lighter as he sparks a cigarette on the other end. He picked up the nasty habit only recently, but never does it around me.

"Sawyer—" he begins, pausing to make sure I'm still listening.

"Yeah?"

"Thanks for calling tonight. I really needed it," he says.

"You called me," I remind him.

"Right. Still...feels good to hear your voice."

"I'll be there in a week, remember? We'll grab that gross coffee at Sweet Tea Junction. Break into the country club pool. Walk down Main a hundred times like always."

"Yeah. I'd like that," he says, words soothing as they settle between us.

"Promise me something?" I ask.

"Anything..."

"Call me the second you need anything. If anything feels wrong, just call. I'll always pick up the phone."

"Yeah. Okay. I'll see you soon, Sawyer," he trails off.

"See you soon," I say.

The line clicks and he's gone. I stare at the screen long after it turns black, something like unease burrowing deep. I lay back and stretch my legs out again onto the couch. The rain batters at the window now. Like a warning. A warning of something I just can't seem to name.

Lacquered pine planks line the ceiling above as the gentle hum of heat flushes through the air. I pull the comforter tight to my chest, slipping into the soothing lullaby of lapping waves. Sunlight peeks into the cabin through open slats in the blinds. The room goes black again as my head sinks back into the pillow, toes wiggling beneath the crumpled sheets. A snore echoes beside me, followed by a short gasp of air before settling again into a deep sleep. I shoot up on the bed, rubbing at the crust that sticks to the corners of my eyes, slowly taking in the room as I float back into consciousness.

I gasp. My hand flies to my mouth, pushing tight against my lips in disbelief. Colt lays on his side, lips slightly parted as his gentle snores settle right back into their slow, rhythmic beat. My head pounds, and my tongue sticks to the roof of my mouth like it's been soaked in sand and left out to dry. My stomach flips, sinking and landing hard as last night's memories come racing back. I chew at another mangled cuticle on my right thumb, leaving the scent of copper trailing in its wake.

Gently. Carefully. I peel the blankets back and swing my feet over the side of the bed, placing each foot quietly onto the floor. My eyes scan the boat's cabin, finally landing onto the crumpled pile of clothes lying just out of reach. My jeans are wrinkled. Sweater half-turned inside out. New coat tossed like some old rag at the foot of the bed. The scent of wood, and *him*, clings to everything, settling deep in my chest. I reach for the jeans, sliding them on with nothing underneath. Pull the sweater over my head, pausing as I catch my reflection in a small mirror that pins to the pine wall.

Hair wild. Lips puffy and raw. A slight flush still blooming across my cheeks. Like someone who let her guard down. And for once, I don't hate what I see. Even a slight smile lingers from my lips.

My father's gun rests at the foot of the bed, shimmering as the morning sun bounces in fractals against the smooth barrel. I tuck it in tight and slip back into my boots, reaching for the new coat and quietly making my way toward the cabin door. Colt gently stirs, flipping onto his other side before slipping back into sleep.

I could just go home now. Pretend nothing has changed. But everything *has* changed. Jay is gone. Daddy might as well be. And Mama will be soon. Something is holding me here. Has me by the throat. I unlatch the door and make my way back onto the deck, boots picking up speed as I head for solid ground.

The air bites a little less sharp than it did before. Sunshine lands warm on my skin. For the first time in weeks, the clouds have pulled back enough for the morning light to streak across the sky. Still, dark clouds peek slowly in the distance, chasing behind like a warning. A bird calls in the distance. I fold my arms against my chest and keep walking until I'm back on solid ground—my ride still sitting just outside Blackwood Social, leaving me pressed to cracked pavement as I rest onto the curb.

His voice echoes in my head. *"You need someone to talk to. To sort out all of this mess you're hiding behind those built up walls."*

My fingers grasp the tiny key still dangling from my neck, curling tight around it.

Home. The word tastes strange, but it presses against my chest in a way that almost feels like hope.

I slip the phone from my back pocket, fingers searching, finally landing on the only name to call. A voice rattles 'hello' on the other end.

"Mama?"

The ride back was quiet. Set to the tune of Kenny Rogers and Dolly Parton on the radio. Mama used to play the album when Skylar and I were little as she took us on trips to the local mall. We all knew the words. Every single note. The song takes me back there. To that place where Daddy was home and Mama still put up a real tree. Pretty certain I caught the hint of a smile tugging at her lips as she turned the car radio up and steered us away from Colt's dock.

She unlocks the front door, keys dangling as they *clank* in her trembling hand. I follow behind, kicking off my boots just inside. She shuffles into the living room, heaving a tired sigh as she plops down onto her favorite chair. On the television, Vera Ellen and Danny Kaye tap dance across the screen in perfect synchronicity .

"There's coffee," she rattles out.

I make my way into the kitchen, past the tiny tree topped with the crochet star. A red stocking trimmed in white fur lays beside it, a card peeking from the top with my name. My head snaps in her direction as her gaze pins to the television, then slowly turns back to the peace offering in front of me.

Pinching the white envelope between my fingers, I slowly slide the card from the top. My name is written in wild, unruly cursive lettering, with tiny ripples from an unsteady hand. I slip a finger beneath the seal, sliding it across and pulling out the card with a glittery Santa on the front. Inside...mostly blank other than a few simple words. "Merry Christmas, Sawyer." Simple words that move mountains in their wake.

I dump the stocking onto the tabletop, its contents spilling out in front of me. Peppermint candies. A milk chocolate Santa with gooey marshmallow fluff inside. And Daddy's old pocket knife he always carried in the back of his jeans. My breath hitches. Something aches terribly in my gut. Maybe it's the memory of Daddy. Maybe it's the loss of someone who sits right here under this roof.

I spin on my heels, stepping into the kitchen where the scent of burnt coffee wafts through the air. A plate filled with cookies sits on the counter. The good kind. Store-bought. Soft with thick red and green frosting, colorful sprinkles scattered like confetti after a parade. I quickly reach for a cookie right at the top, practically swallowing the thing in one greedy bite. My fingers curl around Daddy's favorite old mug, and I pour the black, bitter coffee until it *sploshes* over the top. Salem winds at my feet, gently butting her tiny head into my legs as a welcome home, and I make my way back into the living room, settling into the couch and folding my legs beneath me as the tap dancing duo lands in Vermont.

Mama sits curled beneath a blanket, her body seemingly smaller than it was the day before. "Thought you might be gone for good when you didn't come home last night," she says, eyes never peeling from the television screen.

"No, Mama. I told you I'd be here for Christmas morning. I meant it."

"You got a new boyfriend or something? Who lives out there on the lake?" she probes, wheezing as she draws another ragged breath.

"I'm not seeing anyone. Just visited a friend and the night kind of slipped away, that's all," I lie.

The truth...is that I don't know what Colt and I are. Or if we're anything at all. And I just don't have the energy to try and explain this to her. To anyone. Not until I finish what I came here for. She nods once. Her hand trembles as she slowly lifts her mug into the air.

"Coffee's strong. Not good. But at least it's hot."

"Thanks for the cookies. You got the good ones."

"They were only two dollars at the store. Couldn't pass up the good deal," she says, quickly brushing off any emotion tied to the act.

Silence stretches. We both pin to the screen, though I suspect neither of us is actually paying any attention. Suspect both of us are fumbling our words. Testing the waters with what to say.

"And the stocking..." I whisper low, a slight sniffle escaping. "Thank you."

Nothing. Not even a glance my way. But something moves her. Something that makes her dab at her eyes.

"I remember when we used to bake every Christmas eve," she says.

I startle on the couch. Slowly shift and unfold my legs, pulling them close to my chest as a shield of support.

"You would always lick so much batter off the bowl, you'd have a bellyache all damn night," she grins, eyes finally glancing my way.

I smile. "You let me."

"One time, you had chocolate chips in your hair for days. I'd wash it. Clean you up. And somehow you always managed to find the cookies again. I think your father was sneaking them to you behind my back. But I could have sworn you were just smearin' all that chocolate on your head," she chuckles softly.

It's nice to see her smile. To see the light flicker in her eyes again. Light. Or hope. Something like that. But the mention of Daddy settles deep. Weighs heavier than either of us will admit. She reaches for the remote, clicking until George Bailey stands mid-breakdown as snow falls in quick flurries around his head.

"You figure out what happened to Jay?" she asks.

I still. Her question landing like bricks onto a concrete floor. Just a simple acknowledgment that she believes me. Just a simple gesture that someone actually cares. "I think so, Mama. We're close. Police reopened the case."

She nods. A flash of something like worry pulling at her face. "Be careful, Sawyer. Let the cops handle it. They know what to do," she warns. The way a mother should. The way I always wanted her to care.

"I'm trying not to worry you, that's all. We've almost got them. Then I can move on. Get counseling or something, I guess. I'll figure it out."

I peel myself from the couch, quickly fetching the pile of sugared Christmas magic and placing it between us before settling back into place. She smiles. Faintly. But it's there. I offer her a cookie and take one for myself, frosting sticking to the roof of my mouth like it did when I was a kid.

The movie drones on, but the voices no longer match the screen. I lean in. The sound is all wrong. Warped. Like a cassette tape all chewed up and spit back out. I reach for another cookie. Maybe too much, but it's Christmas day. I sink into the couch, lifting the red frosted treat, stopping just short of my mouth. A tiny ant crawls from beneath, no bigger than a pinhead. Legs twitching like static against the soft dough, scurrying like he has somewhere to be. It curls around a lump of frosting, lifting a green sprinkle above him like a tiny soldier ready for battle.

"You okay?" she asks, green frosting lingering at the corner of her mouth.

I force a smile. Swallow. Nod. Place a finger onto each side of him and pinch his tiny head before flicking him onto the floor.

"Don't worry. I'll save you some for later. You always did like the red frosting the best."

"Thanks Mama," I say quietly.

She peels the flannel blanket from her legs, slowly straightening her spine as she unfolds herself from the chair.

"I think I'm gonna nap for a little while. You gonna be here when I wake up?" she asks.

"I'm not sure," I say. My lips pull tight. Brows pinch.

Something flickers between us. Something different than before. She nears, placing a trembling hand onto my knee.

"You go do what you need to do, Sawyer. But don't you let them break you. Don't let this turn you into something you're not."

I blink. And blink again. "I won't," I whisper. "I promise."

She nods, tears in her eyes, but she doesn't let them fall. "Then go. And be careful."

It lands harder than it should. They're just simple words. A normal exchange for most. But for us, like a sacred prayer. The closest we've come to a goodbye in years. And maybe the first time it actually means something. Her hand draws back as she slowly shuffles across the tile toward her room.

"Merry Christmas, Mama," I call out. One last desperate attempt to save whatever's left.

An exhausted hand lifts into the air with a tiny finger flick as her back stays turned.

"Merry Christmas, Sawyer."

I listen until the door clicks shut. Until the old house settles again. Silent and still. Holding its breath for a family that is never coming home. Or bracing for something that *is* coming. Something unsettling that scratches at the baseboards and crawls behind the walls.

Chapter Twenty-Two

Mama's been asleep for hours now. Her rattling cough quiet. House still other than a few *creaks* and *groans*. Daddy always said it was just the house settling, but Skylar and I never believed it was. We still kept the light on and buried ourselves beneath the covers, legs pulled tight, scared to leave even a foot dangling off the bed. Maybe we were right. Maybe it *is* something more. Maybe something is haunting me...some ghost escaped from the grave, warning of impending doom.

A commercial flits on the television at full volume, something about New Year's Eve echoing down the hall. If the new year is anything like this one, I don't want it. God can keep it. The only thing I want is Bryce Kincaid behind bars where he belongs.

Salem pounces onto my lap, her tiny *meows* burrow into my chest. Gently, I scratch behind one ear. And then the other. She *purrs* a thank you before curling into a ball at my side.

"What do you think, girl?" I ask. "Do we just wait one more day and let it be?"

Her tail flicks sharp, like a warning, before she settles again. I flop back onto the bed, feet dangling as they swing with restlessness and I watch the fan blades spin in endless loops.

"Yeah. You're probably right," I say. "We can just watch movies tonight. Eat cookies until we burst."

But beneath my skin, buried like a secret, something crawls, digs, winds, scratches, grows teeth, and feeds on my every fear. Roots twisting through a cracked foundation. It won't let me rest. Won't let me sleep. Won't let me move on from this place like I'm its hostage. Some kind of sickness without a name.

December dusk rolls in like a bad omen dressed in Sunday best. Feels like the world is holding its breath as everyone gathers around Christmas trees and rain pitters at their doors. I push up on the bed, taking one last look at Salem as she snores at my side.

I won't run. Won't hide. If I go down, he goes down with me. He took Jay. He doesn't get to take me too.

The sky hangs heavy, not quite dark, but not quite light. Just a long exhale of dusk where nothing feels quite right. Rain taps at the windshield again...soft at first, then slowly bleeding into battering rain. I don't bother with the radio. It's nothing but Christmas song after Christmas song anyway.

Broadway stretches long, straight, slick and empty, as heat buries somewhere deep in my throat. Light blurs beyond like halos of amber as the tires hum on a waterlogged road. Past Hooker Street. Past Vine. Past the old, abandoned bank with its half-lit sign. My mother used to take me there. I thought it was the fanciest place I'd ever been, with fake ficus trees in the lobby and dishes of candy on every desk.

My fingers wrap tightly around the wheel, knuckles pure white as a deep chill settles in my bones. I push air past my lips, long and slow, as the car veers onto James Point Drive. Past deflated reindeer and Santas. And far past turning back.

"It's fine, Sawyer. There's no reason to be afraid," I whisper to myself.

The tires crawl to a stop at the curb, just a few beats down from the Kincaid home. Something fast scuttles across the road, sky too dark now to see. The house sits quiet with no light, no sign of life beyond the front door. Something wet runs hot down my cheek as I wipe it with the sleeve of my coat. I'm not sure when I started crying. Guess I was too distracted by Jay's whispers in my ear. I cut the engine, let my head fall onto the back of the seat. My palms slowly loosen their grip as they slip, clammy and warm into my lap.

My chest seizes tight as the cold scrapes it raw, and my head scrambles like meat in a grinder, shredded into something I don't recognize anymore. I lift a sticky palm to the door, swinging it open as rain batters inside the car. Colt's gift wraps tightly around me as I pull the hood of the coat over my hair.

The car door slams...or maybe it doesn't. I can't tell. No time to check. My hands tremble. My knees buckle. And I lunge into the sting of rain like knives on my skin, heart hammering loud enough to split me in two.

My boots shift into a light jog as I make my way toward the side of the house. The driveway sits empty and the gate is still unlocked. Unlatched. Left open like the wound that Daddy left. The kind that never scabs over, fingers always picking until it bleeds again.

Rain batters now. At the windows, at the rooftops, at my brand new coat. I creep slow, shoulders hunched, waiting for Duke to rush around the corner and give me away. But there's nothing. Nothing but the rustle of branches above and the distant sound of thunder rolling through Bartow like something evil turning in its grave. Around the corner is Bryce's room. Nothing but darkness inside as I reach to crawl my way inside. Unlocked. Open. Almost like he knew I would be here, that I was coming back for him.

The sound of quick, eager panting rushes toward me from just beyond the bedroom door as I dig my fingers into the pocket of my coat, reaching for a red frosted sugar cookie saved from Mama's.

"Good boy, Duke," I whisper as I toss it toward him. He flicks his tail in approval, finally settling at my side.

Water drips from my coat and puddles onto the floor as I press myself into shadows, back flat against the wall as breaths come in ragged bursts. Something digs into the back of my head, rattling loudly as it crashes to the floor. A palm flies to my mouth as I hold the air in my lungs, waiting for footsteps or startled voices. But nothing comes. Nothing but something between a grunt and a question as Duke's ears raise at my side. The air settles quiet again as he curls back into himself, closing his eyes, belly filled with his sugary treat. I fold myself in half and crouch low as I grip at the picture frame, glass cracked, jagged and sharp, across the front. Beneath the shards is Bryce, with who I assume must be his parents, dressed in a blue gown with a tasseled graduation cap on his head. I let it fall again, straightening my trembling legs as my eyes flit about the room. Most things are neatly tucked away, only the bedding left crumpled like he left in a rush, and half of a cigarette stumped into a shallow glass on the dresser at its side.

Something reaches for me, wraps its long, creature-like fingers tight around my neck as it steals the air from my lungs. I should let it. Just slowly disappear away from this town. Slip away from the world. A voice whispers low, calling from beyond the bedroom door and stretching down the hall.

I follow the sound. Water drips from the coat's hem, leaving a wet trail as I make my way toward a kitchen in sleek granite and dark wood, and something foul that bites at my nose.

The stench hits first. Overwhelming. Like rotten meat left sitting in the sun. Sick with the hint of metallic, the same smell from Daddy's house and the pig that circled in the mud. I push forward. Follow the rotten scent.

A bowl sits on the counter filled with blackened fruit, shriveled like old leather never conditioned, cracked and beyond saving, nothing now but compost or something rats might pick through. Another step, and then another, until the smell grows stronger like it lives in the fibers of my coat. Shadows cling to the corners as a wet chewing sound grows louder, quickening my pulse until it thrums in my ears. Lights from neighboring houses glow through the window blinds.

Now I see it. Its body pale pink and bloated. Maybe swollen with gas. Maybe swollen with rot. It lays still in the corner, right behind a dining table with carefully placed china and fancy linen napkins set beside every plate. My boots pin. Blood turns cold like ice. It's not possible. I cinch my eyes tight. Hope its disgusting body goes away. I count down from three, take slow breaths, but each one reeks of blood and decay as my stomach twists and settles heavy.

My throat burns as I open my eyes to see him—head tilted with one eye missing, the other clouded with death. Then, a chewing sound. But not from the pig's mouth. A *smacking* that reeks of rotten pumpkins, potatoes and stale bread that reaches through the walls. The blue floral wallpaper ripples in waves that close in on me as he shifts, belly now exposed with a long gash torn open, crusted at the edges as something writhes inside. The mangled thing lets out a high-pitched whimper as my feet inch closer to its rotting flesh. I fold myself in half as the scent reaches its claws down my throat, slithers through my chest, and settles like an anchor that *thumps* straight into my gut. My pulse races, heat trickling down my back as hundreds of tiny maggots feed on its rotting organs, their tiny, white bodies vanishing into cavities that used to be lungs, meat squirming like it's still alive.

Mama's voice echoes in my head—*come lay down, Sawyer. You're not well.*

I choke on a scream as the dead thing pushes toward me now.

No. No God no. Please No.

My back flattens to the wall as it crawls and drags itself my way. But it's not a pig anymore. The thing doesn't even have a face. It's just a writhing sack of meat riddled with feasting larvae that burrow themselves like worms.

"Rot travels fast, Sawyer." the grotesque thing whispers, its voice soaked in Daddy's drawl. "They'll smell it, too."

A gasp bursts from my throat as something wet and warm drips from my hands, creating splashes of crimson that fall thick onto the floor below.

An engine *growls* loud as headlights splice through windows and spill across the walls. A truck, massive and familiar, quiets as its doors slam shut.

Two. I heard two.

Their boots land with *thuds* onto pavement. And their voices carry loud through the cream painted walls.

Shit. There's three.

"She's here!" a voice spits out. "We fucking got her ass now."

My vision tunnels, and I nearly trip over the breathing pile of guts that sits at my feet. I crouch low, practically crawling down the hallway and back into Bryce's room. I press my back into the wall behind the door, turning my palms over to find them clean. No trace of the blood there just moments ago. No trace that the gruesome thing was ever really there.

Footsteps and voices grow closer as lights begin to flicker on throughout the house. I slide a palm around the waist of my jeans, and my fingers wrap slow around the grip of Daddy's gun.

"She's in here. I can smell her," one voice says.

"Don't play with her," Bryce orders.

"It's more fun this way," a third voice taunts, a low growl dripping from every word.

"She's mine," Bryce warns, like something final, the others quieting as he slowly closes in.

The room flutters fast as my breath crawls up my throat. Ceiling. Window. Closet. The edge of the dresser. Crumpled bedding. Back to the ceiling again.

"Little pig, little pig," Bryce taunts, tapping on the walls as he walks, his voice low, playful and cruel. "Let. Us. In."

His voice isn't just a taunt, though. It's a verdict. My fate sealed. Colt was right. God, he was right. I never should have come.

My chest tightens fast, like something ruptures beneath. I can't breathe. Not really. Only short gasps escape, fast and shallow, like a body being pulled into the deep.

They're coming, Sawyer. Goddamnit, move.

My vision blurs at the edges. The floorboard cracks just beyond the door. A footstep.

Three...two...

A sinister laugh.

One...

"Where 'ya hiding, little piglet?" another voice sneers.

Run.

My shoulders push off the wall as I race toward the still-open window, banging my knee hard as I crawl through its sharp-edged frame. My boots land hard onto wet, mushy ground below. Cold air stings like fire on my cheeks as I race back toward the open gate, heart pounding in my ears, each breath echoing in my head.

Don't look back, Sawyer.

I race across slick pavement as sweat drenches the base of my back. Rain pelts at my skin like stinging needles as their vicious snarls pierce through the dark, sinking into every fiber of me.

"She ran out the back!" someone screams. Maybe Grayson or Dane.

My boot slips. Knees crash hard against the asphalt. A gasp tears out of me, sharp and jagged. Pain radiates through my legs as I shove myself up, palms burning, lungs heaving as I force them to keep moving.

Finally, out of breath and out of hope, I reach the car, door wide open and everything inside soaked from rain. I slide onto the seat and slam the door shut. Fumble in the pocket of my jeans for the key. It's buried deep, too deep, and panic rises as I writhe in my seat until my fingers finally grip at its sharp, jagged teeth. I shove it fast into the ignition, and the engine *roars* back to life as my foot presses hard onto the pedal. I peel away from the curb as the tires spin on the slick pavement.

Sobs stutter up my throat as I adjust the mirror, revealing the headlights that chase far behind, but not far enough. The shoulder of the road holds rain in deep puddles that almost look like lakes, and the tires lose traction as my fingers close tight around the wheel. I swallow down the thing choking me. Race forward without looking back.

The lights of town slowly come into view, offering safety in their arms. I stop at the traffic light where Highway 98 and 60 meet, fingers tapping at the wheel as the light stretches way too long on red. No other sign of life. Only the fluorescent lights of torn business signs, still shredded from the last hurricane that rolled through.

Headlights close in behind me. I slam the gas and yank the wheel, peeling hard toward Main. I can't let them follow me home, can't let Mama get hurt. Skylar is out, too. Plus her house is too far from town. Too dark, too remote, and way too much of a risk to take. I grip the wheel tighter now. The car fishtails as it makes the left turn toward the center of town.

Something lies dead in the road, its honey brown fur, matted and flat, with a pool of crimson puddled beneath his head. Still not washed away from the rain. Probably still warmth beneath its flesh. I swerve quick, barely missing the pitiful thing as I speed toward the edge of town. I run two stop signs and two traffic lights, barely missing the car that turned on green.

Lights grow brighter as I reach the familiar store, and cars fill the parking lot to buy last minute eggnog and cheap beer since every other store in town is closed. One space left open in a darkened corner, beneath a light pole that strobes weak, flickering with its last dying breath. The car tires skid into the lot, and I throw the car into park before it fully stops. The key fumbles in the ignition until I want to scream. Finally, it yanks free and I cut the engine fast.

I land firm onto the pavement, each breath clouding like vapor as I slam the car door behind. A group of faces I recognize from Connersville burst through the door, their shrill laughs piercing the air as I hold back in the shadows, waiting patiently until they finally seal themselves into the hum of an electric car. The fluorescent glow of red from the "OPEN" sign washes over the cracked pavement. And my knees tremble beneath me as I walk toward the smudged glass door.

The bell above jingles as I step inside. Just barely. One shoulder in. The other shoulder out. The excitement of Christmas swells around me as a line, ten deep, waits patiently to purchase their goods. A woman with wild hair in auburn curls stands behind the counter, slapping keys around the register with burnt, sizzling hot dogs rolling at her side. The scent of sweating meat mixes with bleach. The heat and brightness hit me all at once. Too much everything. Too damn overwhelming.

A teenage boy startles suddenly as he looks up from his phone. He pins his gaze as he holds a dirty mop at his side.

"Jesus, are you okay?" he asks.

I glance down at my clothes, at the mud-stained jeans and the gash across my knee. Apparently the window frame sliced through the denim, too, leaving sticky, thick blood oozing from the wound.

He glances around before leaning in closer. "Is someone hurting you?" the boy asks, voice careful. "Do you need me to call someone?"

Call someone...

"Ma'am?"

I blink, searching again past the register, hoping he'll appear suddenly like a rabbit out of a magician's hat. But there's no apron. No brown, crumpled hat. No hot dog saved just for me.

"Can I help 'ya, honey?" the woman calls out from behind the counter.

The soda machine hums. A coin *clatters* onto the tiled floor. And that boy, still watches me with concern dripping from his brow.

"Brown—" I gasp, still dripping, hair matted to my cheeks. "I need—I need—he knows me. Please."

"Who, honey?" she asks, smacking on gum like a cow chewing cud.

"Brown—" hangs like a whisper from my lips now.

"You mean that old man that used to run the place?" the boy asks. He stuffs his phone into his back pocket. "He's been dead for like—years. Right after his wife died."

My pulse hammers loud. Mouth opens, but no sound comes. The corners of the store begin to tilt like the floor is going soft beneath me. My eyes flit. Register. Bathrooms. Cooler. Camera. Red light blinking. Empty coat rack that sits by the door.

"You okay?" he asks again.

I stumble backward, almost tripping over the mat. The bell *chimes* again as the door swings open behind me. Then, I hear it. The deep-throated *growl* of a diesel truck engine that gets louder and louder as it nears. I whip around fast.

"Shit," I breathe, heart slamming against my ribs.

My fingers won't move fast enough as I claw through the door, shoulder brushing hard against the man who stood behind me. Blood rushes in my ears as I run fast toward the car, crouching low as the truck corners the pumps. My body wants to collapse. To fold. To lay down right here and die.

No. Not here. Not now.

The front end swings wide, its headlights lighting up the store like a firework display. Doors begin to open as they rush toward the glow of neon, cheap beer and the boy that helped me just moments ago.

I throw open the driver's side door. Slam it behind me. Shove the key into the ignition with trembling hands. The engine coughs. Once. Twice. *Please*. It catches. The tires *screech* on wet pavement as I tear out of the lot, spitting up gravel behind me.

I aim west, toward the bridge, as the rearview mirror fills with light. My fingers reach, curling tightly around the grip of Daddy's gun.

The town peels away behind me, layer by layer, one streetlight at a time. I don't look back. I know they're behind me. Know that they're close. The rain thickens again as mist turns back into sheets—underbelly of the sky split open with the low *groan* of thunder unleashed. Finally, the bridge appears against the inky backdrop of night. I press harder onto the gas. I'm not leading them home. Not where Mama lays sick. I'm leading them here.

This is where it ends.

The tires *hiss* on wet asphalt as the car rolls to a stop next to the silver guard rail that gleams in the dark. The exact place it happened. The place his voice still echoes if you listen hard enough. I open the door and step onto the pavement as rain soaks through and buries cold in my bones.

I slam the door shut behind me as the truck lights grow close.

If this is where I die, at least I take the devil with me. Let them come. Let them see what I've become.

Chapter Twenty-Three

Rain washes in sheets from the sky now. So heavy that it blurs the edges of reality, warps the steel of the bridge into something that it's not. The air tastes like metal. Rain and rust and something foul. Maybe something dead. And thunder breaks through the sky, rolling like a beast awakened from his sleep.

Dead, water-soaked leaves cling wet to everything...the pavement, the guardrails, the slime-ridden steps that lead beneath the bridge. Down there. Down where death took him. Down where his blood still soaks thick into asphalt. The leaves gather at my heels, my calves, at the toe of each boot. Thick. Sodden. Like memories I can't escape.

The cold chases up my spine. And my chest rises and falls with the sharpness dragged from every breath. I stand in the middle of the bridge, boots straddling yellow paint lines, hair soaked and plastered to my face as my arms fall limp at my sides. I swear the bridge remembers. That the concrete still bears the bruises from that night. It swallowed his screams, holds tight to his blood and whispers his name like cold breath against your skin.

The night spins in stuttering frames as glaring headlights pierce through the battering rain. The roar of a diesel engine grows louder and louder until it swallows the storm. It doesn't slow. Comes fast. My hand flies in front of my face, shielding my eyes from the flash until the truck jerks to a halt at the last second, my knees trembling just inches from the grill. Heat radiates off the hood in rising swirls of steam as the engine finally cuts. The world falls quiet again, except for the drumming of rain and the uneven pounding that claws beneath my ribs.

Three doors *crack* open as their boots hit the asphalt hard. I don't blink. Dig my heels in tight. Curl my shaking hands into fists at my sides.

Their shadows stretch like the silhouettes of monsters closing in on me.

"Evening, sweetheart," Bryce calls out.

Grayson and Dane fall behind his shoulders, lips curled at the corners as they look at me like I'm their next meal. Bryce steps closer, grinning wide, a halo from the gleam of headlights around his face.

"You were hard to find," Grayson adds, rolling his shoulders like he's preparing for a fight.

Bile rises up the back of my throat. I swallow, but it sticks. I take one step back. Then another. My knees buckle beneath me.

"Look at her," Dane laughs as he cracks each knuckle one by one. "She's shaking already."

I break.

"I'm not here to fight," I call out. "I just want to go home."

The cold seeps, burrows deep beneath my skin. I carefully drag fingertips slow around my waist.

"No?" Bryce questions. "You broke into my house. That's called trespassing. There's consequences for that...little pig."

His lips pull tight. Pupils go black. Nothing but pure, feral evil that lives to watch things squirm. A pitiless void. The eyes of something that has never felt one second of remorse.

"She's been snooping," Grayson taunts low, raking fingers through soaked strands of dark hair. "Sticking that little piggy snout where it doesn't belong."

I take a step back, leg trembling beneath me. Then the other. They move in closer.

"Why'd you drag us out here?" Bryce mutters, his half-cocked grin twitching. "We could have ended this already. Do you just need attention? Or did you want a show?"

"I—I—don't want anything. I promise."

The three of them move, their boots grinding against the pavement in slow, deliberate rhythm. I can't look at their faces. Those darkened eyes. Those sharp teeth they want to drag through my flesh. Instead, I pin my gaze to their boots, dark leather soaked and heavy, stepping into shallow puddles that ripple like tiny oil-slicked waves. Water splashes outward, then recoils, leaving wet echoes rippling behind. Bits of gravel crunch beneath each step. Leaves stick to their soles as they drag slow, inching closer and closer as I pin with fear.

Bryce closes the distance slowly, taunting, each step ricocheting through me like buckshot through a ribcage. Violent and final. He stops just inches away, Grayson and Dane slowly moving in at his sides.

"You look cold, little pig," he sneers.

I flinch. Take one too many steps. The cold metal guardrail bites into my back.

"Don't tell me you forgot already," he says, drawing out each word like sticky syrup dripping onto a plate. "Little pig, little pig—"

"Stop," I breathe low, leaning into the rail as if there's anywhere to go.

His face lingers only inches from mine, his warm breath reeking of smoke as he whispers close, "let us in."

My fingers twitch at my sides. Eyes dart. Right. Left. No exit. No help.

Don't let them get too close.

The voice is unmistakable.

Jay.

He's here. I feel it.

I shut my eyes tight, but it only makes it worse. His laugh. His bright smile. The big-framed glasses he wore in eighth grade that were much too large for his head. The swimming pool on sticky summer nights. The strum of his guitar as I lay on his bedroom floor. The promises we made to each other that I wish I could keep.

I open my eyes again. But evil is still there. Still only inches away.

"You remember the way he looked when we found him?" Dane taunts, stepping closer toward Bryce. Toward the railing. Toward me. "Head all bashed in. Weak. Pathetic."

"Don't—" I warn, voice cracking.

Evil swims to the surface. Seeps from his every pore like thick tar, slow and suffocating. His lip curls into a sneer. His eyes narrow until there's nothing but black. Like something that swallows light. Something deeper than hate or cruelty. Something that sinks its teeth and tears at your flesh.

His lips move closer, whispering like the devil at my ear. "You should have seen how big his eyes got. All that fear and pleading. Like he was still waiting for you to come back."

My body knows it's true. I can see his eyes in the dark. Wide, wet and betrayed. I double over with nausea as my hand braces my gut. I can't stop it. It rises like a flash flood up my throat. Hot. Acidic. Violent. It comes hard. Splatters the pavement, thick and sour, splashed with bile and bits of frosted Christmas cookies that didn't digest. It clings to my lips and strings from my tongue. My body convulses. Another heave. Then another. Until nothing's left but bitter acid burning up my throat through dry, cracking sobs.

Another set of headlights peels through the dark, and their heads snap in their direction as another truck slowly rolls to a stop. Not just any truck, though. A familiar truck. With caked mud on a dented metal side. Mud the rain can't wash away no matter how hard it tries. I straighten my spine slow as he climbs out.

"Colt?" I croak. Weak. Emptied of every ounce of strength I ever had.

"What the hell's going on?" he yells out, shining a flashlight in our direction as he nears.

Bryce backs up slow. Lifts his palms into the air in retreat. "She's losing it!" he shouts. "Thought you might want to be here."

He doesn't say a word. Just locks his gaze onto mine. His mouth forms into something unreadable. I sway forward. Or maybe that was the bridge. My ribs expand like they've finally been unstrapped.

"Please," I beg, searching his eyes. "Help me."

"Back up," he orders, raising his hand toward the others. "I've got this."

The circling, hungry wolves—Bryce, Grayson and Dane—hesitate, waiting for their alpha's cue. Then finally step aside. Watching. Grinning. Eyes gleaming. Just waiting for their command. Colt makes his way closer and something loosens inside of me. My pulse still thrums, but softer now. The tremble in my hands turns back to a twitch.

"Sawyer—" he begins, softening his voice, "you need to calm down. You're scaring people."

My lip trembles just like Mama's when we can't hide our fear. "Colt, they followed me. They tried to—"

"I know," he says. "Come on, let's get you home, alright?"

The wolves hang back, watchful and still, like an audience waiting for the final act. My body sags with exhaustion, waving the white flag high.

He reaches out a hand. A safety line. A steady warmth that floods beneath my skin. The hope of something good made just for me. I let him take me. Let him hold me. Let every fear melt into his arms.

Then—fingers clamp around my throat.

Breath sears my lungs.

Panic claws at my chest.

"Colt—" I choke.

He shoves my body violently backward, spine hitting cold metal as his other hand clamps tighter around my neck. Every breath is a fight. My vision edges red. His voice drops. Low. Cruel.

"Aww...you thought that was real? That I actually felt anything for trash like you?"

Rain slicks my face. Batters at my eyes. His fingers squeeze tighter and tighter, coiling until my feet dangle inches from the ground. My head pulls right, eyes searching over my shoulder for that blood soaked pavement that calls for me next.

"Girls like you who always thought they were better than me. Always running your damn mouth. And always needing saving at the end of the day."

I claw at his wrist as my vision begins to tunnel. The faces behind him blur. Air squeezes from my lungs.

"You know...their parents paid me good money to make this go away. And I will. I'll kill you if I have to, Sawyer."

Tears mix with rain. My lungs burn. Mouth dries like sand. He lifts me higher. Spine pressed to cold metal and feet dangling. Folding me backward over the railing in the very spot Jay took his last breaths.

You always get yourself into the worst shit, don't you?

Jay's voice. Unmistakable. My eyes search for him, finding him close behind the others. Where the light doesn't quite reach. Soaked through just like me, but smiling. That "I told you so" grin that I said I hated, but would give anything to see again.

Breathe, dummy. Find your way out.

My hands go numb. Claw ridiculously at Colt's forearm.

"I knew you were fucking crazy the second you mentioned that old man from the store," he growls low. "That was sloppy, Sawyer. Should have kept your secrets to yourself. You just might even be crazier than your mother."

Jay's voice again. Clear as it whispers at the back of my neck.

Don't let them take you.

My muscles jerk hard as one last jolt of panic bursts through. My hand shoots to my back pocket. To the revolver. To Daddy's gun. Colt's hand squeezes tighter as my finger, slick with rain, wraps around the trigger. It wobbles. Heavy and uncertain in my hand.

"She's got a gun!" a voice yells from somewhere. Tunneled. I don't recognize it.

Colt jerks. His hand releases my throat as his elbow crashes into my temple. White heat flashes like stars as more bile comes. My grip loosens and my feet crash to the ground. The gun tumbles. Hits the rail. Spins. I dive for it, landing hard onto my belly, dragging myself though water-logged leaves and oil-filled puddles until someone's boot kicks it just beyond my reach. A groan exhales slow from my chest as I lay on wet asphalt...soaked, battered and waiting for death. The rain slows, now only a mist that lays like a whisper on your skin. I cry out, but don't recognize the sound. It isn't my cry. It's something guttural and broken. Wet and ragged. Raw and blistering. Grief-soaked cries that echo like death knocking at your door.

Boots surround me, but I don't have the strength. Just curl into myself. Trembling like a rabbit about to become the wolves' final meal. Helpless and hopeless like something already dead.

"Grayson!"

The shout dies in the rain. A shirt hits the ground with a wet slap, and headlights flood everything white. A tattoo in black ink blooms across his collarbone. That faded cross from Jay's photograph, now inches from my face. Below it, blurred through rain and skin. Revelation 6:17.

My lungs seize.

For the great day of his wrath is come; and who shall be able to stand?

First Baptist Church. Age twelve. The preacher pounding the pulpit, spittle flying, warning us about the end of times. Judgment. I remember being scared to breathe.

Grayson crouches down. Close enough that I can see the way the ink has bled into his skin over the years. The way the verse sits over his heart like a brand. His eyes meet mine. A slow smile cracks across his face.

And that's when I understand. He didn't get this tattoo as a warning. He got it as a mission statement. He isn't afraid of God's wrath. He thinks he *is* it.

Pain. Hot and electric against my skull. Blows from boots. Fists. The night sky spins. A scream pierces the air. Maybe mine. Maybe someone else's. Jay's face fades no matter how hard I try to hold onto it.

I want to go home. I want to go with Jay. I want to let it all bleed out. Let the rain wash me away.

The truck headlights burst into stars as I uncurl myself and rest my head onto a gravel bed.

And then—

Nothing.

270

Chapter Twenty-Four

One eye cracks open as light spills in, searing and sharp like a smear of white that stretches and warps like heat shimmering off fresh asphalt. It feels too close. Too invasive. Something I never invited in. The lid squeezes shut again. My lashes twitch, weighed down with sticky crust that glues my eyes half shut.

A low groan bubbles from somewhere deep, barely a whisper. Just something low and thick that sticks in my throat. The faint buzz of electric pulses somewhere at the edges. It seeps through my skin, into my head, and echoes sharp with every beat. My breaths echo hollow in my ears, distant, but somehow magnified all at once. The rhythm is off, and each inhale stings sharply as it drags its way through with sharpened claws.

One more try. The edges of the room begin to crawl into focus now. Walls stripped of all color, pale and curving inward, surround me. Shapes shift with every blink. Metal rails. A thick, scratchy blanket folded all wrong that rests at my side. Blurred bodies in all white whispering something just out of reach. A sharp smell that clings to the air and burns in the back of my throat. Bleach laced with lemon and latex and something more bitter underneath. Like someone tried to scrub away blood, but missed a spot.

All thoughts slip through like smoke. Intangible. Memories replaced with static. Names and faces just unrecognizable blurs.

A faint voice pushes through the fog. Or maybe it was a door *creaking* on its hinges. It feels distant. Like it's coming from underwater somewhere, distorted and muffled. I try to push myself up but nothing moves. My limbs refuse. They're made of lead. Alien. Not even mine. My tongue rests heavy in my mouth, and a pressure settles over my chest, pressing down, drowning every breath I try to draw. Panic nips at the edges, sharp and sudden, until it's quickly swallowed again.

My eyelids flutter, flickering in and out of focus as the buzz of fluorescent pierces louder now. Incessant, persistent and cruel. I *think* I'm awake. At least my fingers twitch at my sides. The dull pain in my head sharpens as the air slices through me like hundreds of tiny knicks on my skin. The overhead light has shifted, now a pale gray wash. A little less sharp, but still too bright for the cave I'm buried in. The buzz grows clearer. Faint beeps. Muffled voices. The little *squeaks* of shoes across linoleum.

One.

Two.

Three.

My eyes lock on the ceiling tiles. Counting. Tracking. Staying right here.

Four.

Five.

The numbers spin.

Six.

Seven.

Eight.

Shapes flicker and shadows stretch across the panels.

Nine. Ten. Eleven. Twelve. Thirteen.

My pulse hammers with each silent count.

Fourteen. Fifteen. Sixteen. Seventeen.

Panic claws.

Eighteen. Nineteen. Twenty. Twenty-one.

My fingers twitch again in small, useless movements.

Twenty-two. Twenty-three. Twenty-four. Twenty-five.

The ceiling tilts. Or maybe I do.

I shift, try to sit up, but something tugs. No. Holds. My arms won't move no matter how hard I try. My legs either.

Adrenaline shoots from my gut fast. I pull again. Harder this time. But restraints drag across my skin, their thick straps biting into my flesh. Panic doesn't just rise. It explodes. Like water thrown on a grease fire. My breath catches on its way out, emitting some sort of sound I don't recognize. Not a scream, but the animal beginnings of one.

My head snaps side to side with urgency. Gleaming white tiles. White walls. The hum of fluorescent above. A metal sink. Two women in white jackets whispering with clipboards in their hands. And one pitcher of water, slick with condensation, on a table just out of reach. My fingers twitch. My throat sticks with thirst.

Then, there are my feet—thick, grippy socks shoved onto each one. One half-dangling off, the other bunched at the heel. I kick but it's pointless. A blue flowered gown sticks to my chest, drenched in sweat, tied awkwardly around my neck with loose, fraying string.

I whimper, trying to get their attention, but I choke on it fast. I try again anyway.

"Help—" I manage out, though it's barely a sound.

The nurses still pin at the other side of the room, clipboards held tight to their chests. One glances over her shoulder, just briefly, then looks away again. I swallow what little moisture I have left.

"Please—" I beg, my voice finally cracking open. "Water—"

Tears begin to slide down hot...into my hairline and trailing over my ears to the pillow below. I writhe again, full body this time, thrashing with every tiny ounce of energy I can muster. The straps dig deeper, but won't budge even an inch. I buck against the mattress, but it's no use. I'm like an insect, wings pinned down, ready to be mounted on someone's wall.

My breaths are ragged. I can't decide whether to scream or sob.

"Let me go!"

That did it. That one came from somewhere deep. Slammed off the walls and across the room. The nurses jerk their heads, startled. A clipboard clatters to the linoleum. Both women are moving now. Quick, yet composed. Like they've done this a hundred times before.

"No. No please. What is this? Why am I here?" I rattle out, each word panicked and breathless.

The taller nurse approaches first. She hovers with one hand raised, faint smile and pity gleaming in her eyes. "It's okay now. You're safe," she says, voice soothing like a lullaby. "You just need to calm down a bit."

Pictures scramble in my head. First, faded and distant. Then, slowly coming into focus. Mama folded up in the chair watching Christmas movies. Daddy, worn and thin, alone at the edge of town. Birdie's outstretched arms and big smile. Brown. The store. The late-night talks. Lessons on how to use Daddy's gun. It all felt so...*real*. But not all of it was. Not Brown. Maybe not the store. Or the way he looked at me like I mattered. But Jay—Jay was real. His death was real. Mama, Daddy, Birdie—they're real.

Then, my eyes go wide. Breath seizes. Lungs squeeze tight.

The bridge.

The rain.

Their eyes circling me like prey.

And *him*. A shiver races up my spine. Fast. The hands that touched me so gently the night before, the very ones that tried to choke every bit of life that was left.

"Where am I?" I beg, desperately searching her eyes.

"You're somewhere safe," she soothes.

Another nurse joins at the other side of the bed. I'm surrounded. Right side. Left side. My fingers clench at the sheets, twisting them tight to keep from screaming again.

"You know—" she continues. "It's a good thing that officer was there at the right moment. He said you almost jumped. Good thing he managed to talk you down at the last minute. Divine intervention, some might say." She crouches, leaning close and whispering low now. "He said you recently lost a friend at the same spot. I know it must be hard, honey. But giving up is never the right answer."

Her palm rests on my thigh, just above my knee. I squirm in the restraints.

"Why am I tied down?" I screech. I thrash harder. "Why can't I just go home?"

"You're a safety risk, dear," the taller nurse replies. "Those poor boys you attacked were lucky they only came out with a few scratches and bruises."

My ears flush hot as a scream tears from my chest.

"Let. Me. GO!"

She folds herself in half, leaning close to me, soothing like I'm crazy.

"You're having a stress reaction. That's normal. But you need to stay calm so you don't hurt yourself."

"I'm not—" stutters out in a sob. "I'm not crazy!"

My voice breaks again, splintering at the seams.

"I'm not!"

Sudden, white hot heat surges through my thigh. Pinches. Sharp and deep. I jerk, but she's already pulling out the syringe. The second nurse presses a palm to my chest and leans down, whispering gently.

"Don't fight it."

"No, what did you—" I stammer.

My vision blurs as they turn and walk away. My limbs sink into the bed like they're being folded underwater. The panic fizzles, dulled slightly by whatever they shot into my thigh. The room sways gently. I breathe in slow. Breathe out slower.

Then...I see them.

Just beyond the glass. Just beyond the door. The both of them standing, side by side, arms folded as they whisper close.

Colt.

Wes.

Colt seems to be the one giving orders. At least, his lips are the ones moving. Wes stands still at Colt's side, face turned slightly, completely unreadable.

My chest tightens again, not as tight as before, but a slight squeeze. Like a lion teasing and playing with its prey before the final kill.

"Wes," I whisper, though its barely audible, not even to myself.

I try again.

"Wes, please—"

He turns. Meets my gaze. Something flickers across his face, but I can't recognize it. Pity? Sadness? But he turns, too. My only chance at a real friend. Gone. Taken from me like everything else. And Colt. Nothing more than the devil dressed in his fanciest suit. His eyes, unmistakable, as they lock onto mine. The chestnut and gold flecks replaced by something darker than I've ever peered into before. My breath catches and my lower jaw trembles.

"No—"

I try to scream it, but it doesn't carry. The nurses don't even turn. In fact, one slowly makes her way out of the door, smiling and giving a little wave to the other. I shake my head weakly, fighting through the fog.

"Wes!"

He hesitates for half a second, maybe less.

Colt turns. Wes follows. And their frames grow distant as they slowly vanish down the hall.

Gone.

Silence floods the room. The remaining nurse shakes out the rough fabric of the folded blanket and drapes it over me, tucking each side tightly beneath where she can. I close my eyes as a machine flatlines, then resets. And something *cracks*. Not in the room, but in *me*. The truth. Ugly. Raw. Real.

I don't get to go home with Mama. Don't get to see Daddy one more time like we said. Don't get to repair my relationship with Skylar. And the worst...I don't even get to leave this world to be with Jay.

The silence that follows is anything but peaceful. It's just rot. Just sickness traveling fast beneath my flesh.

Just like Daddy said.

Just like that circling pig.

Acknowledgements

As I put the final finishing touches on my debut psychological thriller, *Falling,* there are several people I need to thank for helping bring this story to life.

To my beta readers, you've been *invaluable* in shaping these stories. You help me to see the characters through a different lens, and I could never in a million years do this without you. Thank you for your time, feedback and your support.

To Julian—thank you for loving our family. Thank you for understanding all those nights I spent curled up in the living room chair ignoring life as I created this story. Thank you for reading every rough chapter I send and being my biggest support. You have shown me how love is supposed to be and I am so grateful for you, babe. I love you always. We love you.

I must acknowledge Bartow, of course, the small town that shaped my formative years. I spent most of my upbringing wishing I could get out, and more recent years spent looking back with the sort of fondness that only grows over time. Bartow, you're a beautiful city steeped in history, and in memories that I carry with me still. My roots in this city are pretty much gone, my last tie dying several years ago, but if you happen to drive through, I highly recommend a bite at Mike's Drive In or a visit to Andy's Igloo in nearby Winter Haven, a stop at the LB Brown

House for a rich history lesson from an old friend, or a visit to Nye Jordan or Mary Holland Park.

Most importantly, I have to acknowledge the person this story was written for. Falling is a deeply personal story to me, inspired by real-life events centered around a childhood friend. His loss, only weeks before Christmas, was incredibly difficult for me. I remember getting the call. I was only twenty-one. So was he. He was an incredibly gifted musician and beautiful spirit (you know people who just have a light around them and make everyone feel safe) taken from this world much too soon. The friend I sat across from every single day in the school cafeteria, belting out the lyrics to our favorite Red Hot Chili Peppers song, taken in an instant.

The events that unfolded over the years became the inspiration for this story. Some are imagined, others drawn from truth. But the most enduring element of *Falling* is grief that never lets go. For decades, nothing ever felt final. With the last words written in this book, I hope to finally close that chapter.

"It's hard to believe that there's nobody out there
It's hard to believe that I'm all alone
At least I have her love, the city she loves me
Lonely as I am, together we cry"
— Red Hot Chili Peppers

READ ON FOR A
PREVIEW OF
THE HIT WIFE

A Novel from Jennifer Grant

Chapter One

Some mornings begin with spilled coffee. Today starts with one perfectly wasted casserole—and a dead man at my knees. The stench of tuna chunks and copper hovers thick in the air as Patty blubbers off to the side, arms flailing, panic radiating through her in waves. I rest the gun onto my lap, smearing a slimy mushroom cube across my cheek.

The ringing hits fast—sharp, high, relentless. So loud that Patty's pleas hang muffled and lifeless in the room.

Slowly, the world rights itself again. Patty's hysterics stutter back to life. A *gurgle* stirs low in David's chest. And Dinah Washington sings of *September Rain* through crackled static from the old radio.

Shit. A gurgle.

My finger curls tight around the trigger. I lift the pistol. Aim straight for his chest, just the way Rob taught me to. One deliberate pull. One loud and resounding *bang*. The gunshot ricochets up my spine as Patty's screams warp into another muffled, looping panic.

He gasps. Quiets. Chest stills. I drop the gun into a goopy puddle of mushroom soup on a bed of perfect al dente noodles. Heat and copper cling to my fingers as I wipe them on my skirt. The mushroom smears with crimson, setting fast into the cornflower-blue fabric of the dress Rob bought me on our first wedding anniversary, insisting that it matched my eyes.

"Patty?" My voice slices through the chaos, calm and sharp.

Panic bubbles fast as tears run hot, carving trails down her cheeks.

"Patty—"

Her panic tightens its grip, tears carving tracks down her cheeks. She backs into the wall, knocking down the gold-framed family portrait of Patty with David and her girls in Fort Lauderdale on summer vacation last year.

"Patty!" I yell, finally catching her attention enough for a single goddamn breath.

Her eyes grow wide as her gaze finally pins to mine.

"Club soda. Towel. Now."

Monday mornings are supposed to be a routine. Pack lunches for Rob and Susan. Drop Susan off at daycare by 8:30 a.m. Then home to ready the house for Sewing Circle Tuesdays, where no one remembers the last time a stitch was actually made. Books are occasionally read, but gossip is always the main craft at hand.

I should have left the casserole on the porch and gone. Should have walked away. But after Patty missed two weeks in a row of Sewing Circle due to some mysterious illness, that doorbell tugged at my conscience. Everything else is a blur. The frantic tilt of Patty's head. The glint of David's fist as he lunged from the bedroom. Time slowed. My only instinct was to reach into the velvet-lined pouch of my purse for the little "peace of mind" that Rob gave me after little scare. It ended up just being a few of the neighborhood teenaged boys with nothing better to do than ding-dong ditch on doors during a summer mid-afternoon.

The room is thick with copper, so much that it swallows like pennies down my throat. I scan the room for anything that could stain further, but it seems most of it just coagulates beneath him in a goopy, sticky mess.

Patty returns, falling to her knees at my side, half-empty bottle of club soda laying in her lap.

"Patty, I need you to listen to me.

"I—I can't—I mean, what do we do?" she whispers, eyes darting frantically around the room like some trapped bird.

"We clean. First, we get this stain out of my dress. Then we move him," I order.

Another sob stutters up her throat as her head falls into her hands.

"Patty, where can we put him?"

Her head lifts. Widened eyes find mine. "Put him? Oh God—Liz, I can't!"

"Patty, you can either tell me where we can hide him right now or risk the girls finding their father lying in a pool of blood on the living room floor."

She sniffles. Wipes the back of her arm across the bottom of her nose. "Uhh—" she begins. "Maybe the—deep freezer?"

"Let's move. Now."

I reach for the towel in Patty's grasp and drown it in club soda, dabbing at the crimson stains splattered into blue fabric. Leave it nice and drenched until I can wash it back home.

"Grab the comforter from the spare bedroom," I instruct.

Patty swallows. Nods. Shivers as she obeys. Her movements clumsy and erratic as she disappears through the kitchen and down the hallway before rushing back again.

I grab the comforter from her hands, a satin dusty-rose with tucks and pleats gathered at the sides. I shake it out and lay it across the floor.

"Help me roll him," I say.

Her palm flies to her mouth again as whimpers echo across the room. Finally, she sucks a breath of air into her lungs as she folds herself in half, grunting as she rolls him once onto his stomach, then again onto his back.

"Wrap him tight. Grab his head," I continue, maintaining my composure against her frantic cries.

Patty works quickly, folding the sides of the comforter over him and lifting up her side as I grab him by the legs.

"Garage?" I ask.

Her head shakes. Loose ringlets slipped free of their pins shake violently around her face. She drops his head. It lands with a sick, violent *thud* onto the floor.

"Oh God!" she starts again.

"Patty—"

She sniffles, then composes herself as she picks him up again. "Behind you. The door just over your shoulder and to the left."

Each move is deliberate. Determined. My muscles strain as we shift his weight, arms trembling over the sudden, unyielding heft. Thank God David decided to focus on his health last year—shedding pounds, tightening muscles, sculpting his once-bulky frame into something sleek and fit. Still, he's a load. Heavy and uncooperative. Quite the chore for us to manage, but we do.

The garage smells faint of motor oil and dust. A deep freezer sits off to the side, tucked tightly around the far wall. The freezer hums steadily as we drop him onto the concrete floor, his head landing again with a loud thump as I pry open the lid and lift it up.

I look at Patty again. Her mascara streaks, mixing with tears and sweat, the smell of fear tangling with the coffee that clings to the fibers of her dress.

"He'll fit," I say.

Together, we maneuver David inside. Patty shoves on his shoulders as I fold his legs and cram his knees. I reach for the lid, slamming it down but it pops open again leaving a sliver of a gap.

"We have to take off his shoes."

"What? Oh God, Liz! I can't—"

"You can. Listen—what happens next is simple. We keep this quiet. You don't open this freezer again. Understand?"

She nods. Trembling. "I—I can do that. I think—"

"You will," I say, voice firm, final. "Because you have two girls to think about now."

More sniffles as she sucks in another deep breath of air. "Okay."

But the word hangs in the air as all color is drained from her face.

I imagine tomorrow. Tuesday. The neighborhood Sewing Circle gathered in my living room asking questions about my visit with Patty. If the casserole was delivered. And how did it taste. Morning mocktails with a side of gossip and judgmental looks. My famous sherbet punch with fizzing ginger ale. Knitting needles and spools of yarn and thread that never get touched.

"I'll cover for you tomorrow. But they're going to start asking questions, Patty. They're going to get suspicious."

She finally moves, reaching for David's size thirteen shoes and yanking them off of his feet. They fall to the floor at her side. "Okay, Liz. I'll think of something to tell the girls and promise I'll be there next week."

I stretch again for the lid, gently closing it as it *clicks* securely shut.

"I need a glass of water," Patty whispers, barely audible through her cracked and strained throat.

She disappears again into the house, and I step over toward the window, looking over our perfectly manicured street. Nothing has changed outside. Each lawn decorated with perfect lines from lawnmowers on Sunday mornings. Occasional shouts of small children playing outside. Our mailman, Harry, whistling as he makes his way door to door.

I catch my reflection. Carefully pin slipped tendrils back into place. Curl my fingers around the pearls my mother handed down last year.

A mother. Wife. Hostess. And something else. Something no one can speak of ever again. A cold-blooded killer. A man's blood stained on my dress.